Dark Streets

Phillip Strang

BOOKS BY PHILLIP STRANG

DCI Isaac Cook Series

MURDER IS A TRICKY BUSINESS
MURDER HOUSE
MURDER IS ONLY A NUMBER
MURDER IN LITTLE VENICE
MURDER IS THE ONLY OPTION
MURDER IN NOTTING HILL
MURDER IN ROOM 346
MURDER OF A SILENT MAN
MURDER HAS NO GUILT
MURDER IN HYDE PARK
SIX YEARS TOO LATE
GRAVE PASSION
THE SLAYING OF JOE FOSTER
THE HERO'S FALL
THE VICAR'S CONFESSION
GUILTY UNTIL PROVEN INNOCENT
MURDER WITHOUT REASON

DI Keith Tremayne Series

DEATH UNHOLY
DEATH AND THE ASSASSIN'S BLADE
DEATH AND THE LUCKY MAN
DEATH AT COOMBE FARM
DEATH BY A DEAD MAN'S HAND
DEATH IN THE VILLAGE
BURIAL MOUND
THE BODY IN THE DITCH
THE HORSE'S MOUTH
MONTFIELD'S MADNESS

Steve Case Series

HOSTAGE OF ISLAM
THE HABERMAN VIRUS
PRELUDE TO WAR

Standalone Books

MALIKA'S REVENGE
VERRALL'S NIGHTMARE

Dedication

*For Elli and Tais, who both had the perseverance to make me sit down and
write*

Chapter 1

Old Joe had been on the street for eleven years, toothless, unshaven and unloved. He was known for his affability, passion for reading any book he could find thrown out on the street, and willingness to take money from a passing stranger. If anyone had spent time with him, he would have told them that he was from the Wiradjuri tribe and had been born outside of Mudgee, two hundred and sixty kilometres from Sydney, New South Wales, in Australia.

It was a colourful tale he would recount to those willing to listen: growing up on a mission, a mother who loved him with a passion, a cruel overseer who beat him, and that he was a descendant of noble nomadic warriors, a rich history stretching back into the never-never, but it wasn't true.

Sergeant Natalie Campbell of the Kings Cross Police Station would have told you a different story and that Old Joe, who was fifty-two years of age, had been adopted at six months by a family in the northern suburb of Wahroonga, an affluent area, and that his education had been comprehensive and entitled, as befitted the son of wealthy parents. Not that he hadn't experienced racism and taunts, but he learnt to deflect them with wit and, if unsuccessful, with his fists.

His downfall came when he fell in love with a local girl when he was twenty-two. Neither regarded their heritages as important. But her parents had, and she was shuffled out of the country on a plane to England and university. For six months, they corresponded, but with time and distance, the romance had withered, her last letter explaining that she had found love amongst the hallowed environs of Oxford and would not be returning to Australia for a very long time, if ever.

Distraught, he felt an emptiness he could not understand. To him, their love was eternal, and his people's ways were the best. For ten years, he went on walkabout, a traditional pastime of his people, when they went into the bush, living off the land, hunting and fishing as necessary, a step back into a spiritual place, but Old Joe, back then known as Joe Coster, could not embrace his ancestors. Modern Australia was too deeply ingrained in him to understand the old ways.

He had worked as a farm labourer in Queensland, a miner in Mount Isa, and even prospected for opals in Coober Pedy. But his food came from a supermarket, not from a kangaroo he had killed with a woomera or a fish enticed from a muddy creek. And as for native foods off a tree or a bush, he couldn't tell what was edible or poisonous.

Conflicted about where he belonged, unsure of his Aboriginal heritage, critical of his upbringing with a white family, a feeling of not belonging to either, he had succumbed to the curse of alcohol: beer when he could afford it or cheap bottles of sherry when he couldn't.

Kings Cross, one kilometre from the centre of Sydney, less than two from the harbour bridge and the Opera House, had a chequered history. In the early nineteenth century, mansions were built for the wealthy, but over the generations, a slow and lingering decline to the 1940s, when servicemen on rest and recreation from the war raging in the Pacific gravitated towards Kings Cross, a twenty-minute walk from Garden Island Naval Base.

That's when the seedy clubs, the strip joints, the criminals, and the prostitutes came in. From then on, attempts to reverse what it had become, successive governments imposing legislation, restrictions on hours to sell liquor, and an increased police presence; but then, less than twenty years later, a new breed of American soldiers in Vietnam, rest and recreation in Sydney, desperate for normality and depravity, finding some of the first, plenty of the second.

However, in the twenty-first century, with no wars, at least in the Pacific or the southern hemisphere, Kings Cross had quietened, although the gentlemen's clubs existed down back streets and the trade in illicit drugs and homelessness remained.

Old Joe might have claimed his aboriginal heritage, but his blood was diluted by previous generations of his people impregnated by white settlers, sometimes voluntarily, more often forced. To the casual observer, apart from his slightly-flared nostrils, he looked white with a hint of a Mediterranean tan.

He had never known his blood father and did not remember his birth mother; he thought them dead. There was money, no more than twenty kilometres from where he lay on his mattress outside a vacant shop, two doors from the entrance to the underground railway station, two stops to Bondi Junction, and then a bus ride to Bondi Beach and its trendies.

In the other direction, two stops to Town Hall and the shopping mecca of the Queen Victoria Building, a statue of the great woman outside. Take a tram down to Circular Quay, where the ferries that plied the harbour unloaded the commuters, the ocean liners docked, the Opera House a ten-minute walk, the harbour bridge looming above.

Captain Cook had never seen Sydney Harbour, sailing past it after leaving Botany Bay, but Old Joe had. As a youth, he had surfed, won a few competitions, and saw himself travelling the world, a girl on every beach, but it had soured soon enough. As an amateur, he was good; as a professional, he wouldn't have made the grade.

The local police knew him to be harmless, and whereas they and other civically minded persons would have preferred him to move on with his swag and sleep somewhere else, there was little they could do. Homeless and destitute, the individual still had rights enshrined in law.

Not that those laws prevented his death ten hours after walking from the Wayside Chapel in Hughes Street, Potts Point, after enjoying lunch there.

It was a Sunday, a day of rest for some, a chance to meet with friends, go to the beach, or sail a boat on Sydney Harbour, but it was just another day for Old Joe. Wake up late and stroll around the area, talk to other homeless persons, and cadge a few dollars from those passing by, although he received money from the government. And then, after lunch, more strolling and talking before settling down with a bottle of beer to whet his taste buds and then a cheap bottle of cooking sherry to dull them.

The first anyone knew of his demise was on Monday morning. It was early, a charity helping those on the street, counselling if they were listening, and finding a place to live if they wanted.

Dimitri Smith, his mother was Greek, was committed to the task and six days out of seven, he would drive the charity's van around the areas where the homeless could be found. Not many slept rough on the main street in Kings Cross; one week, up to five or six people; other weeks, two or three. More slept in the nearby park adjoining the El Alamein Fountain, commemorating those who had died in 1942 during World War 11 in two battles in El Alamein, Egypt.

The homeless dying on the street wasn't unexpected. Most hadn't received medical treatment in years nor visited a dentist. And even if the Wayside Chapel supplied an adequate meal, it didn't stop Old Joe and others from foraging in waste bins, and although a bottle of cheap sherry may have settled an alcoholic's needs, it still rotted the gut.

Sergeant Natalie Campbell looked at the body as a medic checked it. He declared the man dead, although it was not for him to venture an opinion about the cause of death. Natalie Campbell saw the blood trickling from the man's mouth and slight bruising to one side of his face. To her, it was suspicious.

Her suspicions were confirmed by Stanley West, the forensic pathologist, twelve hours later. Blunt trauma to one side of the face, probably caused by a clenched fist or a boot, cracking a rotten tooth which caused the bleeding, and then his face held down onto his mattress, causing suffocation within two minutes. It was a homicide.

Natalie Campbell made the phone call to State Crime Command, Homicide Squad. She hoped it wasn't racially motivated, as that would cause complications and raise anger in the local community and division amongst those who held opposing views. However, she felt a sense of elation. It was her first homicide, and she was ambitious. Working with Homicide could only benefit her career.

***

Detective Inspector Gary Haddock breezed into Kings Cross Police Station at 2.30 p.m. He was tall, carrying twenty kilos more than he should and wearing an aftershave lotion that reeked of arrogance. Natalie Campbell took an instant dislike and could see misogynist stamped across his forehead in capital letters.

'Good to see you, Gary.' Superintendent Grant Martin welcomed Haddock with a hearty pat on the back and a firm handshake.

'Confined to the sticks,' Haddock replied.

'Doing your job, leaving you with the glory.'

It was the banter of two men comfortable in each other's presence. Natalie Campbell wondered if she had been premature in her estimation of Homicide's finest. She knew it was her habit to judge people on the first meeting; she had been wrong before. It had been like that with Old Joe, now resting on a slab in the mortuary. The first time she had spoken to him, two years previously when she had joined Kings Cross Police Station, was to warn the man about accosting people on the street, but since then, each time she had seen him, she would stop and chat, ask him how he was, what book he was reading, did he have a family. The last question was always answered in the negative. 'None that I know of,' he would say.

After Haddock and Superintendent Martin had spoken about old times in the latter's office for ten minutes, DI Haddock was in front of Natalie Campbell's desk. 'You found the man, I'm told,' he said.

'I did.'

'Great, then you're the person for me. How about we have a coffee over the road and get to know each other. Not my part of the world, and you know the locals. Tell me what you can, any thoughts as to why someone would kill someone sleeping rough. Tough enough as it is for them, but they can be a nuisance. I'm sure you'd attest to that.'

Natalie could.

Seats were at a premium in the coffee shops, so they sat on a bench near the fountain to fallen heroes. Natalie had a latte; Haddock had a cappuccino and a croissant.

'Missed my lunch,' he said. 'My wife's constantly on about me overeating, can't blame her. Your first murder?'

'It is.'

'Upset, or can you handle it.'

'I can,' Natalie replied. 'I knew the man, often spoke to him. Educated, life had taken a bad turn for him somewhere along the way.'

'It does for all of us. His heritage might have had something to do with it. Prejudice is still out there. It can't be stamped out totally.'

'Serial or a one-off?'

'Can't tell, not yet. Killing the homeless seems pointless, but Sydney's got its fair share of psychos, not as much as overseas, but we've got enough. Soon know if it's serial.'

'How?'

'Timing. Once a murderer's got a taste for it, it doesn't take long for them to commit the next. Three to four days, maybe ten, and we should know. You'll be my eyes and ears around here, okay by you?'

'It is. Superintendent Martin?'

'I've known him for years. A straight shooter, honest as the day's long. More of an administrator than an investigator. As for me, can't stand the paperwork; you, good at it?'

'Better than average.'

'Great, that's another job for you. You're wet behind the ears, no offence. I'll need to throw you in the deep end, and I can lose my temper and might swear at you. Think you can handle it.'

'As long as it's when you're angry or I've stuffed up.'

'Stuffed up, I can handle. Murder can get nasty, progressively more violent, and depraved if serial. Don't throw up over me if you can help it.'

'You've seen a few?' Natalie asked. She liked his style of speech, rapid and to the point, no-nonsense, no rhetoric, call a spade a spade.

'Too many. Remember out west, Fairfield, a couple of years back, a couple of murders, slashed throats?'

'I do. Were you there?'

'I was, saw the aftermath. At your age, I would have thrown up, but not now. You become inured to it, which is not good, makes you callous and unfeeling. You'll have to control yourself to work with me.'

'I will.'

'Great. What can you tell me about the area I don't already know.'

'Edgy during the Vietnam War, prostitutes bussed in to satisfy GIs on R & R, but since then, a slow decline. The strip clubs have gone, a fire took one out, and Covid finished the others. A few gentlemen's clubs around the back streets, rare to see a prostitute on a street corner these days.'

'Organised crime?'

'In the past, and probably there's some around. Mostly it's the homeless, the drunk and drugged fools of a weekend, break-and-enter and car accidents. Although we had a couple of one-punch deaths, which caused the government to lock the clubs and pubs early. That was pre-Covid, decimated the place, and never recovered. Attempts to upgrade the area, a couple of apartment blocks, but not a lot has changed. A few too many empty shops, plenty of places to eat and drink, a market in the park on a Saturday, buy a kebab or get your fortune told.'

'Anyone to watch out for? Known troublemakers?'

'Drug-addicted mainly. No vandalism, mild to be honest.'

'So why kill someone minding his own business, even if he was making a mess by his presence?'

'That's what you're here to find out.'

'Touché,' Haddock said. 'Where to start?'

'The murder scene?'

'Lead on,' Haddock said.

Chapter 2

Eight days later, the investigation had not advanced, Detective Inspector Gary Haddock had his answer, and Natalie Campbell had her first sampling of violent death.

A housewife who chose to stay at home: an honourable profession once, but now derided by many as it was up to both parents to provide income for the family. But Miriam Levine was no ordinary woman. She was a Hasidic Jew, a sub-group of Judaism known for religious conservatism and social inclusion. Her husband was a high-income financial manager with Westpac, one of the major banks in Australia, and it was for him to be the provider. The two children of the marriage, a daughter of eighteen months and a son of four years, were still at home with the mother.

Their house was in Point Piper, four kilometres from Kings Cross. It was in prime real estate territory, with mansions and waterfront properties, jetties jutting into the harbour, and luxury cruisers moored to take their owners and friends out to sea to drink, gorge, and make fools of themselves. But not for the Levines, whose free time, if they had any, was devoted to their religion. No socialising outside of their group, no drinking and gorging, or frolicking vacuously with wanton persons on their boats.

Their Chinese housekeeper travelled four hours daily by train to and from the Western Suburbs. Not to a mansion, but a one-bedroom apartment, where the neighbours played music until late in the night, and the hoons raced up and down the street in their modified Mazdas and Subarus.

She lived a terrible life, but when she left the Levines', she breathed a sigh of relief. Music and cars revving their engines were better than the austerity of where she worked.

Since four that morning, the housekeeper had prepared breakfast for her husband, clean clothes for her daughter to wear to school. She knew that by the time she came home, she would be too tired to spend time with her daughter, thankful that on the Jewish Sabbath and the Christian Sunday, she would not be working.

At 7 a.m., she let herself in by the back door of the Levine's five-bedroom house, careful not to disturb the serenity of the home with her presence. The first item on the agenda was to prepare the food for the day and then, afterwards, to clean the house, although a professional cleaner came in on Wednesdays, and it was now a Thursday. Thankfully, the cleaning wouldn't be too much that day, but changing the bed sheets would hurt her back.

She was making good money, the reason she worked for the Levines, and her husband's Chinese takeaway was in profit, another outlet within the year. And then she would leave the Levines and run the second takeaway in her husband's burgeoning empire, and, hopefully, another child and a deposit to buy a small house for the family.

She worked silently, or as silently as she could, as the floor in the kitchen was tiled, and a utensil dropping off the kitchen sink would reverberate, and opening cupboards and preparing food made some noise. She realised the house was strangely quiet, with no sound of prayers or children running around. And then she remembered the man of the house was interstate at a conference, and the children were with their aunt for a couple of days, and it was only Mrs Levine at home.

At eight-thirty, her work in the kitchen complete, and with no sign of the lady of the house, the housekeeper continued with her chores, moving into the sitting room and then up the stairs to the bedrooms.

With only one person in the house, she could see an easy day; no need to bother with the children's rooms, only the parents'. She knocked on their door twice before unlocking it with a spare key. Once her hands had steadied, she phoned the police.

***

First to arrive was Sergeant Natalie Campbell, twelve minutes after receiving the message from emergency services. Inspector Gary Haddock arrived within an hour. Natalie knew that her earlier opinion of him had been incorrect and that he was a good person. He was overweight and tall, which didn't work in his favour, nor did his looks, as he was not an attractive man, with a bent nose, boxing at school, according to him. Natalie thought it was more likely street fighting as a youth. He had grown up in Bankstown to the west of the city, a working-class area with aspirations of middle. Still home to a few ne'er-do-wells and hooligans. One of those, twenty years ago, a young Gary Haddock, joined the police after he matured from silly-stupid to plain stupid; sufficient time to reacquaint himself with his education, gaining a Bachelor of Policing from Western Sydney University within four years instead of the usual six. More intelligent than others had credited him in his youth, he emerged as the year's top student.

Outside the house, four police vehicles, six uniformed officers, and a gathering crowd of onlookers. Up above, three helicopters, one police and the others from two of the three commercial television stations in the city.

Not a cloud in the sky, the promise of a warm day, although it was decidedly chilly in the house. The woman's husband was returning to Sydney, alerted to the situation by Natalie. She had briefly spoken to the housekeeper, who sat in a foetal position in the back garden. As Haddock had predicted, Natalie just made it out of the bedroom after viewing the body before unloading that morning's breakfast into a flower vase on the upstairs landing.

On his arrival, Haddock climbed the stairs to the bedroom after he had donned protective coveralls, over-shoes, mask, and gloves. Unperturbed by what he saw: a woman in her mid-thirties lying on her back, her throat cut, and a knife on the floor alongside her. He did not need advice from the crime scene investigators; the cause of death was evident, and the woman's clothing showed that the attack had not been sexual. Although he would wait for Pathology and Forensics to confirm before submitting his report on the woman's death.

'Nasty way to go,' Natalie Campbell said. Unburdened of her breakfast, although feeling vomit in her mouth and a lump in her throat, she was in control, unwilling to let Haddock say afterwards, told you so.

'Rules out a psycho bent on ridding Sydney of the homeless or the indigenous population,' Haddock replied. 'Are you alright, or still queasy?'

'I'll survive. You were right; it throws you at first, easy to become blasé with violent crime.'

'Not blasé, unemotional. We're professionals. Got a job to do. Breaking down in tears as the woman is outside won't help. Have you spoken to her?'

'Briefly, her English is not easy to understand, and she's not coherent. Might be a good idea to get her away from here.'

'Where to? Kings Cross Police Station? I don't think so. Spend time with her; make her a cup of tea or coffee if she wants it. Or better, get one of the uniforms to find a nearby café and bring it back for the two of you. Sit down by the pool on a couple of chairs. The police station might freak her out. If, as you say, her English is not good, she might not have been in the country long, and men in uniform might bring back unpleasant memories.'

In the garden, Melanie Chin sat with Natalie. Natalie realised the heavily accented English, interspersed with Chinese, was due to the woman's nervous state after discovering her employer's body.

'Five years,' she said. 'I didn't know them well, did my job and went home. You noticed?'

'I did,' Natalie said. She'd had a Jewish friend at school, who was moderate in her beliefs, whereas the Levines were not. 'Difficult to work for?'

'Demanding. Mr Levine rarely spoke and ignored me usually, but Mrs Levine would occasionally talk, never about herself.'

'Did you like them?'

'Not particularly. My husband and I, we have plans, and we need the money. Mr and Mrs Levine had plenty and paid above average, could afford to, and had trouble with other employees in the past. Not everyone understood them, some were argumentative and thought the Levines odd, but I minded my own business, worked Monday to Friday, and left early on Friday before sundown. That's when their Sabbath starts.'

'You found the body?'

'I did. It was an easy day, professional cleaners were in yesterday, and then I remembered she was alone in the house. I did what I had to downstairs, went upstairs, checked everything was alright, knocked on the bedroom door, opened it, and found her there.'

'Any sign of anyone else in the house? When did you last see her alive?'

'Just before ten in the morning on Wednesday.'

'Before or after the cleaners?'

'Before. I was busy doing the washing. I waved to one of the cleaners soon after, and he waved back. Apart from that, nothing more to tell.'

'Why didn't you see Mrs Levine after that?'

'She wasn't here. Goes out when they're here. She's used to me, uncomfortable around strangers. They paid me every Friday morning, an envelope on the kitchen table, cash inside, which is how I like it.'

Natalie knew why Melanie Chin liked it – no tax deductions. Not that she could blame the woman, as paying tax was a burden the majority bore reluctantly. If the woman could circumvent the tax man, good luck to her.

The arrival of the dead woman's husband at the scene two hours later was a diversion the police could have done without. But the man had his rights. He had been out of the state; he was innocent of the crime. He was dressed in a dark suit and wore a heavy beard and a black hat. Natalie, who had seen him briefly, leaving Gary Haddock with the man, thought him distinguished.

So far, there had been no connection between the death of a homeless man in Kings Cross and a woman in Point Piper, but Haddock was sure there was, as was Natalie, who had researched the subject, and statistically, two homicides separated by four kilometres and eight days had to be tied to each other. Also, the increased violence of the second death allied with Haddock's statement that once a murderer gets a taste for it, he or she will commit more with increasing viciousness.

***

Pathology confirmed that Miriam Levine had died from her throat having been cut, that she had not been sexually violated, and there was no sign of other injuries. As the pathologist, Adil Rashid said when Natalie and Haddock met with him, 'Nasty way to go. Slow and painful, although probably went into instantaneous shock.'

Malcolm McGoogan, who headed up the crime scene investigation team, was as short as Haddock was tall, but whereas the latter was a bear of a man, McGoogan was a pussy cat, slim in stature, clean-shaven, an avid jogger, never failing to finish the City to Surf annual 'fun run' from Hyde Park close to the City to Bondi Beach on the last six times he had competed. Only, to him, the fourteen-kilometre run wasn't fun. It was serious. The reason why he was in the second group off the starting block after the professionals.

'Almost certainly resting in the bed when she died,' McGoogan said.

'Resting or asleep?' Gary Haddock asked.

The three were sitting in a coffee shop, Haddock's preferred place for conducting business.

'Either, can't be sure on that. Somehow, whoever committed the crime could get into the house, climb the stairs, enter the room, and knife the woman.'

'Which suggests?' Natalie asked.

'Either the woman was semi-comatose, sleeping tablets or something else, neither of which we found, or the murderer was light of foot.'

'We confirmed that the cleaning company didn't enter the room, as the door was locked. Clear instructions that a locked room meant no entry.'

'Which means she was dead before they started their work,' McGoogan said.

'Unless someone came in with them,' Haddock added. 'Slipped in an open door, up the stairs, into the room, locked it behind him, killed the woman, and left the house within five minutes. Unlikely, the cleaners were looking too closely at what was happening around them.'

Natalie thought there was credence in what Haddock said. She had paid a company to come in once a week to clean her small unit, and she knew they were not professional; as for cleaning, they didn't understand the word. They lasted for three weeks, with her refusing to pay for the last week after they had broken a vase her grandmother had given her.

Although there was one component that made no sense, apart from the tie-in with Old Joe's death, and that was why the murderer had chosen a modest woman who offended no one and lived in the affluent suburb of Point Piper. There had to be a reason, but it remained hidden.

Haddock had explained it to Natalie. 'Focus on who is dead, see if there is a pattern, geographically, ethnically, even historically.'

'Historically?' Natalie quizzed.

'Maybe not historically, but we've got no motive and no association between an orthodox Jewish woman and a homeless man, and it's unlikely that Miriam Levine or her husband visited Kings Cross, probably never driven through it, avoided it like the plague, Sodom and Gomorrah.'

***

Professional, cleaning, and company: none applied to those that cleaned the Levine house. What Natalie found in Marrickville, an inner-city suburb, was a rathole of a run-down terrace house, rubbish outside and more rubbish inside. A dog growled in the backyard, and a flea-bitten cat rubbed against her leg.

'You clean for Mr and Mrs Levine?' Natalie asked.

'We do,' Petar Parvanov said.

Natalie could see Eastern European, a recent immigrant to the country, attempting to make his way, willing to take any job, try anything to make money.

'You were at the house yesterday, arrived in the morning, left in the afternoon.'

'We've already told you this on the phone,' said Iliana Parvanov, Petar Parvanov's wife.

'You did,' Natalie acknowledged, 'but that was cursory; this is formal.'

'We arrived just after ten, waved to Melanie, and left at two in the afternoon. Not sure of the exact time.'

'How long have you worked there?' Natalie asked. She had pushed the cat to one side and taken a seat. 'Not much of a place you've got here.'

She could see they were decent people, doing it tough, trying to get ahead, the same as Melanie Chin. The rathole was where they rested between the cleaning company and the restaurant where Petar waited on tables at night, and Iliana worked in the kitchen.

'Seven months. This place is a dump,' Petar said. 'The landlord doesn't bother us or care that we run a business from here. Worse than where we lived in Bulgaria, but we don't complain and do what we must. Unlike the Levines, all that money, living close to the harbour and miserable. Apart from the mess of this place, we're happy.'

'We believe that Mrs Levine was murdered between six in the morning and midday. Which means someone got into the house and could have been in that room when you arrived.'

'We didn't see anyone, and clear instructions: if the door's locked, don't enter. Something to do with their religion, or maybe they're suspicious of us, think we're gipsies, out to steal their valuables, not that they've got much of those in the house. Makes you wonder why people want to live like that. This dump is better than their mansion. Here there's laughter and love, not sure they had much of either, and now the woman's dead, and you're here.'

'Do you employ anyone?' Natalie asked. She liked the Parvanovs, decent and humble, but they had come from a tough background; temptation loomed on every corner, especially in Point Piper. She wanted to give them the benefit of the doubt, but she couldn't, not yet.

'Just the two of us, although if one of us is ill, Iliana's got a cousin who'll help. Not that she's been to Point Piper with us.'

'Any communication with either of the Levines on other occasions?'

'Only with her. Criticism if we missed somewhere, but then, too many competing for a slice of the pie, and we're undercutting the Chinese, Koreans, fellow Slavs.'

'Get what you pay for.'

'Exactly. We can give four hours and do our best, no more. Maybe we're not the best cleaners, and they could get better if they paid twice the price, but they won't.'

'Mrs Levine? Any friends?'

'Not that we saw; a couple of children, very young. She'd go out sometimes, not to the harbour or a restaurant, somewhere religious, and her clothes never changed much, drab colours, hardly haute-couture.'

'You know about fashion?'

'Iliana does. She designed clothes in Bulgaria, might do it here again if things turn out alright for us.'

Chapter 3

Gary Haddock had previously worked with criminal profilers, and intelligent analysis had resulted. However, he still believed that investigation at the coal front, out on the street, was preferable to better understand the person they were looking for.

He was willing to concede that with the deaths of Old Joe and Miriam Levine, there was no pattern. Natalie, not as experienced as her inspector, was increasingly convinced that the murders were unrelated, as it had been almost three weeks since the last murder and nothing since, other than a sublime quiet in Point Piper, people fearful of going out at night, women only willing to venture forth with a man by their side. However, in Kings Cross, life continued as usual: late-night drinking, brawling, and the occasional reprobate from a facility for the seriously deluded not more than two kilometres away straying into the area, up Darlinghurst Road, ranting and raving, showing a clenched fist to people on the street, banging hard on the side of a vehicle, receiving a smack to the head from an irate motorist.

Old Joe, with no family he acknowledged and none found, other than a relative from the house in Wahroonga, who lived in England but was not willing to return to Sydney. The Wayside Chapel arranged his funeral, ensured a good turnout of locals to give him a send-off, and offered a free meal to anyone who came, which meant all the homeless in the area.

Old Joe, affectionately remembered by all, with the church's blessing and that of an aboriginal elder. There was even a person to play the didgeridoo, an aboriginal wind instrument which Natalie had tried to entice a sound from back in her college days but hadn't succeeded. And whereas it wasn't musical, not as a classicist would define music, it was appropriate and lent an additional solemnity to the occasion.

Natalie attended, as she had known the man, and she held onto religion, not for its spiritual content, but because it united people, gave them a sense of purpose, a set of behaviours to adhere to. Haddock didn't attend, as he had removed religion from his life, a God-fearing father as a child, a mother browbeaten into submission. For him, faith had connotations that brought back memories he'd rather forget.

Ruth Stein was good: Natalie and Haddock had to agree. She was police approved, with a PhD in Forensic Psychology, a Master's in Criminal Psychology, and a string of qualifications after her name. She was in her fifties, the closest there was to an expert in criminal profiling, well respected and articulate, able to separate the wheat from the chaff.

'Frankly, after studying the reports into both murders, I'm not sure where I can go on this,' she said.

Natalie and Haddock met the woman at the University of New South Wales, on Anzac Parade, near the Sydney Cricket Ground, where Australia had received a drubbing from England three weeks earlier.

'I'm giving a presentation,' Ruth Stein continued. 'It wouldn't do my credibility any favours if I admit this case baffled me. Are you certain it's a serial killer?'

'Instinct tells me it is, and murders are rare in Sydney, the last one in Kings Cross, three years back, Point Piper, none on record. We must consider the serial killer possibility, as killing the homeless serves no purpose unless it's for weird sexual gratification or the person despised them for littering the street. And if you can kill one, why not two?' Haddock said.

'And the other woman? Jewish?'

'Hasidic, affluent, no history of crime, kept to themselves, didn't bother the neighbours, even if some of them could be boisterous, parties around their pools, no doubt a few lines of cocaine.'

'Not easy to understand, the ultra-conservative, but how does she tie in with a homeless man who claimed indigenous heritage? Proven, his heritage? A few stretch a long bow with their claims.'

'Proven, but diluted, but Old Joe only mentioned it, no axe to grind,' Natalie said. 'I knew him, spoke to him on occasion. Educated, lost, nowhere to go, taken to the bottle, rotted his guts and teeth.'

'Inspector Haddock, I've read the reports and noted your comment about serial killers; also, you've encountered them before. You're right that it becomes easier, more violent and depraved. No sexual violation?'

'None, not yet.'

'Might not be, never can be sure, and if you're right, and I hold strong with an experienced police officer's instinct, then whoever is out there won't stop at two. But it's been more than a few weeks since the last person. Either the murderer's incapacitated or waiting for the right person.'

'And who would that be?' Natalie asked.

Credentialed, well respected and highly knowledgeable, Dr Ruth Stein had not helped so far, only confused.

'That's the problem, nothing to tie the two deaths together, not even in the manner of their deaths. The only thing in common is that they're close to each other. And if you try to separate, what do you get? Homeless, open to abuse and random thuggery, but two doors up from the railway station, close to midnight? It's hardly secluded and leans towards another homeless person, the only person who could get close enough without raising suspicion.

'As for the woman, that's a conundrum. I've known a few devout in their faith and community, not given to violence, intimidated some, intransigent in their views; hardly a reason for murder. Usually pacifist, intolerant of other religions. A lot of negatives, but to murder one of them smacks of something more. Any hotheads in the area, rabid fundamentalists?'

'None,' Natalie said. 'Apart from Kings Cross of a weekend, the area's peaceful, and Point Piper is a haven from the world's ills. Go up there looking for trouble, and the locals will press the fast-response security buttons on their phones and in their houses. Troublemakers would stick out like a sore thumb there.'

'Criminal profiling would be looking for commonality, a criminal signature, but I can't find it in the persons murdered, where they lived, or how they died. What do you have? Anything obscure that might have been missed? Inconsequential? If the murderer's teasing us, no idea why. They could be deluded or highly intelligent, obviously psychopathic. Anything?' Ruth Stein said, pushing the enquiry back into Natalie and Haddock's court.

'Lonely, disappointed with life, solitary by nature,' Natalie said. She thought they weren't valid but couldn't think of anything more.

'Not sure if Miriam Levine understood the concept of joy,' Ruth Stein said. 'Old Joe, embittered, could harbour disappointment and sadness, reflecting on his life as the privileged son of wealthy parents, a yearning for his indigenous heritage. And if disappointment and sadness are common points between the two, how would the murderer know this, and why choose them?

'I've applied criminal profiling to both murders. I have looked for a criminal signature, but none appears apparent. However, there are other analysis techniques to explore. Top-down profiling divides the offender into two categories, organised and disorganised. I've correlated all info from the crime scenes, autopsy reports, forensics, witnesses, photographs, choice of witness, and locations, and looked for similar patterns here in Australia and overseas.'

'Any luck?' Haddock asked.

'If you're referring to a homeless man and a Hasidic woman living an affluent lifestyle in Point Piper, the answer is no. But there's more to this than just one component. Organised and disorganised, important to clarify, gives insights into the person responsible.'

'Organised, I would say,' Natalie said.

'You're correct. Were the murders carefully planned? Do the crime scenes reflect control by the murderer? Yet again, I would say they do. Although there are anomalies.'

'This person was certainly in control of the situation, almost sticking his finger up at the police,' Haddock said.

'He or it could be she, might not even consider their actions criminal.'

'They are.'

'Assuredly they are, but we're looking for the person, not his belief in the legal system. Continuing on, were restraints used? None were, but the murderer chose his victims well, a homeless man, drunk from drinking cheap sherry, a woman resting in bed, possibly praying, confused in the house on her own, missing her children, absorbed by her faith, or critical of it.

'A deviation comes in that I would expect the bodies to be hidden, which they weren't. That indicates arrogance or a subconscious signal that the murderer wants to be caught. Can't help you with that. And here's the crux of the analysis, this person is above average intelligence and is following the murders in the legacy and social media. He's obviously got your names, probably watching you. Not sure if that should comfort you, but you need to be aware of this. It could get dangerous if he's cornered or his reason for killing two seemingly unconnected persons makes a connection to a police officer. Are you armed?'

'We are,' Haddock said.

'One final factor is the geographic area. Both locations are close to each other, which means the murderer lives close by. With two, it's impossible to be more precise, but assume he's not within an immediate radius of where the deaths occurred, allow a one-to-two-kilometre buffer from either.'

'The person commits a murder in Kings Cross, another in affluent Point Piper,' Haddock said. 'Does that indicate anything, different demographics?'

'A person who can move in Point Piper without alarm, either a tradesman or a businessman, coat and tie. In Kings Cross, someone who blends in, not in a suit, more likely the clothes of the homeless.'

'A person who changes their appearance?' Natalie asked.

'It seems possible,' Ruth Stein said.

***

Miriam Levine's funeral followed Hasidic custom. Natalie would not be allowed to attend, and Haddock chose to respect their community's wishes and stayed away.

It was now a waiting game, not for a breakthrough, but another murder, aware that with increasing confidence and violence, the attention to detail of the instigator falters, mistakes are made, evidence is left at the scene, and a pattern starts to form.

It was not the way to conduct a murder investigation, but it was their only option. The only positive they had was that someone had entered Miriam Levine's bedroom, killed the woman, and that the CSIs, skilled in finding the minutiae, had failed to find any presence other than the dead woman, her husband, and Melanie Chin. Someone meticulous had killed the woman, which was another factor, although when and where that information would come in useful was unknown.

The housekeeper, now unemployed, was found behind the counter at her husband's takeaway.

Natalie drove out to where the woman lived; Haddock was on a course and would return as soon as there was a development.

'Hungry?' Melanie Chin asked.

'Starving,' Natalie replied.

'Take a seat. The least I can do is give you a good feed.'

'Sounds great. You're working here now?'

'I'm looking for another job, but the former housekeeper of a murdered woman doesn't sound great as a reference, and Mr Levine won't speak for me. Something to do with his religion, or maybe he didn't like me and saw me as a non-believer. Never knew with him, can't say I liked him, but she was okay, a little strange, but decent.'

'No reflection on you, but yes, your past employment will go against you. Can you survive with what you've got here?'

'We can, just that the extra would have come in handy. If I don't get a job, better for the family, and I get to see my daughter and take her to school. You drove out here; try it on the train five days a week, uncomfortable and unpleasant.'

'Did you see any unfamiliar faces in the days leading up to Miriam Levine's death?' Natalie asked as she ate her food.

'I enter the house early, do my work, have lunch in the kitchen, and leave. I rarely go out on the street, and the walls surrounding the house are tall. No, I didn't see anyone, and even if I did, I'm not sure what I should have been looking for. It was a job, do it well, take my money and leave, nothing more. I didn't get involved with the family, didn't listen to their conversations, not that I could understand them.'

'Yiddish,' Natalie said. 'A Jewish dialect, some English words, some High German. You might have understood some, but not much.'

'Virtually nothing and I wasn't curious.'

'We believe the murderer was intelligent and light of foot, careful not to make his or her presence known.'

'I didn't notice anything unusual.'

Apart from the meal, not a lot had been gained from Melanie Chin, and if the murderer was of above-average intelligence and a careful planner, it wasn't unexpected that the Levine's housekeeper hadn't seen anything.

Chapter 4

It was eleven thirty on a cold and wet night when Haddock and Natalie arrived at the site. The body had been washed up on a narrow beach close to Rose Bay Marina, a sliver of sand unsuitable for swimming but clearly visible when a group of drunken revellers had piled off a cruiser after a night of drinking, eating, and whoring. Under other circumstances, Haddock would have envied the men, but the sight of a body floating face down, covered in seaweed and small crustaceans, dampened his ardour and that of the men.

The revellers, now drinking coffee, were a sorry-looking bunch in their fifties and sixties. The six women accompanying them were in their mid-twenties to early thirties. Haddock didn't need a picture painting of what the cruise had been, although Natalie, more innocent than him, didn't understand. Not until he explained it to her.

The body had been covered with a plastic sheet, and the tide was coming in. The crime scene investigators lifted it onto a stretcher and carried it to the marina. Floodlights had been erected as the investigators began their work.

'Young, eighteen to nineteen, no visible signs of sexual intrusion, clothing intact,' McGoogan, the lead CSI, said.

'Death?'

'Unsure. In the water for several hours, lacerations on her legs, probably close to the marina for a few hours, sliced by boat propellers. The crustaceans don't appear to have done much other than a few bites here and there.'

'Drowned?' Natalie asked.

'Can't be sure on that,' McGoogan said. 'It'll need the pathologist to confirm, but at this time, judging by the bruising around the throat, I'd say she had been strangled, bare hands, possibly a rope, but salt water makes it difficult to be sure. Not sure I want to call this one. I could be wrong. May have been dead on entering the water, could have been alive. Ingestion of water will tell.'

'Is there any more?' Natalie asked. 'Any obvious signs that link it to the other murders?'

'Stretching a long bow on that one,' McGoogan said. 'Serial killers have a modus operandi, an identifying style, method of death, knife, gun, asphyxiation, but this is totally different to the other two. Are you still convinced, DI Haddock?'

'Dead certain, excuse the pun.'

Haddock, twenty years plus in the force, could feel a connection, although willing to concede the possibility that it might be more than one murderer. To him, the three murders were connected. He didn't know why or how, but instinct told him they were, an acquired trait that an investigative police officer gains after years of exposure to the worst of humanity.

No more than a handful of years older than the dead woman, Natalie Campbell looked at the body and saw slim, once attractive, straw-coloured hair, either natural or dyed, although she thought it natural. She had thrown up at Miriam Levine's murder scene, but this time the scene wasn't as horrific. She felt calm.

The captain of the cruiser, English and in his thirties, confirmed what Haddock had known and Natalie had not. 'Once a week, maybe twice, rain or shine, late at night, three to four hours a night, a group of men, plenty of money, and what you see is what you get.'

'Expensive?'

'Not much change out of ten thousand. A regular cruise costs plenty anyway, but then they have to pay for the women, and they don't come cheap.'

Natalie looked at the women, standing apart from the men. They might have been stunners when they had embarked on their nautical adventure, but they weren't now. The money was in their bank accounts; they had provided the fun, and the men no longer interested them. And judging by the men, affluent but not all of them attractive, but probably generous tippers, they might have had their fun, but the women had not.

Natalie's suspicions were confirmed when she spoke to one of the women, dark-haired with a short skirt and tight blouse. Natalie was sure the woman's breasts were implants, not that she formed an opinion or was interested in women indulging in such behaviour. She had grown up in an accepting family, not given to comment on the actions of others as long as they didn't cause offence. It surprised her that she felt mild condemnation for the woman and realised she might be a prude.

'All I want to do is get away from here and those lechers, shower to wash their smell off and have a good sleep,' the woman said.

'Not much fun?' Natalie replied.

'Can be, depends on the man, but they were perverts, wanted us to put on a show.'

'That's what they paid for.'

'Sure, not that we complained. Don't have to like it, do you?'

Natalie could have said if you want to whore on Sydney Harbour with men who want to paw you, have sex with you, and watch you with another woman, don't complain afterwards.

However, she didn't. 'I suppose not,' she said instead.

'Anyway, you're not here as the moral police. Get enough of that from my parents. Screwing whoever, what if you get a disease, should wait till you find a good man, that's what they say every time I go to see them, which isn't often.'

'We're concerned about the dead woman. We don't expect you to know her, but we need to know what you saw.'

'Nothing. We left the boat before the men. We didn't want their hugging and kissing, promising to meet again soon. They had that out on the ocean. Back here, a handshake if they're lucky, but give them a chance, they would have a hand up your skirt or down your blouse. Amazing, they think we enjoy it, and they're God's gift to women. Apart from their deep pockets and overdosing on Viagra, they are poor examples of the opposite sex.'

'You're off the boat,' Natalie said, tired of the woman's griping. 'Did you see the woman first?'

'I did, almost kept walking, didn't want to return to the boat. Don't know why I did; civic duty, I suppose. Some morality is left in me. Besides, whore for a living, you come across violence too often. I've had a couple threaten to kill me; one beat me up and put me in hospital. Is she a whore?'

'The dead woman? Probably not. We believe whoever killed her, murder not yet confirmed, did it for pleasure. Sex doesn't seem to be a reason.'

'She was murdered.'

'How do you know?'

'I've seen murder before. I had a friend, lived with her for a while before I wised up, spent money to get to what you see now, and moved from street crawling to a comfy apartment in Darlinghurst and jobs like tonight.'

'She was murdered?'

'Look it up, five years ago, Maggie Baxter. She was twenty-two. A child at fifteen, raped by her brother. She was mixed up. I can't blame her. Whoring was what she did to survive, no emotion, only the money, the next fix, injecting heroin.'

'Are you?'

'Never. I finished school and could have gotten a decent job. I tried but got bored of it and the office Romeos who fancied their chance. Stripped for a while, men in plastic macs in the front row, dollar notes down your bra or undies. Took the money, worked in a brothel, on the street for a while, and discovered the internet. A boom if you have no vices. Two properties now, working on my third.'

'And after three?'

'Who knows. Might find myself a man permanently, might not. Anyway, she was murdered. I can tell.'

'Because of your friend?'

'She had brought this man back, not that I saw him. She did what she had to do, and he threw her out of the window before he left. Into body-building, so I was told. The dead woman looks the same as Maggie.'

***

Haddock spoke to the men, reluctant to give their names and details; anonymity was the keyword for a night of debauchery on the sea. One of the six one was a judge that Haddock knew. Of the other five, one was a doctor, another a solicitor, and the rest were real estate agents.

Compared to the women, who were not reticent about sharing their details, as they had nothing to lose, the men expressed alarm.

'My reputation,' the solicitor said.

'Can't be helped,' Haddock replied. 'Murder's murder. Can't ignore you any more than the others. Embarrassing, I suppose, especially after that sex-trafficking case you presided over. Gave the ring-leaders long prison terms. Grounds for appeal? The judge frolicking with prostitutes.'

Haddock could have been more sympathetic, not condemning the man and the others nearby for their adventure, but the judge had once let off someone he had arrested on a mere technicality. Although sneakingly, he had to admire the men their good luck, having espied the woman Natalie had been speaking to.

The doctor was philosophical when he gave his statement, stating that he was divorced, the children were adults with families, and the family patriarch caught with his literal pants down would cause merriment and a lot of harmless ribbing.

The solicitor was concerned with propriety. None of the real estate agents was worried, as notoriety, good or bad, drew more customers to them.

A small purse had washed up, the assumption being that the dead woman had had it in a pocket of her clothing when she was murdered, and it had fallen out on retrieving the body from the small beach. It was empty, except for a name and a phone number on a piece of paper, barely readable but still legible under a strong light. The dead woman was fifteen years of age and a resident of the area.

At the house, Natalie took the lead. Telling parents that a child has died came hard to Haddock. It was better to leave it to his sergeant, who empathised with the dead girl's father after the mother collapsed. A doctor was called and administered a sedative to the woman.

'How?' Brandon Griffith asked. He was a small man, slightly stooped, in his forties. An accountant, he worked from home, filled out tax forms, and gave advice on negative gearing and retirement planning. The house was a modest single-level dwelling with three bedrooms, a backyard pool, and a cat asleep on a window sill.

'Unsure,' Haddock said. 'It's very late. Did you register her disappearance?'

'She was staying with a friend, a sleepover. We thought she was safe. We heard from her at seven in the evening. We joked about no boys and no alcohol. She was a good girl who made us proud. And now she's dead. Are you certain it's Rebecca?'

'The bag says it is,' Natalie said. 'If you're up to it, we can take you to identify.'

Natalie thought she was harsh with the man, and it always concerned her giving bad news to parents. There had been a street walker in Kings Cross in her early forties, a short skirt that showed what little underwear she wore, and stiletto heels so precarious, a wonder the woman could walk.

And then, one day, the stiletto heels killed her. Walking home down Butler Stairs, named after James Butler, a draper who had lived and worked in the area, an alderman on Sydney City Council who was instrumental in building the stairs. They connected Victoria Street in Potts Point, near where Bridget McElhone had sold her wares in Kings Cross, and Brougham

Street in Woolloomooloo, where she lived in a two-bedroom hovel with another streetwalker.

Two fifteen in the morning, a cloudless night, with only three customers since nine in the evening, enough money for heroin and her week's rent for the hovel. Slowly negotiating the downward slope of the Victorian-era sandstone stairways, one hundred and three steps worn unevenly by the people walking up and down over the years. They were challenging at the best of times, but early morning, a prostitute, worn down by heroin and degenerate men, not helped by the shoes she wore, slipped at the top and didn't stop until halfway down, her neck broken. She was dead.

Her parents, humble people who lived fifteen kilometres from where their daughter had died, took the news philosophically.

'Top of the class at school,' the mother said, a handkerchief in her hand but no tears.

The father, more vocal, stated that she had been their only child, and then, the curse of bad drugs and even worse men, and they hadn't seen her for eight years, the last time, a tearful reunion in a café in the city.

Natalie had seen the sadness on the face of Brandon Griffith, the father of Rebecca.

Chapter 5

Gary Haddock, grateful that he hadn't had to tell the parents of the young and very dead woman, focussed on the area around Rose Bay Marina. He needed pathology to establish the time of entry into the water. After that, tidal flow, entry point into the harbour, and persons who might have seen anything unusual.

One significant factor was that it was possible to see the house where Miriam Levine had died from the marina.

The Levines' house hadn't been waterfront, and access from their residence to the water's edge was through other properties. It was worth considering, but for now, there was another person to interview, the sleepover friend.

Wolseley Crescent, Point Piper, was waterfront, the most expensive street to purchase real estate in Sydney. Homes of the ultra-rich, the titans of industry, money-management gurus, bankers and lawyers. It was a place that Haddock, a small 's' socialist, regarded with a mild degree of disdain. His parents had strived all their lives, so had he, and the most they had to show for their effort was a small fibro cottage forty kilometres from Point Piper. As a detective inspector, the most he could afford was a red-brick three-bedroom cottage built in the forties to the north of the city, amongst the eucalyptus and pine bark.

Standing at the front gate of the sleepover friend's house, he wondered how people who would not have worked harder than his parents had achieved so much, when they had achieved so little. He had read that it was to do with financial management, intellect, and the willingness to take a calculated risk, and he might have agreed up until he met the father of the sleepover friend.

'No need coming in,' a short, balding man said from the other side of the grille on the gate. 'Nothing here for the police,' after Haddock had shown his warrant card.

He knew there was, and this man, whoever he was, wasn't like the others in the area. Some were snobbish, a few turning their noses up at the riff-raff, none rejecting entry to a police officer unless....

The man behind the grille must be involved in something nefarious. Either on the run, hiding out, or had absconded with the money that had paid for the mansion. Nobody rejected a police officer unless they were involved in a crime. But Haddock wasn't there for any other crime; it was a murder that interested him. He wasn't in the mood to take any nonsense.

'Your daughter had a friend staying over?' Haddock said, pushing on the grille, coming up against resistance from the lock on the other side.

'She did, Rebecca Griffith. What's it to you?'

'Your name?'

'Not sure I want to give it.'

It was unusual behaviour, as though the man was expecting a visit by the police soon, someone demanding money, or even criminals wanting to harm him.

'You've seen my warrant card. Do you have the phone number of the local police station?'

'I do.'

'Then phone them up, tell them Detective Inspector Gary Haddock is at your gate, and you're refusing entry. Also, tell them that your daughter's sleepover friend, Rebecca Griffith, is not in your house but with the pathologist, fished out of the water at Rose Bay Marina two hours ago.'

'Dead?'

'Probably murdered, but that's to be confirmed.'

The gate opened.

Inside the mansion was a sweeping staircase up to the first floor, then down a wide carpeted corridor to the bedroom of Rebecca Griffith's friend.

'Sorry about that outside, can't be too careful, threats against the family,' the man said, now identified as Alexey Sidorov, born in Australia to Russian parents, the head of a finance company in Sydney, who had been born poor, but had made himself rich by hard work and a quick mind.

Sidorov had told him that much after the gate opened and that with wealth comes concerns about personal safety. Haddock knew there was more to the story, but it wasn't his concern, not now, but the dead fifteen-year-old was, and her friend was slow in opening the door.

After the father's third bang on the door, Haddock put his shoulder to it and pushed, the door lock breaking easily. So much for security, he thought.

Inside, disarray.

'That's how she likes it.'

It didn't look like that to Haddock. He had a teenager of his own, he knew the mess they made, and this wasn't it. It was a sign of violence.

'Better to wait outside,' Haddock said.

Before proceeding further, he took out his phone and pressed the speed dial. Natalie answered.

'Wolseley Crescent, Point Piper, you've got the address. Send back up.'

'Murder?'

'No idea, taking precautions.'

Ending the call, Haddock turned to the anxious father. 'Stay back. Someone else might be in here.'

The father wasn't ready to listen and rushed into the room.

'Maria, are you in here?' he shouted.

Realising the situation was out of control, Haddock had no option but to enter, his firearm drawn.

A muffled sound from the en suite; inside a bound and gagged woman.

'Where's Maria?' Sidorov shouted, increasingly panicked as he looked around the room, under the bed, and out the window.

Unbound and ungagged and shaking violently, the young woman spoke. 'I couldn't see who it was.'

'Your name?'

'Rebecca Griffith.'

There had been a misidentification of the dead body. Haddock phoned Natalie to update her, although she had been with Rebecca's father. He had seen the body at the pathologist's and knew an error had been made.

'Crime Scene Investigators, pronto,' Haddock said. 'Whoever it is, is making mistakes. No idea why here, and why confront two women and only murder one.'

'Maria, Maria,' Sidorov said. He was slouched on the floor, his head in his hands.

'Her mother?'

'Passed away two years back, cancer. It was just Maria and me. Is it her that you found?'

'Only one way to find out.'

Haddock realised that sympathy was needed, although he felt cold, impassive, and only interested in the investigation.

Rebecca's father was on the way in Natalie's car. Haddock was on his way with Sidorov to identify a body.

The murder investigation had moved forward, evidence was accumulating, and criminal profiling still made no sense. Haddock knew it wasn't the last murder they would experience and that the perpetrator's modus operandi would continue to change. Statistically, it was a man who had committed the murder, but he was making sure to leave no clues.

It was as if the person was intimate with criminology, the law and the police. Also, the person was psychopathic, and the value of life meant nothing, nor did the anguish they caused. This would be a difficult person to capture.

***

Alexey Sidorov was a broken man. A wife who had died of cancer, a daughter who had died from violence. The wealth he had acquired, the luxuriousness of the mansion, and the top-of-the-range Mercedes Benz amounted to nothing.

Maria Sidorov, the apple of his eye, was not as pure as her father thought. Apart from her untidy room, she was rebellious, as was the resurrected Rebecca Griffith. A sleepover at the Sidorovs did not imply girlish talk of boys but the chance to experiment with recreational drugs and watch pornography on Maria's laptop.

In the following days, pathology confirmed that Maria had died before entering the water. There had been no sexual violation, although she was not a virgin at fifteen. Strangulation had been the cause of death, and she had been thrown into the harbour from the jetty stretching out from the back of the Sidorov mansion, in plain sight of other mansions and jetties. It had been late at night, three hours before the body had been discovered, an incoming tide moving the body from Wolseley Crescent down to the marina.

Haddock was unsure of the direction to take in the investigation. The CSIs had found signs of where the young woman had died and a piece of rope, unquestionably the murder weapon. The murderer had arrived by water and left the same way, in a kayak or a small rowing boat.

Multiple skills had been shown by the murderer, and Ruth Stein, the criminal profiling expert, was at the police station in Kings Cross. She had offered her opinion the first time, placing much of it on her years of expertise, and had been right in certain areas but had not advanced the investigation or halted the deaths.

However, Haddock had superiors, and they wanted answers, proof that every avenue was being considered, no stone unturned, and no lead not followed up.

'I take it you've investigated how he arrived at the place,' Ruth Stein said.

'We have,' Natalie replied, siding with Haddock, that out on the street, talking to people, looking for a clue, old-style policing would be more beneficial than theorising.

'It's clearly a man,' Stein said.

'Why?' Haddock asked. He was sure it was, but he needed something that would look good on his reports besides his gut feeling. Senior police officers, confined to their offices, playing office politics, looking to get a lift up in the hierarchy, didn't appreciate gut feelings, but Haddock believed in them. There was something niggling him, something that made no sense.

'Modus operandi.'

Irritated, Haddock responded, 'What modus operandi? Each time, a different type of person, a different method of death, no sexual violence, either.'

'Women don't break into houses, tie up one teenager and murder the other.'

'Don't they?'

'Never,' Stein retorted.

Low-level feminism, Haddock thought, standing up for the sisterhood. But Ruth Stein was married with four children.

'I'd agree,' Haddock replied, 'but no sexual violation is out of character. If the man is out to demean women, that must be the ultimate act.'

'Ordinarily, I would agree. An added complexity. If, as we must agree, psychopathic, no compunction to kill, why stop short of intercourse?'

'He's playing with us, throwing us a bone to catch, grabbing it before we can take hold,' Natalie said. She had read up on the subject in the little spare time she had, case studies from the USA and England, found herself confused on occasions, realised that psychology was a complex subject that required a sharp mind, more than hers, which could be confused at times, subject to thoughts of love and career, the house she wanted to buy, wondering where the money would come from.

'Sergeant, Natalie, you're right,' Ruth Stein said. 'Not only does the man kill a homeless man, but he enters a house through an open door, then breaks into a heavily-fortified mansion, according to Inspector Haddock.'

Haddock realised that both women had revealed an oversight on his part.

'Dr Stein, please excuse us. Natalie and I have someone to talk to.'

'Nothing I said, I hope?'

'It was. Both of you. We know that Maria Sidorov wasn't a virgin, assuming that Rebecca Griffith, the apple of her father's eye, isn't also. Did the two girls plan to let someone in, probably a couple of youths?' Haddock said. 'Two young women on the cusp of adulthood, hormones in overdrive, a building large enough to bring a couple of boys in the back, while the father is out the front sweating over his money.'

'Exactly. And if they did plan this escapade, who else knew? The murderer? But how?' Natalie said.

'Or one of the two is the person we've been looking for. What would two fifteen-year-olds know? The age of ultimate belief in self, trusting too many, convinced they were invulnerable.'

Chapter 6

Rebecca Griffith arrived at Kings Cross Police Station at 9 a.m. with her father.

It was Saturday, no school that day, and the young woman wore designer jeans and a tee-shirt. Haddock thought she looked twenty; Natalie saw through the veneer of the clothes and the makeup and saw a child wrestling with adulthood, unsure of herself, and mentally frail when not surrounded by her peer group.

'Rebecca, good to see you are well,' Haddock said. Softly, softly, was the best approach, his sergeant had told him. Usually, he would have adopted the bull in the china shop approach, but he heeded his sergeant's opinion.

'Sad about Maria,' the softly spoken Rebecca said.

'Good friend?'

'The best.'

'We must ask questions. Answers you will not want to give, but we need to find this person. I hope you understand.'

'We've spoken about it,' Brandon Griffith said. 'I don't expect Rebecca to be the child I believe her to be. No point denying this; we were all young once and did silly things.'

'Still do,' Haddock said.

Natalie thought it a nice touch by the man to show humility and empathy with the Griffith family.

'It's embarrassing,' Rebecca said.

'If you prefer your father not to be in the interview room, we could ask your mother to be here,' Natalie said.

'Mum would throw a fit; Dad will only be upset.'

'Good. First question. Did you have drugs in the room? We didn't find any.'

'We thought about it but decided not to. Maria comes from a Russian background. Her father can be a tyrant, angry if he finds out.'

'Violent towards her?'

'Never. She loved him dearly. He gave her a good life and treated her well. But Russian anger, fire and damnation.'

'Okay, we'll accept that, no drugs. We'll not ask if you tried them elsewhere, certain of the answer.'

'Thank you,' Rebecca's father said.

'You're in Maria's room, the two of you,' Haddock said. 'What were the plans for the night, a bottle of wine, a few movies, silly talk?'

'No plans to go out that night. Mr Sidorov is in trouble, financial according to Maria, not that she cared.'

'Why? It could have affected her lifestyle.'

'Not that I understand, but Mr Sidorov takes risks. Most pay off, and some don't. Even so, he worries about how much money he has, not how much he needs. Reckons it's how the rich keep score, that and the size of their houses.'

'Did he leave the two of you alone in the house?'

'He did. He knows we'll get up to mischief if we can, but he protects us, cameras everywhere, regular patrols by a security company.'

'Not on the water, though,' Natalie said.

'Not there.'

'Which is how you planned to sneak in a couple of visitors. Correct?'

'It was Maria's idea. She can be easy with her favours, back of the bike shed, although we don't have a shed at school, don't even go to the same school as her boyfriend.'

'An old term for a young woman,' Haddock said.

'That's Dad, euphemisms.'

'Where then?' Natalie asked.

'On the way home, an empty boat shed near her house. Sometimes, she would go there, other times at his house.'

'Regular boyfriend?'

'Not that her father knew; throw a fit if he did. Saw Maria as the vestal virgin, but she wasn't, not by a long way.'

'And he was coming over, bringing a friend?'

'Paddle a kayak under cover of darkness, tie up to the jetty, and then Maria would let them in.'

'Were you in favour?'

'Sort of.'

'Which means?'

'The other one, I knew him, but he wasn't my boyfriend, never had one, not like that. A crush on one, but I wasn't like Maria.'

'Here's one for the father to put his hands over his ears,' Natalie said.

'I know the question, certain of the answer. Ask Rebecca; I'll listen,' Griffith said.

'Are you a virgin?'

'Yes. Not that I'm prudish, nothing like that.'

'Then why?'

'I just thought I'd wait until I met someone I liked. Teenage love seems intense, but it's the hormones, lust without love. Maria didn't care. She wanted sex under her terms, not waiting for the right man.'

'Was the boyfriend the right man?'

'Brett Kline, I wasn't certain, but they seemed to have a bond.'

'Did they arrive?'

'No, never did, not even while I was bound in the bathroom. Although they might have. It was up to Maria to let them in, but she was gone.'

'And if Kline's friend had turned up, would you have had sex with him?'

'I'm sure I wouldn't. What we were doing was risky, and if Mr Sidorov had found out, Brett and his friend would have regretted it.'

'How?'

'Not violence, not with him. But he was a powerful man and would have sued Brett's and the other friend's families for all they were worth. He loved Maria, kind to her friends, as long as they weren't rampant males on the prowl, but cross the man, and you were history. Plenty of enemies, few friends.'

Both police officers could see that Rebecca Griffith was a sensible young woman, wise beyond her years, whereas Maria Sidorov, the indulged daughter of a wealthy man, had been emotionally weak and immature. It wasn't a crime on the young woman's part, only an observation of his, and she hadn't deserved to die for her naivety.

***

Natalie could only agree with Rebecca Griffith's summation of Maria Sidorov's boyfriend. A star athlete at his school, he was above average height, eighteen years of age and physically strong, judging by his bear-like handshake; the type of guy she would have swooned over when she was fifteen. His ambivalence over Maria's death and presence in the interview room belied an arrogance of superiority, a belief that he was one of the chosen ones, which Natalie knew he was in the rarefied atmosphere of socially and upwardly mobile Point Piper.

Haddock placed no credence on it, as he was also the son of Justice Kline, the cavorting ocean-going whoremaster who had been reluctant to give his details at Rose Bay Marina.

'Mr Kline,' Haddock said, addressing the younger Kline in the interview room, 'you were Maria Sidorov's boyfriend?'

'I was a friend. A boyfriend indicates permanency. It was casual, free agents.'

'Did she see it that way?'

'She said she did, but I doubt it. Impressionable, immature, finding her way in the world, a dead mother, a dictatorial father.'

Natalie could hear the father coming from the voice of the son. Brett Kline had been versed well in the technique to adopt at the police station.

'We have no reason to believe him dictatorial,' Haddock said. He didn't like the youth, confident that his initial impression was right this time. 'He was, according to Maria's friend and by his own admission, a strong-willed man, adversarial with those he dealt with, generous with his daughter.'

'I should state that I have met with Mr Sidorov professionally,' Justice Kline said.

'In court?'

'Twice I presided over financial disputes that he was involved in.'

'Your rulings?'

'Once, in his favour, once, against him. He is dictatorial, verbally aggressive, and demanding. Professionally, I made the only decision I could. I admire the man; he came from nothing and pulled himself up through hard work and intellectual savvy. My son, Brett, has only known wealth, and so had Maria Sidorov. They cannot understand what he had achieved.'

'Your background?' Natalie asked.

'One of our ancestors arrived in Australia in 1788 with the first fleet, something we are immensely proud of.'

'An officer?' Haddock asked.

'More credit to claim a convict. Our ancestor was sent to Australia for fraud, served his sentence, married a convict woman, and never returned to England.'

'Let us come back to Maria Sidorov,' Natalie said. 'She was murdered on or near the jetty at the back of her house. That night, you intended to visit, to bring a friend for Rebecca Griffith.'

'That was the plan, but it never happened. Peter Regan thought it a waste of time. Rebecca wasn't his type and was unlikely to come across.'

'By "come across", you mean sexual intercourse?' Natalie asked.

'Yes. Not blaming her, but he wasn't about to waste his time, and I wasn't going on my own.'

'Why?'

'The night was young, other fish in the sea.'

'Two-timing Maria?'

'We were open, other people. If I didn't meet with her, there was another.'

Justice Kline interjected, 'My son has been indulged, does not realise his callous disregard for the dead woman. He and Maria have always known privilege, but Rebecca Griffith has not. She comes from a good, moderately wealthy family but has known difficult times. You will also find that Peter Regan is a good person. Do not judge my son and Maria as you would them.'

It was a humble summing up by an experienced judge, full of rhetoric, short on substance. Impressive and well-spoken, it didn't advance the investigation into the murders of three persons.

Unimpressed with the lecture, Haddock allowed the eminent arbiter of justice and part-time lecher some leeway.

'Coming back to the night in question. Brett, you did not paddle up to Maria's house,' Haddock asked.

'Not that night.'

'Would it have been far?'

'Ten, fifteen minutes, not difficult.'

'Your kayak and the one used by Peter Regan?'

'At our house, on the other side of Point Piper, not used on the night, securely locked up.'

'Can you be sure?'

'I used mine in the morning, paddled down as far as Rushcutters Bay.'

'Witnesses?'

'Not at that time. I often paddle it.'

'What time did you hear about Maria Sidorov's death?'

Haddock realised there was an anomaly. Justice Kline had been at the marina. He had seen the dead woman. Even though she had been in the water for a few hours, she was still identifiable, although if the man had been exhausted, he wouldn't have studied the body, face down when washed up and soon covered with a sheet.

'Later that day, at school. The news filtered through that Maria was dead, and Rebecca had been bound and gagged.'

'Yet you made no attempt to contact the police.'

'With what? I wasn't there. Sure, I thought about it, but what could I have told you?'

'Your imminent arrival was why Maria had latched the door instead of double-locking. It was important to know why, and you had the answer.'

'Maybe I did, but I hadn't killed her. How was I to know that the police wouldn't suspect me? After all, I should have been there.'

Once again, vital evidence was delayed due to the natural reaction of innocent people not to become involved and not to reveal specific facts for fear of suspicion.

'Justice Kline, did you know the Sidorov family?' Natalie asked the question that Haddock had wanted to ask.

'As I've already told you. I knew Alexey Sidorov. I didn't know his daughter, although Brett had told me of her, not that he was slipping around to her house of a night time. If I had, I would have advised against it.'

'Due to Sidorov's nature?'

'He was a contentious man, easy to anger, ever easier to apply his prodigious mind to bring those who interfered in his and his family's life to heel. As I said, I admired the man.'

Chapter 7

The second of the young Lotharios intent on paddling to the Sidorov mansion, Peter Regan, was as Justice Kline had described. He was shorter than Brett, not as athletic, and certainly not as attractive, although he had an endearing personality. Polite, where Brett Kline had been arrogant, holding the door for Natalie to pass through, not attempting to flirt or to make sexist comments.

His visit to the police station had been a formality, as neither of the two young men had made the trip that night, but someone had. And if, as Rebecca had said, it still required Maria to open the door from the inside, how had the person entered?

Too many variables, too many unknowns.

'Brett was keen, but he had Maria,' Peter Regan said. 'I know Rebecca, like her as a friend, but no more. Brett didn't care who he went with; Maria wasn't the only one. Not sure if she knew.'

'In this liberated age?' Natalie said.

'I'm not criticising, but I'm told she used to advertise the wares at school, always smiling at the male teachers, seductive-like. Get her into trouble one day, although I suppose that's inappropriate to say now.'

'Do you suspect her of an inappropriate relationship with a teacher?'

'No. Sure, it happens, but her school is strict, and Maria wouldn't have had the opportunity, and the teachers knew of her father.'

'Peter, you were willing to kayak up to his house, aware of what would have happened if you'd been caught.'

'Brett didn't care, thought he was invulnerable, the law on his side.'

'Justice Kline wouldn't have used his position to personal advantage,' Haddock said. 'I've had dealings with the man, honourable, above reproach.'

Although he had not considered that the man had risked serious professional embarrassment after his night at sea with a group of easy women. That fact was likely to be revealed at a murder trial, even if it wasn't relevant, but the defence would look for every angle to get their client off the hook, and a compromised judge would lend weight to their lack of impartiality of the judicial system.

However, Haddock did not consider such matters. His job was to apprehend the murderer, to present the police evidence, to stand up in court and be questioned, answering factually as the prosecution eased him through; as the defence attempted to get him to contradict himself, and generally tease the jury with not only judicial impartiality, but police bias too.

Haddock knew that a conviction for what this person had done was inevitable, but they were dealing with someone smart and devious, Ruth Stein had said, leaning towards genius-level intellect, brilliance verging on madness.

It was a possibility, Haddock thought, but in Point Piper and the adjoining suburbs, high intellect was often assumed.

Regan continued. 'I had an early night; not sure what Brett did. He might have had another woman, might not. Truthfully, he's not that keen on females, but you know his father. A champion sportsman at school, head prefect next year, it wouldn't look good if he was not the stud he pretended to be.'

'Are you suggesting Maria was the only female?'

'Might be. Can't say I knew him well. Only with me, he knew I wouldn't betray his trust.'

'You are now,' Natalie said.

'Maria's murdered. I owe it to her. Brett didn't kill her, but it's a murder investigation. The truth invariably comes out.'

'It does,' Haddock said, impressed with the young man.

Natalie thought Peter Regan and Rebecca Griffith were a matched pair, wise beyond their years, sensible at an age when sense wasn't the driving force.

'Did you speak to anyone as to your plans?' Natalie asked. 'Only someone else made the trip out to the Sidorov house.'

'No one. The kayaks were at Brett's house, backs onto the water, no jetty, though. Did the person use one of the kayaks?'

'We can't be sure, and we've checked the Kline house. Access is not so easy. His father has security and alarms in place.'

'Which means someone saw us from a distance, but he would have needed to know about the arrangement with Maria.'

'Rebecca said that Maria was easy. Is that true?'

'Possibly, not that I can be sure. Flirtatious, always making suggestions, but she was a decent person, just a little wild. Enjoyed the notoriety as the daughter of Alexey Sidorov, the mysterious Russian; thought it sounded romantic, his background in Russia.'

'He was born in Australia,' Haddock said.

'She knew that, and so did we. But Maria liked to talk, and she was good at it. She was in the debating society at her school, debates with ours, convince anyone with her arguments.'

'We didn't see her as academic. Rebecca is.'

'With Maria, it came easy, the daughter of a smart man. Rebecca's a hard worker, studies, and does her homework. Maria just breezed through, no challenge for her, probably why she made up stories and chased Brett.'

'Did she know he wasn't the macho man he pretended to be?'

'I don't think they slept together that much, but in your teens, you've got to be seen as promiscuous, easy with your favours, something to do with the allure of the unknown, grown up and mature. But we're just kids; think we're not.'

'You're refreshingly honest,' Natalie said.

'Have to be with the police. And besides, I owe it to Maria, to Mrs Levine.'

'You knew her?'

'Not really, nobody did. I've seen her around and said hello in passing. Nothing against her or her husband. They minded their own business, didn't interfere with others.'

***

Haddock could see that the investigation focussed on Point Piper, although Natalie had to remind him of Old Joe in Kings Cross. If he, as the more experienced officer, continued to believe that all three murders were the work of one person, then one modus operandi, Point Piper, was not valid. The perpetrator was multi-suburb, multi-wealth, and multi-variable in how the murders were committed. Although someone had known about Brett Kline and Peter Regan's proposed visit to the Sidorov house. It was essential to know who, a vital clue, in that they weren't only observed, but had been overheard by the murderer, and two teenagers weren't likely to discuss it with an elder, certainly not their parents, nor their teachers, but their peers was a possibility. The reason why Brett Kline, Peter Regan, and Rebecca Griffith were in a restaurant in Darlinghurst with Natalie.

It had been Haddock's idea, a neutral location where the three would feel calm with an officer they could relate to. Natalie looked young and fresh; Haddock did not.

Natalie arrived early, casually dressed, wearing jeans and a loose-fitting blouse. The other three came after fifteen minutes, a table in the corner, the restaurant owner primed to give them space to breathe.

'Inspector Haddock?' Brett Kline said as he sat down, not before looking Natalie up and down. Natalie wasn't sure about Peter Regan's comment that Kline wasn't the macho man he portrayed.

'Not today. We need to talk, just us four, nice and cosy. I'm not much older than you; remember when I was your age, thought I was invincible.'

'So did Maria,' Regan said.

'Smart, confident, sleeping with Brett, I'm sure she did.'

'Not much sleeping,' Brett Kline interceded.

'Today, Brett, no loud mouthing. This is serious. Better order first.'

It was early morning, just after eleven, and the restaurant didn't open its doors until midday, enough time to speak and to eat. The two men ordered steak, and Rebecca ordered a salad.

'Vegetarian?' Natalie asked.

'Not particularly,' Rebecca answered.

Natalie ate a salad. Too many late nights, too many hurried meals, and she had noticed she was gaining weight.

'Here's the situation. I'll explain it in detail; hopeful you'll find it interesting,' Natalie said.

'All ears.' Brett had to offer an opinion.

'Shut up, Brett,' Rebecca said. 'Maria was my friend.'

'Sorry, can't help it sometimes. I'm sure you understand, Sergeant.'

'Natalie, no need for titles,' Natalie replied. 'Let me start. There have been three murders. Old Joe in Kings Cross, Miriam Levine and Maria Sidorov in Point Piper. If this was a big city, multiple homicides, we'd be inclined to say they were unrelated, but statistics tell us that there is a common thread that unites all three.'

'How do you know this?' Peter Regan asked.

'Inspector Haddock's instinct. He's gained it through years with the Homicide Squad. Admittedly, the thread is weak, and we could find a link between Miriam Levine and Maria, both residents of Point Piper. Old Joe is more complicated. Homeless, indigenous heritage, but he didn't go on about it. I knew him and spoke to him occasionally. Educated, grew up with a family in Wahroonga and attended a good school. Alcohol was his curse. But what we need to do is to focus on Maria.

'Someone knew of Maria and Rebecca at the Sidorov mansion. This person also knew Brett and Peter intended to visit, and they later decided against it. We need to know how; a clue that might lead us straight to the murderer.'

'Are you saying we were being watched?' Brett said.

'It's an assumption, although it's more complex. The murderer is organised and doesn't leave anything to chance. He wouldn't have been hanging around on the off-chance. That person knew exactly what was happening.

'Rebecca, you first. Who did you speak to, social media, texting, phone call?'

'Nobody, honestly. Maria wouldn't have told anyone, or I wouldn't have thought so. Could never be certain with her, as she did like to show off.'

'Brett.'

'I might have bragged about it at my school, but that means nothing. We all do, acting big, showing off, as Rebecca said.'

'Unlikely to be another pupil. It could be a teacher or an employee at either school. Anyone you can think of? Anyone who looks suss?'

'A few teachers and Maria could be flirtatious, rolling her eyes at a couple of them,' Rebecca said.

'Employees, janitors, handymen, administrative staff? A lot of gossip in a school, not difficult to overhear something,' Natalie said.

'We don't reckon the employees at our school. Cranbrook has new employees vetted,' Brett said. 'Tend to ignore them.'

'Because of their lowly status?'

'Some are contemptuous of our privilege. Some are recent immigrants, don't have sufficient skills in the English language to better themselves, and others are unambitious or slovenly. The school pays them minimum wage, but none would follow us or care what we did.'

'That's what I thought,' Natalie said. 'Teachers?'

'One or two are strange, but murder is something else,' Brett Kline said.

Natalie could see that underneath the false bravado, there was a decent person but that, amongst his peer group, he was unwilling to show it. Haddock would have said like father, like son.

'Specifics, anyone we should focus on. Who did Maria roll her eyes at? We believe this person to be secretive, academic, could even be the most innocuous person you would meet: polite, social, possibly a benefactor of the church.'

'A saint who murders,' Rebecca said.

'Could be, can't be sure. Murderers come in all shapes and sizes. I need names.'

Natalie left the three to compile a list of who they would consider and why. Brett Kline and Peter Regan would focus on Cranbrook in Bellevue Hill; Rebecca would concentrate on Kincoppal-Rose Bay on New South Head Road in Vaucluse.

***

Due to the sensitivity of approaching each school, Haddock set up a team at State Crime Command in Charles Street, Parramatta, twenty-four kilometres west of the harbour. The city was only ten months younger than Sydney, first settled in 1788, the furthest navigable point inland on the Parramatta River from Sydney Harbour. Originally it had been intended for farming, as the soil close to the small settlement in Sydney Cove was salty. Two centuries later, it had burgeoned into a metropolis no longer isolated from Sydney CBD. It was where the Homicide Squad was based and where Gary Haddock felt at home.

Natalie, who had accompanied him that first day, thought the building lacked charm. She preferred the intimacy of Kings Cross Police Station, its location close to the El Alamein Fountain, a short stroll to the cafes and the restaurants, and not far from the rowdy drunks of a weekend.

'We've got five names, two from Cranbrook, another three from Kincoppal,' Haddock said. 'We need to know everything about these people, no forewarning any of them. Internet use, websites they've watched, pornography, violent activist sites, and fundamentalism. Also, focus on their searches on young girls, specifically those at Kincoppal. Four days maximum, burn the midnight oil.'

Natalie could see the young constables were not enamoured of the task ahead, but she knew that Haddock was correct. If this person was whippet smart he would also sense a rat if she or her inspector were closing in. Better to act as though they were floundering, which they were, than go in empty-handed, asking dumb questions, receiving equally dumb answers in return. If the person was at one of the schools, it still left Old Joe out on a limb, and Natalie had begun to doubt Haddock's conviction that he had died at the hands of a serial killer.

'One issue we haven't considered,' Haddock said as he and Natalie drove back to Kings Cross.

'What is it?' Natalie asked. It was late in the afternoon, and the traffic was leaving the city, heading back to the suburbs that stretched out from Parramatta for thirty kilometres in any direction. The two police officers encountered little traffic, entering the office within thirty minutes. Natalie wanted an early night, a chance to meet friends, drink a bottle of wine and put her feet up.

'We assumed the murderer knew Kline and Regan wouldn't be there.'

'But he did.'

'Why?'

'He wasn't interested in them, only one of the women.'

'But, remember, he killed Old Joe, and neither woman had been sexually violated. When have you encountered violent crime against a woman when a sexual act hasn't been committed?'

'I've not had the experience you have. Sure, sex is a factor. We've even had prostitutes raped, and they're available for a hundred dollars off the street.'

'What if the murderer's modus operandi had changed again? What if he intended to kill any of the four or all of them? It places a different emphasis on Maria's death.'

It did, Natalie knew, but she couldn't buy into it. Mass murder wasn't a serial killer's style, although when had this murderer acted predictably: an old man, a devout housewife, and a teenage girl.

'Assuming there's validity in what you're saying, we still have to find out how this person knew. If we do that, we probably have a murderer, but what if he made it to Sidorov's mansion? Two women, but he was after four. Not so easy to subdue two young men, one physically strong, the other no slouch. And how did he get in, and why choose Maria?'

'Questions to be answered. Just a possibility, and I would agree it sounds implausible.'

Natalie left the station soon after. Haddock was off home, or was he, as he had driven off in the wrong direction. It wasn't for her to worry. The man was old enough to make his own decisions, but policing placed heavy demands on a marriage, and many had been seduced by alcohol and fast food, others by different distractions.

Chapter 8

Ruth Stein felt she had the measure of the killer, which she presented to Natalie and Haddock in a long-winded presentation at Kings Cross Police Station. Natalie was impressed by the thoroughness of it, unsure as to what it actually meant. Haddock had no difficulty with it, just thought it was intellectual babble, an attempt to gain credibility for providing nothing worthwhile other than the murderer was intelligent – didn't need a degree to know that, Haddock thought – and that the murdering spree wasn't over yet.

In short, Haddock decided that the investigating team was down one person, its criminal profiling expert. To him, it was pressing the flesh, sticking their noses in where they weren't appreciated, and walking the beat.

Early morning, the unlikely figure of Inspector Gary Haddock in a tee-shirt and swimming shorts. The first time he tried to enter the kayak, purloined from a local kayaking club, he had nearly tipped it over until Natalie grabbed him. On dry land at Rose Bay Marina, a kayaking aficionado showed him how to enter the kayak and gave him rudimentary tips on paddling.

Natalie needed no instruction. She had rowed for her school, and kayaking was second nature to her. The aficionado offered to come, but Haddock was polite but adamant.

'Need time to think and observe. Best done with just the two of us.'

Natalie wasn't sure the aficionado was appeased by Haddock's explanation, but he smiled and wished them both well. 'Watch out for the bull shark,' his parting comment as he waved the two off.

Haddock had outlined the plan. They were to paddle up to where Maria Sidorov had entered the water. The belief was that the murderer had also used a kayak, although Natalie wasn't convinced. Haddock couldn't believe that anyone would swim in a wetsuit with a waterproof bag tied to them.

It took a laborious twenty-five minutes to reach the first waypoint on their watery adventure, the Sidorov jetty. It jutted out into the harbour, longer than most, shorter than some. In a part of Sydney where substance often triumphed over style, Haddock knew it would have once been of concern to Alexey Sidorov. The noble cruiser that had been moored there, named after the dead daughter, was gone.

Since Maria Sidorov had died, her father had become reclusive, and then he had gone overseas, and now the mansion was for sale. Natalie was sad to see it in darkness. The only sign of life was a security guard who stood on the jetty. He was armed, which concerned Natalie.

'What's your game?' the guard shouted. Haddock recognised the accent and the man's surly attitude: Eastern European.

'Detective Inspector Haddock, Homicide, and my colleague is Sergeant Natalie Campbell,' Haddock shouted back.

'Identification?'

'Not on me, not dressed like this. Phone the local police station, certain you've got it on speed dial. Licence for that gun?'

'Mr Sidorov is wary of uninvited strangers. I've got a licence. Check with my company. They'll confirm.'

The guard made the call. After that, his attitude changed. The two police inspectors stood on the jetty; both had a hot drink in their hands, courtesy of the guard.

'Russian?' Haddock asked.

'The poor cousin.'

No further comment was needed. Those with the money always ensured employment for a relative, no matter how demeaning and poorly paid.

'Did you know Maria?'

'She worried Alexey sometimes, her wild behaviour. But they were devoted to each other, especially after his wife, her mother, died.'

'No worse than many others,' Natalie said. 'I went through the phase.'

'No doubt you did, but you didn't live in Point Piper. It makes a difference.'

'How?'

'Maria wanted her freedom, a typical Australian teenager's freedom. No problem with that, but Alexey upset people, dangerous people, and Maria could have been leverage.'

'No leverage in murder,' Haddock said.

'He worried about kidnapping, something nasty happening to her, rape, that sort of thing.'

'We always believed he was an honest man who played a hard game.'

'He was honest, but he didn't get this mansion, nor his lifestyle, by being a pushover, not that it means much to him now. He's a broken man.'

'You saw him when he left the country?'

'Took him to the airport, wished him well, kissed him on both cheeks, Russian style. He won't come back here.'

'He'll stay in Russia?'

'He took mementoes of Maria to bury in the family vault. One year, maybe two, and he'll be in it.'

'Ill?'

'Broken heart. He'll pine away.'

'And this place?'

'Who knows? It's for sale, but the debtors and his so-called business colleagues will be sucking his bones dry. No one to stand up to them other than his lawyer, but he's a bloodsucker. Sell his soul to those picking over Alexey's bones. Make sure he gets a slice of the pie.'

So far, Haddock and Natalie hadn't travelled far, but they hadn't expected to meet one of Sidorov's cousins. The man might have knowledge that only an inconsequential member of the man's family would know. Although how that would relate to Old Joe and Miriam Levine wasn't clear.

Haddock realised they wouldn't be paddling further that day, for which he was thankful. Natalie called the aficionado and asked if he would come up with another kayaking devotee and paddle the kayaks back to Rose Bay Marina.

Natalie changed out of her seafaring clothing, which caused the poor cousin to take a glance her way. He liked what he saw.

She should have been embarrassed but could only smile. Not the easiest of lives, the poor cousin of an exceptionally wealthy individual.

'What do you reckon?' Haddock asked.

'Of Maria?' the guard replied.

'What else? Do you reckon someone came by water? You must know the house better than the police.'

'Worked here on and off for three years. Sometimes, no security other than alarms and cameras. Frankly, they're sufficient, and I'm here because he worries that someone might get in and look for incriminating evidence against his business interests.'

'Doesn't sound like someone who's gone to the old country to die,' Natalie said.

'He'll die. Before he left, he said, "Dima, I'll be back; see you, right. Look after this place for me while I'm gone; move in if you want."'

'Have you?'

'A small bedroom at ground level.'

'He acts like he's not given up, but you're saying he has.'

'We grew up together. Proud people, wear our hearts on our sleeves. His pride wouldn't allow him to show what he thought, but I knew him better than he knew himself. He thought he was a Western entrepreneur and acted the part, but blood is thicker than water, and the pull of the old country is still there. After a month, he'll be drinking vodka, sitting in the village square with the elders, and eyeing up the young women.'

'It sounds idyllic,' Natalie said.

'Romanticised. Freezing cold in the winter, mosquitos in the summer. Poor and backward, but Alexey will embrace it.

After all, what has he here? People after his money, a wife and daughter cremated. What would you choose? What would anyone choose if they could turn back the clock, go back to a simpler time?'

Haddock knew the cousin was right. He, a police inspector, lived in a red-brick three-bedroom house. He had grown up in a fibro shack with a lawn at the front, a vegetable patch at the rear, and church on a Sunday. He was happier then but could not go back, but Sidorov had.

'Born in Australia?'

'Russia, until I was ten, came out when it became difficult. My father's dead. He tried to make a go of it and loved Australia but could never master the language. My mother lives in the Blue Mountains near the escarpment, wakes up to the sound of magpies carolling, and goes to sleep with the kookaburras laughing. As for me, a one-bedroom apartment in Chippendale, inner-suburb drab and dreary.'

'Not got Alexey's talents?' Haddock said. He was sitting down on a chair in the garden. The sun was rising, and his muscles ached from balancing the kayak and paddling.

'Not many have. Either you're born with it, or you aren't. I did well at school and could have done better, but I'm lazy and unambitious. Alexey never stopped and would have worked himself into an early grave, but he's got that now. Only it's the sadness that will kill him.'

'What's your take on Maria's death? To us, it doesn't make sense. Why risk running into the two women, Maria and Rebecca, and then the young Lotharios, Kline and Regan.

'Maria used to get up to mischief in the boat shed near here. Alexey knew.'

'Knew or suspected?'

'Knew. Alexey doesn't work on assumptions. He would have seen her there, or someone was paid to watch out for her.'

'Paid, private investigator?'

'Security. She wanted freedom, but he had someone close by most of the time.'

'The poor cousin?' Natalie asked.

'Famous or infamous depends on who you're talking to. Russell Harding.'

'We know him,' Haddock said.

'Well, I don't,' Natalie said. She wasn't about to keep quiet while two men discussed another. She wasn't that proud she couldn't admit to a defect in her knowledge of local villains and heroes, confident that the security guard's statement indicated the man could be both.

'Celebrities in town from overseas, the vacuous and the plain stupid, the types that adorn magazines and reality shows.'

'Burly and beefy?'

'Neither. Harding's a short man, knee-high to a grasshopper. He's behind the scenes, checks out a hotel before they enter, a restaurant before they sit down, and the chauffeur before they sit in the car. Protects them from unwanted intrusion, hidden cameras and microphones.'

'Snooping for Sidorov, part of his job?'

'Maria was,' the guard said. 'Alexey worried about her, but he knew it would be impossible to curtail her enthusiasm for making a fool of herself, and Kline was tolerated. Alexey had the father on a short leash, don't ask with what, I don't know, probably wouldn't understand. If another young stud had come sniffing, he wouldn't have got far.'

'So, we have the father worried about his daughter and Russell Harding keeping a watch out for her. And then she's murdered at the back of the mansion while the father is at the front. If I was suspicious, I'd say something was amiss.'

'And you'd be right. This place is Fort Knox, with alarms and cameras front and back. If Kline was coming, Alexey chose to let it happen.'

'Makes no sense,' Haddock said.

'Alexey was a complex man, not easy to understand. A tyrant with others, a pussy cat with his daughter, and she was as fiery as him. A firm hand with her, gentle and loving, ease her through her stupidity, and she'd be fine, take over the business from him in time.'

'You're very knowledgeable,' Natalie said. 'More so than a security guard.' She was suspicious of the man. Too good to be true.

'I observe and learn from the man, but I'm not ambitious, only want to survive. What Alexey had looked impressive but came at a cost, his wife and daughter.'

'But she died from cancer.'

'His wife, exhausted by the demands of maintaining the pretence of the perfect hostess for the social climbers around here.'

'Did Alexey know?'

'He set high standards, not that he was the perfect husband, had a mistress.'

'And the wife knew?'

'She would have expected him to. She was from the same area in Russia and understood.'

'He drove her to an early grave?' Haddock asked. He was also starting to have suspicions about the guard, not that he had yet spoken to Natalie about it.

'He placed demands on her, not that she would have objected, but she needed rest. She wouldn't blame Alexey, not with the life he gave her, but sometimes there are other considerations.'

'Maria, did he place demands on her?' Natalie asked.

'He expected her to take her education seriously, play when she had to, and take responsibility when demanded.'

'And as the future Sidorov overlord, she was allowed a great deal of leeway.'

'There was no son, only a daughter. She also understood the reality and that her father would allow indiscretions in her youth.'

'Not a mistress, but other men if she was married.'

'It would have been expected, and Kline was controlled by the father. Talk to Russell Harding, and push him hard. The man's a weasel, but he's no fool, knows the dirt on people other than the Sidorovs.'

Chapter 9

Further confusion occurred one day after Haddock and Natalie's adventure on Sydney Harbour.

It looked like an accident. An elderly woman had fallen over a balcony, a drop of ten metres onto concrete. A retirement home in Vaucluse, another enclave of the wealthy, less than seven kilometres from Kings Cross Police Station, less than four from where Miriam Levine and Maria Sidorov had both died. The murderer was moving east, and if he continued in that direction, he would soon have to turn south towards Bondi Beach, easy pickings with the backpackers, the tourists, and the crowded beach of a weekend.

Ruth Stein wanted to offer an opinion, but Haddock had done with intellectual theorising; he was out on the street, observing, postulating, attempting to get into the mind of a killer. He had done it before, a gruesome murder out to the west of Sydney: Mount Druitt, working class, humble immigrants and citizens. Those in the rarefied atmosphere of affluent Point Piper and Vaucluse wouldn't understand, but it was where Haddock felt comfortable. Out there, fifty kilometres from Kings Cross, there was another world, edgy, petty crime, hoons in loud motor cars, people trying to survive, to make enough money to put food on the table for the family, to deal with religious intolerance and bigotry.

Two warring families separated by four houses in Sydney, united by a village in Calabria. The son of one, eighteen and argumentative, a potential scholar, but ingrained with the violence and feuding back in Italy, had killed the other family's son in a heated argument outside a shopping centre. It had been late at night, warring hoodlums, bored with the monotony, taking drugs, acting big, one drawing a knife on the other, lunging forward, egged on by others, a dead youth on the ground.

Haddock had arrested the youth, enough witnesses to ensure a conviction, and enough anger in the offender to own up to his crime: 'He had it coming to him.'

Three days later, a bullet was fired into the house of the offender, his ten-year-old sister, an innocent casualty, as the bullet slammed into her head as she was doing her homework.

After that, others in the areas, three families he counted, taking sides, jostling in the street, shouting vulgar insults, and threatening.

Haddock had read up on feuds in Southern Italy and understood how so much anger could remain, not helped by the impoverished conditions in which the two primary families found themselves. Life had been tough in the old country; it hadn't improved in Australia. He spent time with both families and found he had empathy, not that that prevented him from arresting the drive-by shooter and charging him with murder. Although, after six months, an uneasy truce was brokered by Haddock and counselling. He understood the rationale that drove people to commit heinous crimes against others. He wondered if the same could be applied to the current case.

Initially, it seemed an elderly woman had lost her footing while looking over the balcony. It had been the crime scene investigators who had found an error with the initial conclusion.

'The balcony railing was too high, the woman too immobile. The angles are wrong; if she had slipped, she would have gone backwards and smashed her head against the railing. No doubt about it, she was grabbed from behind and thrown over; a nasty way to go,' the CSI said.

Mary Otway was eighty-three years old, a champion sportswoman in her youth and an entrepreneur later. Wealthy enough to have afforded the nursing home, she had never married and had no children; a brother flying down from Queensland and a cousin coming up from Melbourne.

Of the building's two hundred and forty-one persons, one hundred and eighty-two were permanent residents; the remainder were ancillary staff and administrators.

Natalie conducted a count and reasoned that only twenty-six residents would have been able to commit the crime but all the ancillary staff and administrators could.

However, it was complicated because visitors came in and out regularly and weren't thoroughly checked.

Gary Haddock left his sergeant to it. He had come to trust her, ambivalent at first: too young, wet behind the ears, didn't drink beer or swear. But he had been wrong, as she was bright, picked up the fundamentals of a murder investigation quickly, and was trustworthy. Unlike his previous offsider who had run a red light while drunk, hit by a prime mover, dead at the scene, she wouldn't let him down. Once this investigation was over, he'd bring her into Homicide if she was interested, which he was confident she was.

CCTV at the retirement home had been checked. Cameras on every floor, corridor, and at the home's entry and exit points. The exit concerned the retirement home more, as those residents cognisant of the reason they were there, hostile in some cases, would occasionally make a break for the freedom outside. Those with dementia tended to wander off, and one a few years back had managed to get as far as the busy road before being hit by a car; one less resident.

Natalie waited for the brother to arrive, spoke to him, and asked him to identify his sister; he agreed. After that, she left the building with no more to do or additional evidence for the police to work with.

***

Haddock remembered Ruth Stein's opinion that serial killers don't live within a one- to two-kilometre buffer zone of a murder but would live close by. However, these murders had not radiated out from a central point but had almost been in a straight line from Old Joe in Kings Cross – strike one Stein theory. Also, she had focussed on the modus operandi, a similarity in how the deaths had occurred – strike two, and that the crimes would become more violent – strike three. He realised that the forensic psychologist / criminal profiler did not have a good track record with the current murders. The only point he would agree on with the woman was that the murderer was intelligent, able to kill a homeless man, a devout Jewish woman in her house, an indulged daughter of a wealthy man, and now, an old woman. In summation, he realised he had nothing to go on, no theories, no thoughts other than to tread the pavement and see if there were anomalies.

One thought came to him as he stood outside the retirement home, which he had seen once before. On the balcony where the woman had fallen, Haddock stood and looked. In the distance, the Sidorov mansion was clearly visible. He had observed from the Sidorovs' that he had seen the roof of the Levines' house; although he had not looked from Kings Cross over to the Levines', he knew he would not see it, and even if he did, what would it mean? Murders weren't committed based on their visibility from each other. He dismissed it as errant nonsense.

The weather was cool; he felt fitter than he had for the last few weeks. In the car, a pair of runners, a feeble attempt at keeping himself healthy. Complaints from his wife about his poor physical condition and from another about his inability to satisfy her. He realised his wife didn't deserve deceit, but life was hard, and he needed the diversion. It was an excuse he intended to continue to use, disappointed in himself that he had to, aware that Sergeant Natalie Campbell knew, not that she had questioned him, but she would. And what would he say? The spirit is willing but the flesh is weak. It was a lame excuse. He would be ashamed to use it, but he would.

His career had stagnated, his senses blunted by too much societal malignancy, and now an old woman was dead. Although what saddened him the most was the fifteen-year-old girl on the cusp of adulthood, two months older than his daughter. She was calmer, or he thought she was. Maybe she wasn't, but he didn't have Russell Harding, only himself, and he couldn't spy on his child, regardless of his concerns.

He covered two kilometres down New South Head Road, heading back to where Maria Sidorov and Miriam Levine had died, and realised that the day was becoming warmer and he was sweating. It was a pointless exercise, good in theory but poor on reflection. On the way back to the retirement home, it was uphill, and he had neither the energy nor the inclination to walk back. Instead, he hailed a passing taxi, surprised that it was vacant, even more so when he sat in the front seat alongside the driver.

'Long time, Haddock,' the driver said. 'Don't remember me, do you?'

Haddock never forgot a face, although the youthful glow of the driver had been replaced by a heavy-set man with a voluminous beard. 'Colin Keys,' he said. 'Five years, Long Bay Prison, robbery with menace.'

'You arrested me, ensured I went to prison. Not that I hold it against you after all these years.'

'How long ago? Thirteen, fourteen years.'

'Fourteen years, served my time, met my wife due to you.'

'How?'

'Social worker. She used to visit me in prison and was assigned my case on my release. We've been married for ten years, three children.'

'Crime?' Haddock asked. He remembered the man from before. Apart from the crime, he had been charismatic, agreeable, and not demonstrative or criticising when arrested and had taken his punishment as a man.

'No reason. Back then, times were tough for a lot of us. A downturn in the economy, no skill other than manual labour. But with prison and then Julia, my wife, I sorted myself out, make decent money driving taxis. You're involved with these murders?'

'I am. No leads to go on, dead end at this time. I thought I'd pace the pavement, try to get a new perspective on the murders, convinced it's the one person. No idea why, and my sergeant's not convinced.'

'Why are you?'

'Instinct, a police officer's best tool. Also, statistics. Homicides are rare, and now four in the area, almost a straight line from one to the other. He's playing us for fools, making a good job of it.'

'Inspector Haddock, buy me a coffee. You did me a favour once. I owe you one in return.'

Belle Café on the corner of Laguna Street and New South Head Road in Vaucluse; two men, one a police inspector, the other a former criminal. Haddock treated himself to bacon, eggs, and a latte; Colin Keys ate cheesecake and drank orange juice. It was two men who should have had nothing in common, a seething condemnation from the one who had been sent to prison courtesy of the other, but instead, bonhomie.

'The favour?' Haddock said.

'I drive around the Eastern Suburbs, six days out of seven, the occasional late-night shift. Taxi drivers are like police officers. They see a lot and sense when something's not right. It was a few weeks back, eleven in the evening. Business was quiet, and I thought to go home, sleep, and be out on the road early the next day, pick up a few forlorn people standing at a bus stop.'

'Something happened?'

'I had pulled up to a taxi rank in Kings Cross, although virtually every job comes from a phone app these days. I'm just sitting there, and there's a knock on the taxi's roof. A drunk, I thought, but if he's coherent and he's got the money, why not.'

'And then?'

'He was medium height, in his forties, not that I could get a good look at him. He says he's on holiday and would I drive him around. It's late at night, nothing to see in the dark, but he's adamant and it's easy money. Drive past the Finger Wharf in Woolloomooloo, then along New South Head Road, take in Rushcutters Bay, Double Bay, Point Piper, past Rose Bay, up through Vaucluse and down to Bondi Beach.'

'You gave him the tour?'

'I did. It came to over two hundred dollars. He paid cash and gave me a fifty-dollar tip. I don't think he was a local. Thought no more about it that night, although it was weird. From what I could tell, he wasn't drunk.'

'Where else did you drive, apart from where you said?'

'We diverted a few times, up this street, down another, passed close by every location there had been a murder.'

'Why didn't you come to the police before about this?'

'What would they say? You're straight, Haddock. A lot aren't. A few would have said I was an ex-con out to make trouble. And, besides, I didn't make the connection until you got in the car.'

Unfortunately, Haddock knew that Keys was correct. A convicted man offering the police information to solve another crime would have been regarded with suspicion.

'You're right. Good that I hailed you,' Haddock said.

It wasn't only instinct that a police officer acquired with time. There was also being in the right place at the right time; the visibility gained on the street, not in a police station. Others would say it was luck that he had encountered Colin Keys, but Haddock didn't believe in the concept. He had persisted and been rewarded.

'Busy day?' Haddock asked.

'Not particularly. I can spare a few hours.'

'Two questions. Would you recognise this man if you saw him again? And, apart from the tip, why did you think he wasn't local?'

'Nobody tips, not in Australia. That was a giveaway.'

'Unless he'd been overseas for a long time, a damn nuisance in some countries.'

'I might recognise him, but he wasn't special, and it was late at night; only the other cars' headlights lit his face. He sat in the back seat and asked me to show him the highlights. Everyone asks for Bondi Beach, but it's up the back streets where you see how the people live. Kings Cross didn't interest him. He commented on the homeless, much less than overseas, he reckoned. Which means he could have spent time overseas.

'I drove past the Levines' house, knew the wife, as sometimes she'd take a taxi. Also, Sidorov's mansion in Wolseley Crescent. And then up here, down Laguna Street; I told him it was the best retirement home in Sydney, which it is. A two-hour trip, and I was home by one-thirty in the morning. No more to tell you.'

'Accent? Australian?'

'Australia or New Zealand, certainly not English, Irish or Scottish, and not foreign.'

'Local? Or might have been once?'

'Can't be certain. He made out he wasn't from around here. As I said, weird at the time, but then I get the occasional crazies in the vehicle, tend to not think about them after they've paid their money, too many people in and out.'

Haddock could sense he was onto something. He phoned Natalie to join them at the café. She was only five minutes from where they sat.

Keys recounted his story to Natalie, corrected by Haddock when he embellished it. An attractive woman, Keys needed to elaborate; factual with a grizzled police inspector. But facts were significant, and, with additional recounting, hidden details from the recess of the mind would reveal themselves.

'Put Colin in prison,' Haddock said. 'Reckons I did him a favour.'

'Doesn't sound like a favour,' Natalie said.

'It was,' Keys said. 'Look at me now, Sydney's premier taxi driver, helping the police. In Long Bay, you'd be lucky to not get a thumping for snitching.'

'For helping to solve a murder?'

'After the event, they might apologise. But it's the young girl that sticks in the throat. Do you reckon the person I picked up might have killed her?'

'We need to find him, our best lead so far. Where did you drop him off? Back at Kings Cross?'

'Bondi Beach. Said he wanted to walk on the sand and dip his toes in the ocean. It was a ruse, wanted to get rid of me. Last I saw of him, he's on the Esplanade.'

Haddock and Natalie noted what Keys had told them, but for now it would be on the backburner, not because it didn't have relevance, but late at night, a mysterious stranger, almost impossible to find. Neither police officer gave much credence to what Keys had told them, other than it had been a welcome diversion on a trying day.

Chapter 10

Natalie had heard mention of the man: insignificant and short. She thought the security guard's and Haddock's comments about the man were derogatory and incorrect. It was a surprise when the two of them met him.

Russell Harding was short, not a dwarf but below average height. He was dressed in a suit, off the shelf from what Natalie could see, a white shirt and tie, black leather on his feet. He was Mister Insignificant; Mister Average. He was forgettable.

'Is this about Maria Sidorov?' Harding said. The three were in Harding's office, located above a shop in Rose Bay. It was as insignificant as the man, lacking any touches that transformed from functional to pleasant. A small light to the back of the man was the only light in the room, apart from a window that looked out to the harbour.

'It is,' Haddock replied. He had heard of the man but never met him. In fact, hardly anyone had. A house in Bellevue Hill, a Mercedes to drive when he ventured into where the wealthy lived, a nondescript Toyota of indeterminate vintage when he didn't.

Natalie could see he was comfortable in his skin, with no intent to emulate those in the area. Sidorov, she thought, had chosen his man well.

'Official?'

'It is.'

'Very well. What do you know?'

'Questions we should be asking you.'

'I need a reference point, somewhere to start. You're here because my name has been mentioned as an associate of Alexey Sidorov. Am I correct?'

'You are.'

'Few people know this, so I assume it's that stupid cousin of his. Correct?'

'We didn't believe him to be stupid, but yes.'

'Unimportant. Alexey asked me to watch out for his daughter, to inform him if she overstepped certain boundaries.'

'Did she?'

'Apart from an unfortunate relationship with Kline's son, rarely. Alexey was a realist and understood he couldn't keep her under lock and chain, not that he wanted to. He was devoted to her; she to him. They were alike in many ways, pushing the limit, encountering resistance and backing off or pushing through.'

'You mentioned associate,' Natalie reminded Harding.

'I watched Maria, not day and night, but occasionally and discreetly. Alexey did not want her to feel harassed.'

'Did she know?'

'I believe so, not that I ever spoke to her. I never even met her, only watched from a distance. Those he dealt with in business wouldn't touch her, but others might. I don't believe her murder is related to her father, but another reason.'

'Nor do we,' Haddock said. 'But you're a man who observes, sees the minutiae that others don't.'

'People see more than they think but don't focus or remember; I do. Maria was involved with Kline's son, an adolescent romance.'

'Sexual intercourse,' Natalie said.

'Yes, but it was brief, in a boat shed or at his house. There were no weekends away, no chance of her getting pregnant. Alexey knew, didn't like it, but told me to not become involved and to report back to him. She was underage, and Brett Kline was guilty of a crime, but his father was under Alexey's control.'

'That's the second time it's been mentioned,' Haddock said.

'The security?'

'Yes.'

'I told Alexey that he couldn't be trusted. Alexey would tell me whenever I broached the subject, "Harding, he's a cousin. You'd not understand."'

'I understood. It was a weakness of Alexey's to trust his relatives. But this is Australia, not a Russian village in Siberia or wherever. Alexey had been born in Sydney, and the guard had lived here since he was young. Alexey held onto the old ways, not certain the guard did, too poor to maintain traditions.'

'You've not answered what associate meant,' Natalie reminded Harding.

'Maria was his primary concern, but he had competitors, people he dealt with. He needed to know their peccadilloes, whether they could be coerced, and who was behind them, violent or otherwise. Frankly, his life wasn't one I would choose. I prefer to be secretive and aloof.'

'But you're not that here; more verbose than mysteriously silent.'

'This is official, and I saw how she handled herself with her friends and the young studs. She was Alexey, a worthy successor. Also, I do feel guilt over her death, not that I saw the possibility, never saw suspicious characters lurking, and it wasn't my job to watch her 24/7.'

'No guilt to you,' Natalie said.

'Even so,' Harding said. 'What do you have? Is it tied in with the other deaths?'

'I believe they are,' Haddock said. 'Sergeant Campbell is not so sure. No common link to them.'

'Apart from the fact that homicides do not occur that often in Sydney. Inspector Haddock's right on this. Not sure what the connection is. Levine was an oddball but harmless. The old woman, nothing to say about her, kept to herself most of the time.'

'Did you know her?'

'I've been in this office for the last thirty-two years, not many people that I don't know of. I knew her by sight, doubt if I ever spoke to her.'

'We've not released her name,' Natalie said.

'Unimportant. I knew her name before you did, ears and eyes.'

Haddock knew what Harding was referring to. From the small office, Harding knew people who knew people, who would gossip and pass him knowledge as needed.

'If you believe there might be a connection, it would help if you were forthcoming.'

'You're the police. I'm just a private investigator looking in windows, peering through keyholes. Why should I know more than you?'

'No more keyholes; find more on the internet,' Natalie said.

Natalie found the man intriguing, if elusive, as though he was playing with them, that he knew more but wouldn't reveal it. There had to be a reason. 'Why are you holding back?' she said.

'I have suspicions, nothing more. Speculation based on what I know and have gleaned over the years. Besides, Inspector Haddock had never met me, and you hadn't heard of me. I'm not sure I should trust you,' Harding replied.

'You have a civic duty to assist,' Haddock said.

Natalie thought he was more forceful than he should have been. Russell Harding was not a man to respond to a threat or a plea to his soul. She could see he was an impassive man who was not given to anger or joy and maintained a detached demeanour.

'Civic, you might say. I would not. I don't get involved with the police and do my job confidentially without any criminal intent or act. I choose not to become involved, aware my credibility would be compromised by those who trust me.'

'Even so, we're floundering, and you know something.'

'I'll tell you a story,' Harding said. 'How you deal with it is up to you. But first, we will eat. I will order for us; we will eat in the office. Is that acceptable?'

'It is.'

Even though the office was austere, the food wasn't. It was delivered by the restaurant, complete with plates and cutlery.

It was haute cuisine, and Natalie loved it. Harding would have preferred takeaway, but he still ate with relish. A fine bottle of red wine was shared by all three.

At the end, a waiter from the restaurant arrived and cleared away. After what seemed an eternity, Harding returned to what he had been talking about.

'I could say, once upon a time, but I'll resist the temptation. Let me say that this is off the record; no names will be mentioned.'

'Understood,' Haddock said, although he didn't.

'We're going back twenty-five years, maybe longer. A woman took a younger man as her lover.'

'Toy boy?' Natalie said.

'Not so much a toy, but they were enamoured of each other for a while. Not known by many, this romance lasted for eighteen months until she was tired of him. It was one of the few romantic interludes in the woman's life.'

'Anyone in particular?' Haddock asked.

'It's a story,' Natalie reminded him, hopefully giving him a hint to keep quiet and to let the man continue.

'This woman went on to success. The man did not. They did not speak to or see each other after the romance ended. Others knew of the relationship; some secretly approved, some were ambivalent, and several were opposed.'

'Opposed interests us,' Haddock said.

'The story continues,' Harding reminded him. 'In time, both got older, and one sank into despair, the other ceased to remember. Yet those who opposed never forgot, either due to their love for the woman or her money. Although there is a complication. Others who should not know could be suspicious, and they might talk, and then all would be revealed. None wanted that.'

Haddock knew the man was giving them a lead, but without names, he would not be implicated and not held accountable in a court of law. It was a strategy that he approved of, although it was frustrating.

'Others knew of this relationship,' Harding continued. 'As I've said, they wanted some of the woman's money, if not all. But there were other claims, some financial, some emotional.'

Haddock and Natalie realised Harding's convoluted way of giving information questioned Haddock's conviction that it was a serial killer. One person committing murder for reasons valid to him wasn't serial, psychopathic, or malignant, although it was still murder.

Natalie was convinced by what Harding said. Haddock wasn't. To him, it would be weeks of laborious investigation to find out what Harding could have given them in ten minutes. However, he resolved not to show his frustration with the secretive man and wished him well with a firm handshake.

***

Haddock had the unenviable task of explaining to his superior at State Crime Command in Parramatta that the time and the cost of solving four murders would be extended due to a recalcitrant man who wasn't willing to give them the whole story.

His superintendent, blustery, red-faced and an arse-licker, Haddock's opinion of the man, banged the table. 'Pull your source in, threaten him, get him to speak.'

Haddock listened to the man bluster, puff, and blow, threatening to blow the walls down, aware he would eventually run out of steam. Before heading up the Homicide Squad, Superintendent Payne had been out in the bush, back of Bourke, dealing with glue-sniffing teens and layabout farm hands. It wasn't the same as dealing with an educated man in the Eastern Suburbs. Not that Haddock agreed with the superintendent's behaviour at his previous station, but the man had been proud of it. Threaten Harding and pulling him into the station would end up with a conviction for police harassment, and he and Natalie Campbell would be out of the police force. Careers dashed, his marriage in tatters, not that it was in great shape as it was. He didn't want it to get any worse.

Haddock absorbed the man's wrath, filed his report, ensured he had the budget and returned to Kings Cross.

The first person that he and Natalie met was Ruth Stein. The serial killer angle appeared to be in shreds.

'It sounds logical,' Ruth Stein said. Even though she had proved of little worth, both police officers were glad of a third person to unburden with details of the current investigation.

'The link is tenuous between the four,' Haddock said.

'The young stud, lover of the dead woman at the retirement home. You suspect it's Old Joe?'

'We do,' Natalie said. 'He would have been an attractive man once, and we know the woman wasn't a shrinking violet, had the occasional lover, never thought to marry any of them, can't blame her there.'

'The voice of youth,' Stein said. 'Wait till you get old, my age, the dead woman's age. A young stud will look appealing. I could fancy one myself.'

'But you wouldn't?'

'Married too long, but the woman wasn't, had it made, footloose and fancy-free. Work hard, play hard, that was her life, not so unusual these days.'

Natalie knew she had the first, not the second, not after Christmas day the previous year when her live-in had moved out after a blazing row about a workmate he had kissed at his office party one week earlier. It was a day of revelations, her telling him about losing her virginity at sixteen; him, at nineteen, made up for the lost time until he had met Natalie. Both drunk, tongues and clothing loosened. A drunken romp on the floor, and him admitting that the office party was more than a kiss; her sobering up and then the tears and the anger and him storming out, only to return three days later, contrite, wanting to move back in, lipstick on his collar, a love bite on his neck.

Since then, a couple of one-night stands, both unsatisfactory, both leaving her feeling sad. She understood where Ruth Stein was coming from.

'We need your insight,' Haddock said. 'If all that we've told you is true, why kill people for something that happened long ago?'

'Have you found out what happens to her money?'

'Not yet. Her brother is in Sydney, and another relative is coming from Melbourne, but she is unsure when.'

'Could Old Joe be the beneficiary of the woman? Her long-lost love condemned to the street while she went on to fame and fortune.'

'It seems a weak link,' Haddock said. 'Doesn't resolve Maria Sidorov or Miriam Levine.'

'Not yet,' Natalie said. She understood where Ruth Stein was coming from; Haddock didn't. She knew he had taken umbrage with Harding, a man who knew more about the murders than he did, and now Ruth Stein was lecturing on how to conduct a murder investigation. A proud man, Haddock could listen to advice and appreciate the assistance, but a lecture he didn't want, and Ruth Stein could drone on.

'Dr Stein, the murders have been committed from Kings Cross to Vaucluse, almost a straight line along the harbour foreshore. Does this tell us anything?' Haddock said. Natalie knew that using the woman's formal title when Ruth would have sufficed was an attempt by the inspector to wrest control of the discussion. She wasn't sure it would succeed.

'If it's serial, no. If it's due to the old woman's money, that presents a different set of circumstances, undefined, open to conjecture and analysis. Whoever's killing these people might be rational, never committed a crime before, no anger, possibly some remorse, but determined.'

'A former lover?' Natalie asked.

'It could be. What about the brother? Any reason to suspect him?'

'He's in his eighties, confined to a wheelchair,' Haddock said.

Ruth Stein sat, placed one hand on her chin and closed her eyes. Haddock took it as a sign that the woman was confused, out of her comfort zone, and experiencing an intellectual challenge she couldn't answer.

'Assume it's not the brother. How about the cousin? Any reason this person might have a claim? Male or female?'

'Female. We're checking her out, coming up with blanks so far,' Natalie said. 'Apart from her and the brother, there doesn't seem to be any other relatives.'

'Lovers? Do you have a list?'

'We've got people working on it, interviewing her friends, those still alive from when she was younger. Cut quite a figure on the social scene twenty to thirty years back. Nothing in the last fifteen.'

'Alzheimer's?'

'Age. She was cognisant of her surroundings and knew that balconies were for looking over, not falling.'

'Cameras?'

'Not on the balconies. Those who run go out the front door, don't try to shimmy down a drainpipe.'

The idea of one of the residents attempting to leave by a drainpipe amused Haddock. He smiled, which eased the tension in the room.

'Ruth,' Haddock said, informality resumed.

'Inspector,' Ruth Stein replied. Informality halted.

'Time out,' Natalie said. 'We need a breather, coffee shop across the road.'

Chapter 11

The coffee shop option had not proven successful, and after twenty minutes of back and forth across a small table, Ruth Stein made her excuses and left.

'You blew it,' Natalie said.

'I was willing to listen, but these murders don't need a criminal psychologist,' Haddock replied indignantly.

'Agreed. The relative option is feasible.'

'How about the checks into the staff at the two schools? What happened there?'

'Dead end. Interviews were conducted, and internet usage was checked, as were political allegiances. One of Kline's and Regan's teachers is a naturist on the weekend. At Maria and Rebecca's school, a couple of lesbians keep it to themselves, but they're low key, not the butch haircut. A few are left-wing, wanting to overthrow the tyranny but not bringing it to the classroom. Besides, has the situation changed or are you unsure?'

'I'll agree this is not a psycho, but financially motivated. Seems logical, although instinct tells me differently. It might just be an itch I can't scratch.'

Natalie Campbell had never held firm with the serial killer option, although her inspector's experience and expertise had caused her to go along with it. But now, she could see another option.

'Have you considered that the four deaths are unrelated?' Natalie said, unsure of Haddock's reaction.

'I've considered it; make me look a fool if I tell Payne that we've spent weeks chasing our tails for nothing.'

'Not for nothing, but he'll not understand. Is the man as bad as you make him out to be?'

'He came from the bush, back of Bourke, the outback. More like the Wild West than Sydney. It toughened him up and made him cynical and aggressive. Not a lot going for him, but he's in charge, and I need to play by his rules. If it's proved that these are isolated killings, that means a new approach; not sure how we go about it.'

'A day in the office, go through what we have,' Natalie said.

'I still hold that the answer is out on the pavement.'

'So do I, but we need a reference; need to solve one murder, focus on the second.'

'The easiest?'

'Which is?'

'No idea. We've reached a nexus. Pick a murder.'

'Literal? Pin the tail on the donkey, something like that?'

'We need the woman's last will and testament. Need to know if the Old Joe connection is valid. We have Harding's statement that it might be, but he could be stringing us along: give the dog a bone, make it go away.'

'You don't trust him?' Natalie asked.

'Not for one minute. The man's slimy, squeaky clean, mud doesn't stick.'

'If he's got the dirt on people, does he use it? Or does it afford him protection? Remember his comment, associate of Sidorov? A faux pas or intentional?'

'Veiled threat? It could be, not that we can do much with him. He might have fed us a line, deflecting us from the investigation, making us go away. He won't be as agreeable the next time.'

'Willing to confront him again?'

'At the cost of my career, yes,' Haddock said.

'And your marriage?' Natalie thought it was time for her partner to open up. A close working relationship requires honesty, even if not detailed. He had to protect her back; she had to protect his. Secret liaisons complicated. Incurious otherwise, not given to criticising, but she needed to know.

'Took you long enough to get around to asking.'

'None of my business, but I must protect you if you're about to take on Harding. Can't do it if you keep secrets. They'll find out if they come after you, and then all hell will break loose.'

'Rocky, a few years now. Our daughter's growing up, the difficult age, Maria Sidorov's age. Might be getting into trouble, wouldn't know, but she's difficult; closed door, don't enter her bedroom, ever. Places pressure on the best marriage, and ours isn't. Too many hours on my side, too much anger on hers dealing with me coming home late at night, incommunicative, only wanting a whisky and to watch banal rubbish on the television. She wants to discuss renovations, the dog biting the neighbour, and our daughter. Not sure I can take much more, can't see a way out.'

'You and the majority, struggling to make headway, feel you're going backwards, life passing you by. You're not unique, but what will you do about it? This other woman? Important?'

'She works out at Parramatta, one floor down from Homicide. It's casual, could be serious, but I don't want it. I would prefer to solve crimes during the day and relax at home at night. But that's not possible. Not enough money to improve the situation; enough to scrape by.'

'I don't need more details. Just enough, in case...'

'In case we fall into a big hole we can't escape from,' Haddock said.

'We could. Old Joe doesn't appear to have much importance unless we make the connection with Mary Otway. What about his early life up in Wahroonga? And when did he go off the ropes, and why? If there's no connection, he either saw or knew something, but no one would listen to a homeless drunk, no credibility.'

'Has Kings Cross been canvassed? Was anything missed?'

'Nothing missed,' Natalie replied. 'Most don't want to talk, but some did. He had been in the area for a long time, drank his bottle of cooking sherry at night, and had his hand out during the day unless his face was in a book. Contradictions, but they all have a story on the street. But he was unique; not sure I understood why, but I didn't pry. I was there to keep the peace.'

'And now, you're solving murders.'

'Attempting. Haven't solved one yet.'

'You will. Fancy working for Homicide, get out from Kings Cross?'

'As a colleague, yes.'

'Nothing more. You're skin and bones, not my type.'

Natalie knew that Haddock had given her a compliment in his awkward style. Parramatta didn't excite; State Crime Command, Homicide Squad, did.

***

Her star in the ascendancy, Sergeant Natalie Campbell, not as wet behind the ears as she had been before meeting Detective Inspector Gary Haddock, felt the need to shake up the investigation.

She understood that Haddock's situation wasn't good: a fragile marriage, a blustering superintendent. It was up to her, the reason she found herself sitting in a café on the street outside Russell Harding's office.

'Surprised you had the nerve to phone,' Harding said. 'I could destroy your career in an instant. You must know that.'

'I do,' Natalie said. 'Inspector Haddock is not naïve, believes you know more than most, and that you have subtle influence across all strata in Sydney.'

'He's right, but that's not how I operate. I'm not fuelled by ego or ambition. I have enough money to satisfy.'

'Then why continue?'

'Pride in a job well done. Do you, as a police officer, take pride in what you do?'

'I do, not that it makes a lot of money.'

'Money is only the tool that allows people to do what they want. Most don't ever reach that point in life, struggling forever, and others make too much, destroying them.'

'Alexey Sidorov?'

'What he did was worry. About his money, his house, and his daughter. The last one I can understand; the other two, I can't.'

'You were circumspect when we met the other day. You inferred but didn't expound.'

'Two police officers, I never will. Those in authority keep their distance, realise that my assistance is selective and not for gain.'

'Why hadn't I heard of you?' Natalie asked.

'I maintain a low profile, available to a select clientele; some I like, others I loathe.'

'Did you loathe Sidorov?'

'On the contrary. A man of good values, tough to deal with, paid me well.'

'An associate?'

'They all are. Don't read something that isn't there. Your inspector, honourable, honest?'

'I've not known him long, but I believe he is. Troubled by life, a dedicated officer.'

'Some aren't. You do know that, or are you still finding out?'

'I've had no personal knowledge that some aren't, but there must be some. The police service is no different to any other organisation. A core of competency, a peripheral few who aren't. Hard to tell who is and who isn't. Do you know?'

'Of some, but I will never reveal. Safer to keep it to myself.'

'But I'm here, talking to you. Wouldn't that be seen as suspect?'

'A sergeant from a local police station, no. And besides, you contacted me. It takes courage to do that, knowing I could destroy you.'

'Verbiage or fact?'

'Fact, transferred to the back of beyond.'

'Are you going to help?'

'I do this for Alexey and his daughter, not for you and your inspector,' Harding said.

'Why get involved? Your discretion is legendary, according to Inspector Haddock.'

'Focus on Maria Sidorov. The others are unfortunate but not my concern. Talk to Alexey's security guard, Dima Ivanov.'

'We have, at Sidorov's.'

'And what did he say?'

'He said to talk to you and that Brett Kline's father was compromised.'

'Interrogate Ivanov, kid gloves with Justice Kline. One's got some brains; the other can't keep his trousers on.'

'You know?' Natalie said.

'I know nothing, never told you anything. Is that clear?'

'It is,' Natalie said. Harding was spoon-feeding the investigation, which made little sense to her, but she would comply if that was how he wanted to play it.

***

'Too easy,' Haddock said after he had blasted Natalie for meeting with Russell Harding.

'We've got to check it out. Ivanov gave us the lead, and we didn't follow up,' Natalie said. She had taken a risk with Harding; it had paid off. She was sure that Haddock was more upset that it hadn't been him in Harding's confidence.

'Where's the poor cousin? No doubt you've checked.'

'Chippendale, twenty minutes. I've made the appointment; I thought you'd be pleased.'

'Natalie, let's get this straight. You've had a win; good on you, but you must be careful. People are dying, and whoever's behind the deaths isn't a fragile wilting flower, but a malevolent killer; as easily kill you as push an old lady off a balcony.'

It wasn't something she had considered. Whoever committed the murders was calculating, planning in advance, and calm in execution. She knew her inspector was correct. Next time, she would tell him what she had planned.

'Not much of a place,' Ivanov said when Natalie and Haddock entered the small apartment. It was up two flights of stairs and then along a dark corridor, on the left at the end of it.

'Moved out of Sidorov's place?' Haddock asked as he pushed a copy of a girlie magazine to one side before sitting down.

'Open for inspection for those with the money. The real estate agent's taken control, getting the place tarted up. Some of the artworks moving out. They didn't want me there, and Alexey must have agreed.'

'They have contact with him?'

'Through his proxy. I can contact him, not that I often do. He's told me he's not coming back, unpleasant memories.'

'His empire will collapse,' Natalie said. She had seen the dishes in the sink, a half-eaten meal on the table. She understood why the agent didn't want an untidy man on the premises.

'Collapse? Why should he worry? He's dying, told me so.'

'With what?'

'He said cancer, but I know the truth. What worth is money if you have no one to spend it on?'

'Do you have someone?'

'Ex-wives, two of them, three children. I do what I can, not that it's much, the reason I'm in this hovel.'

'We spoke to Harding, inferred that Brett Kline's father was compromised, suggested we talk to you,' Haddock said.

'I only know what I overhear. Alexey never took me into his confidence. I never saw Justice Kline at the mansion, only heard Alexey speaking on the phone to Maria about him, not sure if it is of much use to you.'

'We'll decide. Tell us what you know.'

'Alexey tolerated the younger Kline, realised he couldn't do much about it. Three weeks before Maria died, they were in the house. Maria wanted to go on a camp with the school, but Alexey's not a fool. He makes a phone call, Harding probably, finds out the truth. He tells Maria she has absolute freedom within certain parameters. The first one is that she doesn't lie to him. The second is that the school doesn't have a camping trip organised, and he knows she intends to spend the night with Brett Kline.

'I'm around the other side of the house. A couple of hours later, Alexey is on the phone, and the speaker is on. I can hear what's been said. Alexey's calm, his temperament doesn't change often, and Justice Kline is on the other end.

'Alexey tells Kline to take his son to task and that he's got the goods on his father, and if one falters, the other pays.'

'Pays what?' Natalie asked.

'Career, life. I don't know, only that the elder Kline's frightened. I can tell it in the tone of his voice. "I did it for you, had to," Kline pleaded, but Alexey wasn't interested. He'll tolerate a lot, but if it's to do with his daughter, no leeway and the young Kline crossed that line.'

'Yet he still planned to come to the mansion with Regan,' Haddock said.

'What happens when you tell a dog on heat to back off?'

'Takes no notice,' Natalie said.

'That's it. The father couldn't control the son; otherwise, Alexey would have.'

'But Alexey allowed that visit?'

'He did, don't ask me why or how, but Alexey stayed bitter towards the father. One night, the two of us were down by the water's edge, and he started to talk. Sometimes he liked to talk in Russian. "Dima, sometimes I worry, sometimes I must do things I regret. Maria, she's all I've got. I would kill for her if anyone came between us or upset her." I knew he was truthful. If you speak Russian, you think Russian. If Brett Kline had upset his daughter, the father or son would have suffered.'

'Did you regard his threat as serious?'

'I did. Maybe not death, but something else, more precious.'

'Justice Kline treasures his reputation above all else,' Haddock said. 'I know that for a fact.'

Chapter 12

Haddock could see progress, although he still believed the murders had a common point. What it was, remained unclear. Natalie had phoned Old Joe's relative in England, a foster brother in Wahroonga, but he hadn't seen the homeless man in over thirty years. The reason was plain enough. He had lived in England for thirty-two years, married an English woman, and carved out a career. Life was good in England, and the lure to return to his roots in Sydney hadn't been strong. The man made it clear that he had no issue with Joe Coster, but they had not been close, fought at times, and once argued over a female. If his family's foster child was dead, it was a long time since he had thought about him.

She wasn't sure if she had been told the truth by the relative, and she would get others to check. Bringing the relative from England by force was impossible, and little would be gained.

Haddock had a more serious problem: his wife. She had found proof of what she had long suspected, but not the woman. Her initial reaction was to believe that his sergeant was the person he spent time with, professionally and recreationally. A heated argument outside Kings Cross Police Station, close to the El Alamein Fountain, while the woman hurled insults against Natalie, accusing her of sleeping with her husband, a tart with a badge, a seductress.

In the end, Natalie grabbed hold of her and forced her to sit on a park bench.

'Listen,' Natalie said as she held the woman firm. 'I'm not involved. It's not me.'

The riled woman maintained her anger. 'Let me go,' she said.

Haddock's wife was strong. If she had had the opportunity to consider, Natalie would have said she was attractive, starting to show her age after rearing her child and dealing with a difficult husband.

'It's not me. Please, this doesn't help.'

The woman calmed; Natalie released her grip.

'Then who?'

'I don't know, and that's the truth.'

'But you know?'

'I know that you need to talk to your husband. He's a good man, under a lot of pressure. I'm not making excuses for him, but he's committed to you. I know that.'

'Men, they're all the same,' Haddock's wife said.

Natalie had to concur, remembering the live-in boyfriend who had cheated on her and then wanted to come back, evidence of his indiscretion visible.

She didn't see herself as a marriage counsellor, but she respected Haddock, and he had already made representations on her behalf to State Crime Command, and she had met the superintendent that gave him strife and found him polite, if brusque. She thought animosity between the two men had tainted Haddock's objectivity, although time would tell. Agreeable with a mid-twenties female police sergeant wasn't the same as dealing with a hardened male police inspector.

Horses for courses, the manner of the superintendent adapting to the situation, and she had heard of policing out in the far west of New South Wales, the need to be culturally sensitive to the indigenous population, forceful enough to deal with a recalcitrant few who had fallen victim to alcohol and sniffing glue or petrol fumes, addling the brain. Old Joe had suffered from the curse but not the excess.

A café across the road; a manager who understood. A glance from Natalie and a table at the rear of the café became available. Open enough not to cause comment; secluded for Natalie to conduct an informal discussion with a person of interest: keep it friendly, low key, a chat, not an interrogation.

'Are you aware of the pressure we're under?' Natalie said.

Both women drank a latte, and a selection of cakes on the table, courtesy of the management. Not a bribe, but the manager, a woman in her fifties, Italian at birth, Australian by inclination, knew that maintaining friendly relations with the law was handy.

'The murders, yes, I am. Doesn't help that my husband is making a fool of himself.'

'It doesn't, but I confronted him about it, needed to. We're treading on feet, important and influential feet; I need to protect him if the proverbial hits the fan. Sorry about the language, but that's how it is.'

'Apologies not needed. Not that I hold with swearing, strict Baptist upbringing, but mixing with the criminal class it must be unavoidable.'

'It's avoidable but sometimes necessary. We're rattling chains, bound to hit a brick wall at some stage and be told to back off. I need your husband behind me; me behind him. Do you understand?'

'He's a good police officer, husband, and father until the last few months. What's changed?'

'He's feeling his age and sees life slipping by. He wants more, but he's not the person to fight for it. Arrests the criminals and ensures their convictions, but he doesn't play the game, doesn't know how and never will. Might make superintendent, no higher.'

'Suits me, but I want him back.'

It surprised Natalie that a woman who would have scratched her eyes out thirty minutes earlier could be so agreeable now. But then, Russell Harding had opened up to her when he would not have with Gary Haddock. She wanted to believe it was due to interpersonal skills but knew it was not. With her inspector's wife, it was two women united in a common cause. With Russell Harding, it was because she was young, female, and attractive. She could have said Harding was sexist but disagreed with the modern take on societal inequalities. Gary Haddock might be comfortable as an inspector, but she would not. She realised she had the ambition for the two of them, but only one would see the benefit.

***

Four hours later, Natalie and Haddock met Mary Otway's brother. It was clear, Haddock had explained earlier to his sergeant, that the brother could not have murdered his sister, as he had seen when he met him at the morgue where he had identified his sister.

In a wheelchair, an old man sat. He was as old as Mary Otway had supposedly believed herself young. 'I've told your inspector,' Geoffrey Otway said, 'that I rarely saw my sister, and not at all for the last nine years, not since I was confined to this damn chair and she to that home.'

'Apart from that,' Natalie asked, 'were you friendly?'

'As children. We drifted apart, phone calls at Christmas and on birthdays. Not a lot in common. Mary was full of life and lived it to the full: successful, partying, and a socialite. I'm sure you've checked on her.'

Natalie had. She had surfed the internet and looked for references to the woman: a fashion label she had established, standing next to a Range Rover at a charity event, paying thousands for something worth hundreds. Also, a grainy newspaper picture of the woman with a younger man, his arm around her. She hadn't shown Haddock the photo yet. Instead, she had handed it over to Forensics, digital enhancement, superimposing the dead Joe Coster's face onto the younger man. It would be three days before they had a result. In the intervening time, there was plenty to do. First, she had to save a marriage, and second, she had to ensure her transfer to State Crime Command was approved, but third, she should have said more important but wasn't sure it was, which concerned her, they had to apprehend a murderer or murderers. One person responsible for all was not firmly established, and her instinct, not as good as

Haddock's, which took years to acquire, was that it was multiple murderers, not a lone wolf.

'Any reason someone would want her dead?' Haddock asked. It was a cliched question, heard on any cop show on the television, not that he ever watched them – too structured, too perfect, too many white teeth and made-to-measure suits.

'I wouldn't have thought so. Popular when young, even more when older.'

'Lovers?' Natalie asked.

'Only what I read in the papers and what she told me. She lived life to the full and told me that she had someone, but our conversations were always short. Unlike my sister, I lectured at a university in Brisbane, busied myself with academia, and lived well enough. I'll stay here and bury her. After that, I'll return home, a house in Kenmore, comfortable, paid for. Another year, and I'll see if it's lights off or a halo on a cloud. Professionally, I believe it's the first; personally, I hope it's the second.'

'Your discipline?'

'Philosophy. Esoteric, not for Mary. She was for doing; I was more for thinking about it. I'm sorry to see her go, but she was eighty-three and could have tripped on a bar of soap or caught a cold.'

***

The situation was serious and exceedingly sensitive. It took Natalie and Haddock two hours to convince Superintendent Martin of the importance of what they had to do and another three hours to convince Haddock's boss.

For three days, Inspector and Sergeant sat at the back of Kings Cross Police Station, preparing the presentation for both men, long on evidence, short on proof.

After one week and further grilling by legal at Parramatta, the all-clear was given. Justice Kline would be summoned to appear before Haddock and Natalie at a place of Kline's choosing. It was to be kid gloves all the way, and there would be uproar, a pushback from Kline and the Supreme Court of New South Wales, headquartered in Phillip Street, Sydney, across the road from the Rum Hospital, not far from the New South Wales Parliament House, a stone's throw from Hyde Park.

Due to the man's importance and the weight of the evidence relating to Maria Sidorov's murder, the legal department would prepare the summons and present it to Justice Kline. He would then be allowed to contest it, ask for more time, submit a counter, state one statute after another, and drag it out for months.

Haddock expected the man to squirm; after all, his nautical adventure was on record and would be revealed. It would end the man's career: an honourable retreat whereby the Supreme Court would acknowledge his contribution, wish him well, pay him off, and then firmly lock the door behind him. Natalie wasn't confident she was up to the task, but Martin and Payne had been adamant. 'It's you and Haddock, don't stuff it up,' Payne said at a meeting of those involved. The legal department at State Crime Command had five in the conference room at Parramatta. Haddock and Natalie on one side of the long table, Payne at one end, Martin at the other. Victoria Adderley sat on one corner, carefully positioned to observe everyone. Natalie was nervous; Haddock was primed and ready. He thrived on conflict; she did not.

Payne kicked off the meeting. 'Inspector Haddock, Homicide Squad, and Sergeant Campbell, Kings Cross Police Station, have presented evidence and facts relating to the murders of four people in Sydney, the first in Kings Cross, the last in Vaucluse.

'Inspector Haddock believes that the murders are probably tied to each other, but that is not confirmed. However, we've all seen the evidence, read the statements, and find that the death of one victim, Maria Sidorov, a fifteen-year-old resident of Point Piper, the daughter of Alexey Sidorov, points to a relationship between her and Brett Kline, the son of Justice Kline of the Supreme Court of New South Wales. Brett Kline has admitted to the relationship, verified by Dima Ivanov, Rebecca Griffith, a friend of Maria and present in the Sidorov residence at the time of her death, Peter Regan, a friend of Brett Kline, and Russell Harding, private investigator and security adviser.

'There is irrefutable evidence that on the night of Maria Sidorov's murder, Justice Kline was on a boat in Sydney Harbour. You've all read Inspector Haddock and Sergeant Campbell's report and the interviews conducted at Rose Bay Marina, near where Maria Sidorov died. Unfortunately for Justice Kline, one of the departing persons from the boat saw the body of Maria Sidorov in the water. Otherwise, we would not have known of his presence. The boat carried a complement of middle-aged men and female escorts. The purpose of the cruise was prostitution. I'm not sure we can couch it any more delicately than that. I'll ask Inspector Haddock to speak, but first, does anyone have a question?'

'Just one,' Victoria Adderley said. A lawyer, she had worked with State Crime Command for five years. Haddock had had no reason to interact with her before the current murders, but her reputation in the building was that she was efficient, hard-working, and regarded herself as a cut above the rest in the legal department.

'Carry on,' Payne said.

'What Inspector Haddock and Sergeant Campbell have submitted is in order, and legal has no issue with proceeding. However, one anomaly concerns us. Maybe Inspector Haddock could answer the question.'

'If I can,' Haddock replied.

'Inspector, I'm not sure that is a suitable response.'

Natalie could see the subtle putdown, legal exercising itself over a police inspector.

'Very well, I will.'

'Good. Justice Kline is on the harbour. He's acting in a manner unbecoming of his position. However, it's not a crime. It's established that his son is having sexual intercourse with an underage female, Maria Sidorov and that her father is aware of this, and that Justice Kline is as well.'

'That's what has been presented,' Haddock said.

'No issue with the thoroughness of what you and Sergeant Campbell have presented, but I believe that I am to be the devil's advocate. Justice Kline returns to the Rose Bay Marina late at night, and there is a body in the water. He's reluctant to give his name but does, hopeful that's the last he'll hear of it.'

'Professionally embarrassing.'

'That would be an assumption. This is where it becomes difficult to understand, and Justice Kline will realise this and use it to his advantage. What are the chances of a body appearing as Justice Kline steps off the boat and that, based on the time of the boat's departure and the woman's death earlier in the evening, you believe he might have been involved in her murder?'

'I can't say luck, don't believe in it,' Haddock said. 'However, the facts are before you. Proof of a dispute between Justice Kline and Alexey Sidorov, the possibility of an incorrect judgement where one was presiding and the other was the plaintiff or defendant.'

'Even so, serendipity doesn't bode well in a police investigation or a legal department. It's a set of coincidences that stretch the imagination and will not hold up in a court, nor should they. You've presented solid facts. A different time and place would be enough for a probable conviction, but here you've got lucky, which doesn't work for us, nor will it for Justice Kline. A presiding judge would rule against a conviction based on your presentation.

'I agree,' Haddock said.

Natalie was impressed; the man was holding up well. Even with his domestic problems, he was able to compartmentalise. It was an admirable trait, not something she had honed. After the live-in had cheated on her, she had been a nervous wreck for two months, still shed the occasional tear, and thought to get a cat for company, but knew she didn't have the time to be responsible for it.

Superintendent Martin felt the need to speak. 'I believe Inspector Haddock is aware of this,' he said.

'Even so, rattling a sabre at the Supreme Court of New South Wales might invoke a response that the police don't want,' Victoria Adderley said.

'It's a homicide,' Natalie said. It was the only thing she could think to say. It was a lame response.

'Agreed, but we all know that the investigation must conclude quickly. Bringing into question the Supreme Court, regardless of whether Justice Kline is a murderer or not, slurs them. They will fend off criticism through legal means and public relations if they have to, but they won't forget. Approaching Justice Kline casually, can that be done?'

'Are you suggesting a whitewash?' Superintendent Payne rose from his seat.

'Not at all. I'm just reiterating that the Supreme Court has some of the best legal minds in the country. They could tie us up in knots.'

'To protect a murderer?' Natalie asked. A better response this time.

'Not to protect, to lessen the blame on their august collective selves. Think of subsequent court cases, the defence arguing that those presiding are not fit to judge. Legal malaise, the courts hamstrung by public opinion.'

'Will you issue the summons?' Haddock asked. 'Ensure that we meet with Justice Kline?'

'Devil's advocate. We all need to know where this could head. Even so, my colleagues and I are behind you,' Victoria Adderley said.

Natalie wasn't so sure.

Chapter 13

Mary Otway was buried on a Wednesday, her brother looking increasingly frail at the graveside. Natalie had attended; Haddock had not. He had more pressing issues, a disconsolate woman at State Crime Command and counselling for him and his wife.

He had thought his sergeant presumptuous when she told him about her confrontation with his wife, but now he had reconciled that she had done what was best. The momentary pleasure of a new love affair paled against a long-term relationship with a woman who'd always be there for him through thick and thin.

Natalie had looked for unexpected faces at the church and then at the graveside – she had seen none. So far, the link between the woman and Old Joe had not been made, and the digital enhancement of a grainy photo had been unsuccessful. Not that she understood technology, but she thought it unusual that it took so long. A nerdish, long-haired individual in dirty jeans and an open-necked shirt had tried to explain and spoke about resolution and pixels. She had faith in the man, as she had met nerds before. If they came with a collar and tie and a short haircut, they didn't qualify. The dirtier the better for her, and she still held out hope, refusing his request to meet out of hours to discuss.

A more recent photograph of Old Joe would help, but she only had one. Old Joe had few distinguishing features. He had claimed aboriginal heritage but showed no signs of it, other than in his youth, when he had gone on his first walkabout at sixteen, reappearing at the breakfast table in Wahroonga six weeks later.

'Where have you been? his foster mother had asked. She had loved the boy, not so much the young man.

'Walkabout.'

'Where to?'

'Here and there.'

After that, his schooling suffered; the need to reacquaint himself with his past had overridden his need to learn. The brother in England had brought Natalie up to speed on a video conference.

'Something to do with his heritage,' the brother said. He was a squat man, although Natalie thought that might be her computer. She hadn't fully understood resolution and pixels, but she understood YouTube, Facebook, and Google.

'Diluted,' Natalie said. 'Can you believe it was that?'

'No. But it was around that time, constant debate for reconciliation with the native population and a formal apology. Joe took it on board and started to believe he was oppressed. Hell, he had a better bedroom than me, and our parents cared more for him than us and saw it as their charitable duty to do the right thing. Not that it helped when he walked out of the door at eighteen, suitcase in his hand, a pack on his back, gone for three years before he returned. Cleaned himself up, went to university, and got a degree. He was very bright and knew a lot about Australia and his people, which was how he referred to them.'

'Did he tell you where he went?'

'No. Although I think that's how it is. You go, come back, and don't explain or say where you've been or what you've seen. Did him good, made a man of him.'

'When did you last see him?'

'Long time ago. I went on my own walkabout, backpacked around Europe, ended up in England, and have not returned to Australia. Our parents had died before I left, never saw the reason to return. Nothing against the place, but it doesn't tug at my emotions.'

'It's worth the trip,' Natalie said.

'Kings Cross? Still as seedy? Women on the street for hire?'

'Not as much, empty shops, the strip joints closed. A couple of gentlemen's clubs around the back. Old Joe, what else? Into women?'

'There was one when he was seventeen. He was keen on her, but that was a long time ago. Married a lawyer, from what I know, which isn't much.

'I've kept in contact with a friend from school. He's in England once or twice a year. We meet up for a meal and a few too many drinks, not that my wife complains, although my head does the day after.'

'Does he know more about Joe?'

'He might. I'll message you the number.'

Haddock arrived at Kings Cross at two in the afternoon. He looked exhausted.

'Alright?' Natalie asked. She didn't think she should ask too much and allow him to speak if he wanted to; he did not.

'Good day?'

'I've got a contact, someone who knew Joe Coster, Old Joe. He lives in Pymble, Bungalow Ave. I'm meeting him later today, a couple of hours, office to yourself.'

'I've got an office out in Parramatta, don't need yours in Kings Cross. Your transfer's sorted, the week after next. Payne's impressed. Thinks you're the next Miss Marple.'

'Don't know why. Barely said two words at the meeting. Victoria Adderley, given Justice Kline the bad news?'

'You're dying to ask.'

'Don't want to pry.'

'You did that before, chummy chat with my wife.'

'I thought we'd moved on from that,' Natalie said.

'We have. I don't see myself as an attentive husband. I'm what I am, can't change, might want to, not so easy.'

'State Crime Command, how's she?'

'Upset. Called me a snivelling coward, a few other words I can't say to a lady. But then she was, and she still called me them.'

'It'll blow over in a couple of months. It did with me.'

'The live-in?'

Natalie had told him the story the day she had told his wife about the other woman. It had seemed the right thing to do then; now, she wasn't so sure. Some things need to remain secret.

'Still no tie-in between Old Joe and Mary Otway. I'll be back later today or might go straight home. Depends on what the friend has to say.'

'Don't come back. I'm off home. I need to talk with my wife. I prefer to be with her, but policing, the death knell of any relationship, and you know it.'

Natalie did. Apart from the two one-nighters, she'd had a few other dates, one of the men she had liked, but at the mention of police and officer, he had bolted. The other, a friend of a friend, thought he was on a sure thing, the hands of an octopus, until she had told him that she was experienced in unarmed combat, and if he didn't want a broken arm, he'd better back off. Not a good start to a relationship, not that she cared about him, but the other she had, although, on reflection, his fear of the police caused her concern. She had checked him out the next day and found out he had a conviction for sex with a minor, time spent in prison, and his teaching career dashed.

Bungalow Ave, Pymble, was prime real estate, although Barry Birch didn't live in prime. 'TLC it said in the advert, not that I believed it. I've got plans with the council, knock it down, build a five-bedder, pool in the back, make a fortune.'

Her live-in had been full of big ideas. The last she had heard of him, he was out of the city, living on a farm surrounded by snakes and spiders but no livestock. His aspirations had amounted to nothing, but Natalie thought Birch's might. In the driveway, a late model Mercedes, Biturbo on the back. A police officer needs to know cars, and it was expensive and horrendously fast, too fast for her, as she had a lead foot. Police training, a skid pan, advanced driving techniques, how to spin the car around if the road ahead is blocked, and control at high speed. She had aced the course, top of her class at the driving academy, but on the open road, unless the sirens were on, it was keeping to the speed limit, no abusing the privilege, no breaking the rules, or else.

'Joe Coster, I knew him. Decent guy, but it was unfortunate that some were prejudiced. Great rugby player, best the school ever had, but sometimes, he'd wander off.'

'Walkabout?' Natalie asked.

They were sitting on the back porch of the renovator's special. Birch, in his fifties, the same age as Old Joe, was eager to talk. Natalie enjoyed sitting with him, a can of beer in her hand.

'Not walkabout. Vague. Nothing to worry about, but one moment he's talking to you, and the next he's not. I had no problems with him. I saw him as a regular guy. Travelled a lot in my twenties, a few countries I wouldn't recommend, seriously dangerous; a few idyllic, sandy beaches and dusky maidens.'

'Which do you prefer?'

'Sandy beaches and dusky maidens sound great, but it's the dangerous countries that I remember. Sydney's great, safe and organised. People mind their business, everything works, but it's bland, one day the same as the next.'

'Do you intend to go overseas again?'

'Next week, meeting up with Joe's brother in London, do the round of the pubs, talk nonsense, get a splitting headache.'

'And a dusky maiden?'

'Not me. A bachelor free. I'm a loner. I don't need company. Enjoy it when it's there, don't miss it when it's not. How about you?'

'Nobody at present. Policing keeps me busy.'

'Sounds like an excuse.'

'It is,' Natalie admitted.

Anyway, Old Joe,' Birch said, not before he had thrust another can into Natalie's hand.

'We need to make a connection. You knew him, seen him in recent years?'

'Not for a long time. Joe found alcohol, or it found him. He was adamant he wouldn't drink when he was younger and reckoned his people didn't have a tolerance, not that I would know. I've drunk more than my fair share. If you hadn't turned up, I wouldn't have bothered. Could I use that as an excuse if I'm pulled over for drink-driving? The police drove me to drink.'

'I wouldn't try it. What about Joe Coster? I knew him, not well, but the alcohol had gotten to him. Cooking sherry of a night but didn't deserve to die on the street, two doors up from the train station. What about this girlfriend he had at seventeen?'

'Died a few years back, cardiac arrest. I went to the funeral but never told Joe's brother. He was keen on her, but she wanted Joe. But her parents were against it, not Joe per se, but they were young.'

'Prejudiced?'

'Not them, worried for her. Besides, she was the same age as Joe, too young to get serious. Joe, couldn't tell him apart from anyone else, but any children could have been whiter than white or, well, you know. Sounds bad saying it.'

'It's still prejudice.'

'I know it is, and so did the parents and their daughter, but they were too young to contemplate marriage. He had offered, but they shipped her off somewhere.'

'Pregnant?'

'You weren't told? No idea why his brother didn't. Anyway, never saw the baby. The mother arrived back in the area ten years later, and not a word was said by anyone. By then, she had a husband in tow and a degree in her back pocket. Nothing to be gained by talking to her, even if you could.'

'We're struggling for a better photo of him, forensic analysis, see if he's the same person getting around with Mary Otway, the retirement home death, twenty-five years ago.'

'You've come to the right place. My hobby at school, president of the camera club, not that it means much, there were only three of us, got hundreds of photos of the school and the students, bound to have one or two of Joe and his brother, also the mother of Joe's child. Do you want to see them?'

'I would.'

***

Eight in the morning, the next day, Natalie presented Jimmy Rogers, the digital-enhancing nerd, with a stack of photos and negatives. He was delighted, fascinated with ancient technology, as he referred to them.

Mid-morning, she was in Melbourne, a flight ten minutes after nine from Kingsford Smith Airport, named after Charles Kingsford Smith, who had made the first trans-Pacific flight from California to Australia. The airport, fifteen minutes from Kings Cross if the traffic was light, thirty-five if it wasn't, was on Botany Bay, the scene of another epic trip: Captain Cook, who in 1770 saw the bay but sailed past Sydney Harbour where 'a Thousand Sail of the Line may ride in the most perfect Security', as described by Captain Phillip in 1788.

At Tullamarine, she picked up a rental and drove into Melbourne and up to Spring Street, meeting with the cousin who had breezed into Sydney, attended Mary Otway's funeral and left back to the airport and home. There were questions, but the woman had absconded. Natalie needed to know why.

The two women sat in one of the numerous eateries on Spring Street. Natalie enjoyed the culture of Melbourne but preferred the beauty of Sydney and the harbour. Sheila Cross did not. To her, Melbourne was home and Sydney was too brash, and besides, her cats needed her at home, not in Sydney, answering questions for which she would not have an answer.

Natalie saw a peevish woman with horn-rimmed glasses, a severe haircut, and a tweed jacket. Her dress style was post-war, early fifties. Natalie had seen her at the funeral, briefly spoken to her, and the woman had been dressed in black. Her eclectic dress style wasn't noticeable, nor had her hair been, covered by a large black hat.

'I couldn't stay, don't you see?' the woman said.

Natalie didn't see. The woman hadn't killed her cousin, no reason to, as Mary Otway's money had been left to charity, apart from a small amount to her brother, but none to Joe Coster. It had revealed nothing of worth to the investigation.

'Thirty minutes, no more,' Natalie said. 'That was all I wanted. Did you keep in contact with your cousin?'

'I always sent a Christmas card, never got one back.'

Natalie could imagine the woman with a pile of cards, signing each one, writing a few words of good cheer, a brief update on her life, and then licking the stamp, placing it on the envelope and posting it.

'No contact with her?'

'None. I only came because of Geoffrey; I thought I would see him one more time.'

'How long since you last saw him?'

'Ten, maybe eleven years. He came to Melbourne before the stroke put him in a wheelchair. An impressive man once, now he looks like death.'

'Married?'

'Me? Once, a long time ago. He took off with my best friend. I never saw either of them again.'

'Tell me about Mary?'

'Not much to say. We were friends as children, lived on the same street. Our mothers were sisters. Hers was bossy and domineering; mine was placid and servile.'

'Someone pushed Mary.'

'I should be sad, but I'm not. I went to the funeral for Geoffrey, not for her.'

'You sound embittered.'

'Who did you think was my best friend?'

'Mary Otway.'

'We grew up together and moved into a small place in Surry Hills, near Central Railway Station. It was a long time ago. I became a secretary, but she had aspirations, constantly discussing this and that.'

'You weren't impressed?'

'It was her mother, constantly preaching about bettering oneself. Mine would tell me to find a nice man and settle down, which I had. And then Mary decides she wants him, something to do with her credo, take what you can, steal if you have to. She was more attractive than me and more worldly.'

'You said you never saw the best friend again.'

'I didn't. I forgave her years ago, but Mary wasn't interested in forgiveness, only herself. The tyrant in a skirt, I used to call her, not to her face, never saw her again.'

'If she had answered your cards?'

'I would have been polite; I might have scratched her eyes out. Destroyed my life, destroyed others. Geoffrey didn't see her often, disagreed with what she had become, can't blame him, not after what she did.'

Geoffrey Otway had been noncommittal when he had been interviewed. He had not been derogatory about his sister, only stating they had drifted apart. And now, Sheila Cross, a woman who had a grievance with the woman, told a police officer that Mary Otway had been a tyrant who had taken another woman's man.

Natalie realised that more research would need to be done on Mary Otway. She had spoken to people in Sydney who had known her when younger: tough businesswoman, generous to those in need, gave to charity, a friend. Also, two sergeants from Homicide had canvassed others, compiled a report on the woman, checked her real estate holdings, and received an update from her lawyer and accountant, proof that she paid tax. In short, there was no black mark against the woman, but now, a different story.

Natalie wanted to believe the woman she sat with. If it was confirmed that there was another side to the dead woman, it could give an additional motive, other persons to consider in the investigation into her death.

'What did she do to Geoffrey?'

'Geoffrey had staked her when she set up her business, gave her fifty thousand, pre-decimal, worth over a million today.'

'What happened?'

'He trusted her, thought blood was thicker than water. After a few years, she sends him a cheque, his original stake plus interest. The business was worth a lot more. His contribution should have been adjusted based on the business, not the bank interest rate.'

'What did he do?'

'No paperwork. They didn't have contact for years, but Geoffrey's a pushover and forgave her in time, and so did I. More fool us, but I don't want to be like her. She never loved anyone but slept with a few, including my husband. But love and Mary, no way.'

'Geoffrey never mentioned this. Anyone else she cheated?'

'No idea, must have. I read about her occasionally, but Geoffrey wouldn't say anything, even if he knew. So, the answer is I don't know.'

'Your former husband?'

'She tired of him after a year. The last I knew of him, he went overseas; in his late seventies, if he's still alive.'

'Since then, another man?'

'Never. I settled into a time warp, never moved on, a comfortable rut.'

'We believe that Mary had a romance with a younger man. This would have been twenty-five to thirty years ago. Do you know anything about this?'

'I wouldn't be surprised. Unless it was in a newspaper or a magazine, I'd know less than you.'

Chapter 14

Regardless of Superintendent Payne, who gave him hell, Inspector Gary Haddock thought the investigations were progressing satisfactorily. He was confident that one of the Klines, the younger or the elder, had more to reveal and that Maria Sidorov's murder would be the first solved.

Confidentially, Victoria Adderley had told him that taking on Justice Kline was brave, and she admired both him and his sergeant.

Sheila Cross's statement gave new impetus to the murder investigation, and there was a team in Parramatta checking Mary Otway's business dealings, men she might have known, and an attempt to find Sheila's missing husband, but that was thought to be a long shot.

Jimmy Rogers was like a kid in the toy shop, developing negatives, scanning them into his computer, running digital analysis software, adjusting the parameters, and attempting to improve the quality. He had phoned Natalie a few times; made it known that he was available for a casual romance, but she had pushed him aside with a humorous riposte. If she filed a complaint against police officers who misbehaved or said something that could be construed as sexist, she would have spent days on unnecessary paperwork. Besides, a police officer needed a thick skin and an even thicker stomach for murder and its aftermath.

Miriam Levine's murder had upset her, the most violent of the four; Maria Sidorov's had saddened her, a waste of a young life, but Mary Otway's had only left her numb.

'We're moving on three murders,' Haddock said. It was their favourite restaurant, where the manager looked after them and ensured they had the best seat, the largest slice of cake, and the largest mug of coffee, although both officers ensured they paid. The occasional freebie did no harm, but if it was assumed that it would always be free, that was corruption, and neither wanted to be accused of the crime.

'Maria Sidorov's doesn't tie into the others,' Natalie said. 'Nor does Miriam Levine.'

'Nor does Old Joe, not unless your over-amorous friend comes up with something.'

Natalie had observed ease existed with her inspector and that she could be open with him and he with her. He had told her about his marriage and the other woman, and that counselling was helping. And if you deal with violent murder, going home of a night time to hear about your daughter and the cost of the food in the supermarket and her next door wasn't as exciting as a woman in State Crime Command, who only spoke of love.

She had told him of the live-in who had cheated, the one-night stands that had left her sad.

They had become a team, and they were invincible. She knew that he was right. The murders would be solved, and there would be a breakthrough that would rocket the investigations into the stratosphere, and it would be when they least expected it.

***

Natalie's optimism was not to be realised two days later when Victoria Adderley sat across from her at Parramatta. She was still officially attached to Kings Cross Police Station; unofficially, she was a member of the Homicide Squad out in Parramatta. As expected, more than one police officer had tried to chat her up, but they had been civil. She knew it would not last, although working with Inspector Haddock, seeing the bodies of murdered people, had toughened her. In the past, she had laughed off the crude attempts at sexual harassment; she wasn't sure she would the next time, more than likely to give them a piece of her mind and make it clear she wasn't a pushover. She was their equal, and if they wanted to avoid trouble, they'd better change their attitude, or she would have a word in the ear of Superintendent

Payne, who was exceedingly polite to her. However, she couldn't be sure about him. Superintendent Martin had never gone over the line, but Payne might.

'Justice Kline's thrown a wobbly, subtle threat against the legal department out here,' Victoria Adderley said.

She was older than Natalie, in her early thirties. Not a woman to take abuse or innuendo from a man, and Natalie found that she liked the forthright woman.

'Wobbly, a legal term?' Natalie replied.

The two had found a quiet office, away from the hubbub outside.

'Appropriate. We followed the procedure, dotted the Is, and crossed the Ts. I expected we would have trouble, wasn't proven wrong.'

'You handed it to him?'

'Two of us met him at his office in the CBD, not at the Supreme Court. Courteous when we entered; abrupt when we left. Important people don't take it favourably when a junior takes them to task.'

'His response? Does he intend to fight? Or is he damned? Public knowledge that we're investigating him, questions that need answering?'

'Not yet. Unlikely it will stay hidden for too long. Too serious to be swept under the carpet, conduct unbecoming, cavorting with prostitutes, nights on the harbour, the death of his son's girlfriend.'

'And that we have reason to believe he might be guilty?'

'Can you prove it?'

'No evidence. We suspect him of affecting the outcome of a trial involving Sidorov, but we are unsure which one or if a judgement went in his favour. That's the problem. We know a lot about the Klines and the Sidorovs, but nothing tangible or illegal, apart from the son with the fifteen-year-old daughter, but he's young. Should know better, but he's got a chip on the shoulder, probably gets it from his father.'

'Would you like me to do some research?'

'You've got the time?'

'Not the time, but the interest. He was verbally rough, no bad language but legalese, know his type.'

'Legal profession, the same as the police? Too many think a young woman is there for getting coffee and stroking their egos.'

'More than their egos. Filed a complaint once and got the man transferred. Male chauvinism is out there; there's not much we can do about it.'

'Officially, we can; unofficially, we're stymied. Get the man transferred and he reappears elsewhere. Unjust world.'

'It's not only women. The world's always been unjust, with one tyrant or another, wars fought over nothing. Don't complain or file a complaint. Just be better than those who try to put you down.'

'Justice Kline?'

'I've seen him in action. He's an impressive man, no idea why he's messing about with Alexey Sidorov or on a boat with prostitutes. But then, we've all got hidden sides. His is that he can't resist an easy woman. He must have known the risk, and now's he been caught out, unsure what to do. No doubt checking his law books, looking for precedence, won't find one.'

'You've looked?'

'It's tight, what he was presented with. If we hadn't done this, he would have pulled in a few favours, the old boys' network. This way, he can't. Don't know who else knows of him and Sidorov.'

'Some know of him on the boat. One's a solicitor,' Natalie said.

***

With Justice Kline playing hard to get and Jimmy Rogers enjoying himself with photography, Haddock focussed on Miriam Levine, who, by any stretch of the imagination, didn't tie in with the other three murders.

He found her husband at home, spending time with the children and praying more than usual.

'My sister has moved in,' Levine said. 'It's been a difficult time. Unsure if I can deal with the situation. I might go overseas and ask my sister to raise our children.'

'In your faith, not an impossibility,' Haddock said.

'We will always help each other. She will treat them as her own. You've found no one for what happened?'

'Not yet. There have been four murders, tenuous links for the other three, no reason for your wife.'

'She was a good woman.'

Haddock thought the man was older than when they first met, but it was impossible to be sure. Dressed in black and bearded, he had never looked young.

'Were you always religious?'

'Always, although Miriam came from a more liberated family. She struggled with the lifestyle and would have liked more freedom to travel, to go out to restaurants, but life is a struggle, isn't it?'

'For most of us, it is. But you have plenty. A big house and money to live.'

'Our religion is our life. Miriam was starting to understand.'

'Her past? Any relevance with what happened?'

'Inspector, the past belongs back there.'

'Not to the police. We need to solve your wife's unfortunate demise. I need your help.'

'You have it.'

'If I give you some names, could you respond if you know them?'

The two men sat at a table in the garden at the rear.

'Alexey Sidorov?'

'I know of him, seen him drive down the road, not spoken to him.'

'Justice Kline, eminent judge of the Supreme Court?'

'I met him, professionally, three years ago. When we had a terrorist attack at the synagogue. I was a witness, saw the man, tackled him to the ground.'

'Which makes you a target for retribution.'

'He died in prison,' Levine said.

'I remember, unfortunate accident, fell from a landing. Even so, his colleagues would remember. You're not invisible, proudly show your religion.'

'Not proudly, no vanity involved. We are pious people who do not interfere with others, pacifists unless provoked.'

'Yet you don't have security.'

'We do. A high fence, the windows and doors are double locked, a panic room in the house.'

'Which your wife never used.'

'No, she didn't.'

'Russell Harding?'

'He works with our community, conducts security scans, and advises on potential areas where security could be breached.'

'Unusual that you would use him.'

'Why? He's the best.'

'True, but I would have thought Israel is renowned for its security services.'

'We are in Australia. We are not unpatriotic to this country, do not shun technology, and employ the best, regardless of their religion.'

'Does he have a religion?'

'He's never been asked.'

'Yet two people have died in houses where he has been.'

Haddock thought he was clutching at straws and that Levine, polite as his religion dictated, did not intend to say more than necessary. He was wrong.

'Maria Sidorov is known to me,' Levine said.

'How? And why didn't you mention it when I gave you her father's name?'

'She came here for a school project, studying religions. I answered your question and realised that you would mention his daughter. I did not intend to be obtuse, given to factual, not verbiage.'

Haddock realised that an orthodox Jew would not be verbose; he had to credit the man for his explanation.

'What else?'

'She phoned my wife, explained the school project, and asked if she could come and talk to us.'

'You agreed?'

'I did. It would have been impolite to refuse. We found her to be intelligent and curious. I realised that she was indulged, possibly sexually active and probably flirtatious.'

'How?'

'Observation. We try to maintain a distance from such provocation and grow up differently, but we live in a cosmopolitan society, impossible not to be aware of those around us.'

'Did you confront her on her lifestyle?'

'We did not, but we liked her, not that we approved. She showed us the essay she had written for the school. It was sensitive and accurate. I was sad when she died.'

'You didn't come forward.'

'With what? She came to our house on three occasions and spent one to two hours each time. We spoke of our religion and our beliefs, not of her life. I knew of her father, nothing good or bad; he was successful. How that success was achieved, I don't know, but Miriam liked Maria, and so did I.'

'After the project was finished?'

'She came once or twice, but no more. Sometimes we would see her, talk to her in the street or shopping centre. But she had other friends, not as accepting as her, who would have criticised. She had the vanity of youth and needed her peers' acceptance. We are not unaware that our appearance frightens some and upsets others.'

'Could Maria's visits to this house have something to do with your wife's death?'

'I don't know, but it could. I have nothing specific to say, only hope it isn't true.'

'And if you met this person who killed your wife?'

'I would kill him. Does that shock you, Inspector?'

It didn't, not to a police officer. Man is made of flesh and bone and emotion. A religion might suppress, but it doesn't destroy hate and anger. Haddock knew that if his family were threatened, he would react the same way as Moshe Levine.

'It doesn't,' Haddock said.

Chapter 15

With further revelations, although none had been proven and comprehensively evaluated, Haddock, who had had a rough few weeks, felt the need to celebrate. It was the day he ended up in Parramatta in an apartment with the woman from one floor down at State High Command. It was the prelude to an even rockier period in the man's life. It was for Natalie to take action.

She had phoned his wife late that night, assured her they were staking out a possible murderer and that her husband would be home by two in the morning. After that, she had driven to the Jezebel's two-bedroom unit, grabbed a sober and remorseful Haddock, taken him to her apartment, ensured he scrubbed down with a long, hot, lingering shower, and removed the smell of the other woman from his clothing. She then shoved him into a taxi and gave the driver the address. She hoped it was worth it. The deception did not rest easy with her, and Haddock's wife deserved better.

After Haddock had left, she had sat down and cried, not for Haddock and his wife, the Jezebel or those that had died, but for herself. It had been over a year without a man, close to two with a man she had loved. She was lonely, determined to resolve it, unsure how and with whom. She would accept it if it was a one-night stand but wanted more than carnal. She needed love; she didn't have it. It was unnatural, and it was because of policing, the reason many of the men ended up drunk or forming inappropriate relationships; the reason that some of the women, bent on climbing the slippery ladder of promotion, ended up alone.

She looked at the clock. It was three in the morning, and she had not slept for nearly twenty hours. She had a sleeping pill in the other room, next to the bed, but she had to be in the office by six.

Her phone rang. She half-expected Haddock to be on the other end, to thank her for her help, but it was not.

'Meet me today, ten thirty in the morning, at Catalina Restaurant, Rose Bay. Off the record, let you decide how you want to proceed. Don't bring Haddock.'

She knew she had to accept, aware that it was unusual, not according to the book, and if Superintendent Payne found out about it, he might throw a fit. But then, if he knew about Inspector Haddock's amorous adventures, he might throw another.

Unsure of how to proceed, she knew she would go. She woke Victoria Adderley.

'Early, Sergeant, too early for me. I hope it's important,' a sleepy voice answered.

'It is. Grab a coffee. I need you awake.'

Natalie realised it could be another long day and that she might have napped before the last phone call. At the other end of the phone, she could hear another woman.

Each to their own, she thought, although she had not pegged the legal eagle for lesbian.

'Coffee in hand. What is it? Hope it's worthwhile.'

'Victoria, Justice Kline phoned, wants to meet me, off the record, just the two of us.'

'Not sure how to proceed? Or have you made a decision?'

'I'm going, need advice. Not strictly by the book, and Kline could play me for a dummy, state that I have prejudiced the investigation, or give him a clear way out from under.'

'He's smarter than either of us, smarter than Haddock or Payne, slippery as an eel; not sure you would use that analogy with a Supreme Court Justice.'

'You can. I'm out of my depth. I intend to go, need someone to back me up, defend me if it goes pear-shaped.'

'Which it will, very quickly. The man's up to something. If you're determined…'

'I am. What do you reckon?'

'Professionally, I'd advise against it. You need him in your area of control, not his. But if you don't go, he could use his experience and knowledge to twist it, make out that you and Haddock have a vendetta against him, bring the police into disrepute, and then you know what will happen.'

'Strung out to die, defamed, ridiculed, incompetency proven, drummed out of the force.'

'For starters,' Victoria Adderley said. 'Give me ten minutes. I'll phone you back. In the interim, phone Kline and tell him it's on, but it can't be off the record, and you'll need to take notes.'

'If he'll go for it.'

'He will. He's squirming, trying to deflect blame from himself. You're his best hope. He thinks he can twist you around his little finger, which he can. Are you up to this?'

'I am. Need to tell Inspector Haddock.'

'Not until later. Plausible deniability for him. It might damage his confidence in you. Hope you've got enough brownie points with him.'

Natalie knew she did. She had just saved his marriage; he owed her one.

Kline listened to Natalie, said little, and agreed to her demands, as Victoria had said he would.

For some reason, Natalie was able to sleep. She woke up at nine in the morning, enough time to get dressed and go to Rose Bay. She was excited but apprehensive. A Christian at the Colosseum. It was her against the lion, and the lion had a name.

***

Ten minutes before meeting Justice Kline, Victoria Adderley phoned. 'Continue. There's surveillance, not that you'll see it. If he is a murderer, keep your distance, his suave manner belies a ruthless personality.'

'Inspector Haddock?'

'I've phoned him. For some reason, he went ballistic, worried that you were out of your depth; not seen it before. In the past, he hasn't cared for others he's worked for. Hope nothing is going on there.'

'There isn't. Superintendent Payne?'

'He's aware of the development. I don't understand why Kline's taking a massive risk, but he could be psychotic; never tell with people like him, with anyone, I suppose. Not my area of expertise, but I read that psychopaths often act rationally, are polite and caring, love animals and babies, and kill without feeling. You reckon he's one of them?'

'Could be.'

'Best of luck.'

Natalie looked around the area and saw the seaplane base and Catalina Restaurant, named after the flying boats from the late thirties that landed there. It was Australia's first international airport back then, thirty stops to London and ten days on the 'Kangaroo Route' with fifteen passengers and five crew.

Those who dined at the restaurant were descendants of the affluent few who could have afforded the trip.

Kline arrived on time. He was casually dressed, with no wig and gavel, no exhausted look from the last time they had met, but that had been to look at a body and for him and the others to make a statement.

'Guilty?' he said.

'Not yet,' Natalie said. She had decided not to be subservient. In Rose Bay, he was her equal, but she knew she was treading on eggshells; break her guard, and he would control the situation.

'Are you recording this?'

'You said not to. That's the agreement.'

'It is. Lose the phone. I don't want us tracked.'

'How?'

'In your car. The police can track phones, and I don't want someone smart switching on the microphone. It can be done. That Jimmy Rogers friend of yours could do it.'

'You're remarkably well informed.'

'Have to be. You want to grill me about Alexey Sidorov and his daughter. Somehow, you believe I used my judicial powers to his advantage and murdered his daughter out of spite.'

'Something like that, but we've no proof.'

'We can stand here talking, watched by whoever. I know you're keeping to the agreement; others aren't. They'll have the restaurant bugged, but you'll have to trust me. Tell you what you want to know and some more.'

'Not trust, not after the marina. You're a suspect, the only one we've got. I might be walking into a trap, and you're smarter than me and more powerful.'

'Scout's honour, you're safe. If you ask Haddock or Payne, they'll not agree. It depends on how important your career is to you. This could make or break, dynamite.'

'But why? A judge of the Supreme Court frolicking on the harbour with prostitutes?'

'I'm imperfect. I'm not alone; special dispensation for those in power or in the know. Surely you must have figured that out by now. I'm untouchable by you, Haddock, Payne, and whoever else. Take the plunge, live dangerously, a good feed at the end of it.'

She was cornered, but to walk away would have made no sense. To stay could bring death. There was only one choice. 'Lead on,' she said.

Haddock threw a fit; Superintendent Payne blew his top and screamed at Victoria Adderley, who sheepishly said nothing, only to mutter under her breath, 'You stupid woman.'

Haddock arrived at the seaplane base after fifteen minutes, only to be told by the manager, 'Two passengers and a pilot, Cottage Point Inn, Kuringai Chase National Park, twenty-minute flight, back by three thirty.'

Five minutes later, Superintendent Payne received a phone call. 'Off the record,' a man said. 'Give Kline time with your sergeant. She's in safe hands.'

Payne recognised the voice. He was on the phone to Haddock. 'Back off. Don't rally the troops. She's safe.'

Unaware of the drama below, Natalie looked out of the plane's window and saw the harbour below: Manly in the distance, the Sydney Harbour Bridge, tourists climbing up one of the arches, the aboriginal flag on the top, the Australian flag alongside. The sun shone on the Opera House sails, and yachts bobbed on the water. Ferries heading up the harbour, oblivious to her in a plane with a potential murderer. She thought she should be nervous, but she wasn't. She was elated, as if climbing a mountain or jumping out of a plane, both of which she had tried. There was an adventurous streak in her; she couldn't deny it.

The plane travelled north, hugging the coast, the beaches down below, surfers in the water, and others on the beach getting a tan. Close to Palm Beach, the plane headed west over Pittwater, down below Scotland Island, before landing in Cowan Creek, a tributary of the Hawkesbury River. She had previously paddled from Berowra Waters and seen the restaurant from the water but had never powered up to it in a plane.

'It's all arranged. Use my phone, phone Haddock, tell him you're okay,' Kline said.

Natalie felt like saying, don't worry, but made the call and received advice that the cavalry wasn't coming and she was in safe hands. She didn't ask why. If Justice Kline wanted to elaborate, he would. To her, this was policing at the cutting edge.

'Why here?' she asked.

'Neutral ground. Two people conversing. No axe to grind, calm and relaxed. Haddock's a decent police officer, but he wouldn't understand.'

Natalie did. She was female, young and attractive, and Kline was a wolf in sheep's clothing. 'I know of your reputation, but I've seen you in the flesh. You're a lecher, Justice Kline.'

'Well said. I don't proposition vulnerable young women or take them to fancy restaurants by plane. I take pleasure with women who take my cash, fair exchange, nothing more.'

'Not the behaviour I would expect from a person in your position?'

'Why not? If I am cut, do I not bleed? I uphold my position with dignity; I misbehave with abandon. There is no crime, only an eccentricity.'

'It could be used against you.'

'It could, but professional etiquette would not allow it. In a court, it's the facts, not about those practising the law.'

'Then why come here?'

'I enjoy female company, and I enjoy this place. Two birds with one stone. What are you drinking? Red or white?'

'White.'

'Let me choose the vintage. Alexey had no hold over me. He might have thought he did, but I was circumspect. Brett was spending time with his daughter. I had warned him off, told him that Sidorov was dangerous and could cause trouble for him, not me.'

'How?'

'Ensure Brett didn't graduate from school, prevent him from getting into his university of choice. Sidorov wasn't a criminal but knew how to wield power and get his way. Nothing I would have been able to do to stop him, and I wanted Brett to stop seeing her. Nothing against her, but trouble lurked.'

'If you didn't kill her, who did? The evidence, circumstantial at best, points to you.'

'I knew that on the night at the marina. I warned Brett off going and knew Alexey would have seen him. He might have done something about it or might not.'

'Who killed Maria? Do you have proof?'

'There's only one person, or haven't you considered the possibility?'

'Rebecca Griffith had suffered a wound to the head, tied up in a corner.'

'Was she? She could have hit her head against something, taped her mouth, and tightened the cable ties.'

'Are you suggesting she killed her?'

'I know she did.'

'How?'

'I didn't think about it then, but we were out on the water, distracted. But later, I remembered seeing a scuffle at Sidorov's as we went by.'

'And you thought it might have been Brett or Regan?'

'I couldn't be sure. Too much to process, but then Brett told me he wasn't there, heeded my advice. It has to be Rebecca.'

'Similar height, hair colour, I'll grant you,' Natalie said. 'Why didn't you come forward before?'

'How? I needed time to think. I'm compromised, a trip out on the harbour. Not criminal; it probably won't affect my career, but embarrassing. Nobody wants their dirty linen aired in public, the fodder of legacy media, jokes on the internet, the whoring judge. You know how it is.'

Natalie understood, unsure if she had been fed a line by a man used to controlling conversations.

'Miriam Levine?'

'I can't help you there. It could be Rebecca, jealous of her friend, who thought she was better than Maria.'

Natalie thought she was safe. After all, they weren't the only diners. The plane was moored, the pilot sitting not far away. It had been an unusual day: saving Haddock's marriage, a phone call from someone they thought was a murderer, and then a plane flight, a phone call to tell her she was safe. It was surreal, too good to be true, and probably wasn't. But she had decided, and Justice Kline had given the investigation a possible alternative.

It still didn't prevent her suspicion. The poor cousin of Sidorov, Dima Ivanov, had inferred something different and that it wasn't what Sidorov could do to Kline, destroy his reputation, ruin his son's chance at university, but there was a hold over Kline for services rendered.

'The homeless man in Kings Cross?' Natalie asked.

'Joe Coster.'

'How do you know his name?'

'Supreme Court of New South Wales, a judge. I keep abreast of what happens in this city.'

'Any more to it than that?'

'I knew him a long time ago. It would have come out at some stage. Surprised you hadn't made the connection before.'

'We hadn't. How did you know him?'

'Rugby, interschool competition. He was on the other side, met him several times over the years.'

'You remember him?'

'Vaguely, the name. I went through my papers, old photos, and found him. I must have tackled him to the ground a few times and shared a drink with him, but no more than that.'

'Mary Otway?'

'Sergeant, Natalie, Sydney is not that big a city, and if you're fortunate enough to be wealthy or influential, there's always one gathering or another where you meet each other.'

'That's a speech, not an answer.'

'You're right, waffling. I knew her very well, admirable woman, but she got old, as we all do.'

'She had a younger lover twenty-five years ago.'

'Several, but she was discreet. For some reason, she ensured her privacy. Allowed the public persona, dynamic businesswoman, pillar of society. But she was like many others, a darker side to her.'

'The same as you and easy women.'

'There are always skeletons, and you've found mine. Mary had hers, as did those she mixed with. Do you believe these people are any different from you and Haddock? They fall in love, fall out, find out they've been cheated on, suffer heartbreak.'

'Not what the glossies would let you believe. You're a judge, an upholder of the law, not a celebrity; expect that from them.'

'And a man. We all have a hidden side; allowances are made.'

'Did Sidorov know of it?'

'He did. Thought he could use it to his advantage, but he never understood. He believed that strength of character, a forceful attitude, and the dirt on someone was the way to conduct business. He didn't understand subtlety, the power of an intelligent, enquiring legal mind. He never understood the de facto power that a judge has.'

Natalie took a drink. The alcohol was starting to take effect, and the food was divine. It was refreshing to be in the company of such a man, but knowing that it was inadvisable. One day, she may be involved in a criminal case he would adjudicate – conflict of interest, case thrown out, a retrial. If that happened, and his impartiality was in question, she knew what the smooth-talking judge would do. He would throw her to the wolves.

Chapter 16

Natalie shook the man's hand, thanked him for the day out, and walked away. It was three thirty-five in the afternoon.

Justice Kline of the Supreme Court of New South Wales had been a perfect gentleman, not once taking advantage of her relaxed state as she drank expensive French wine, not once looking at her in a leering manner. There was only one immediate concern, and even though she had taken no notes, she remembered it clearly: 'They fall in love, fall out, find out they've been cheated on, suffer heartbreak.' Was that an oblique reference to her live-in? Did he know? Had he had her checked out? And if he had, by whom?

It didn't seem important but could be, especially as the man had given them their best lead, deflecting Maria Sidorov's murder from him to Rebecca Griffith.

Natalie had grown up believing that the police were decent and honest in doing a difficult job and that the legal profession would be as well. And now, Kline, a senior judge who frolicked with prostitutes, did deals with Sidorov, or was in his debt, and police who were corrupt and chauvinistic.

She saw a cesspit where once she had seen a field of clover. She opened the door to her vehicle, a parking ticket on the window.

'Good day out?' a voice from the passenger seat.

'Inspector Haddock, very nice, thank you.'

His presence was a surprise; she was glad to see him.

'Kline, thumbscrews and the rack? Did he admit to killing Maria? Or did he squirm? Tell you about his deprived childhood, look for the sympathy vote, put the hard word on you.'

'A perfect gentleman. Not sure that I trust what he told me. And you?'

'She smelt a rat, said nothing. It's a drug, not so easy to give up, the same with Kline, need an outlet, the chance to let off steam.'

'More than steam with her at State Crime Command. I need a walk, drank too much, woozy after the flight, the plane had more noise than go.'

'Fear of flying?'

'They lost a plane a few years back, near where we had lunch. Strange that people don't remember.'

'Not strange, human nature. We can't dwell on the negatives; life moves on.'

The two walked along the seawall up to Rose Bay Marina. Natalie told Haddock what Kline had told her.

At the marina, the two sat. Over in the distance, the Levine house, further around the headland, Sidorov's mansion.

'Firstly, Kline wouldn't have met with you, treated you to a slap-up meal unless he knew all about you and me. Secondly, it had been planned in advance, not only by the man, but he must have had help, the phone call to Payne,' Haddock said.

'Who phoned him? Precise timing. Why the dramatics? Justice Kline could have phoned and met for a coffee, or met in his chambers.'

'I don't know who phoned him, suspect it was another judge, senior to Kline. Better not report that or mention it to anyone. These people are smart, protect their own, and we're irritants to them, come in handy at times, forgotten at others.'

'But why the subterfuge, and then so open?' Natalie said. She realised talking to Kline was hard work and needed focus to maintain control. But with Haddock, it was free-flowing, an open exchange of ideas, no need to pretend or lie.

She knew which of the two men she preferred.

'If the proverbial hits the fan, he's got plausible deniability. He hasn't officially spoken to the police, but he has. He could state that you were a willing partner, acting provocatively, attempting to proposition him, that you slept with him.'

'There were witnesses.'

'Were there? Do you think the restaurant will risk its liquor licence to protect you? Or the pilot, subject to investigation over his flight log? What about the seaplane base? Negative publicity, one accident, planes not serviced, flight logs not maintained.'

'Not even Kline could nobble all of them.'

'I agree, but the possibility remains that our case against him is weakened, and he's not the only one up to mischief. Rally around Kline, protect the troops. Superintendent Payne's a pragmatist, understands how it works better than us.'

'Rebecca Griffith?' Natalie asked. She had liked the young woman, and so had Haddock, but an accusation had been made. It would need to be followed up.

'Doesn't work for me. Get Ruth Stein to check her out, the standard tests, see if she demonstrates violent tendencies, psychopath, sociopath, or any "path" she can think of.'

'We'll need her parents' permission.'

'I know just the person to get it,' Haddock said.

'Thanks,' Natalie replied as the two returned to where the car was parked.

***

'I could make a presentation at the school, conduct tests of the pupils, the young woman included. Not so difficult to arrange. I know the headmistress,' Ruth Stein said.

Natalie met the woman at a conference in Sydney. She wondered when she found time for her practice.

'Great idea, but even if you could do it without the parents' permission, it's inadmissible evidence. We've got to do this by the book.'

'Up to you. I'm free next week, the first three days; one session to conduct an initial evaluation, a second one, the week after.'

'That long?'

'No way around it. It's the brain we're dealing with here. We can't use an X-ray or open her up. It's how she responds to my questions. She might be hostile. People don't react well to psychiatric evaluations. The school would have been a game to her, but if it's a no-go…'

'It is.'

Natalie realised they didn't have the time required and that it was strike while the iron was hot, not wait until it was tepid or cold. She also understood that psychiatric evaluation was subjective, and the results were open to question. And Rebecca Griffith, who portrayed solid family values and came from a stable environment, might be able to control herself with Ruth Stein. In short, Ruth Stein stated two weeks, but it could be much longer, and the resolution to Kline's inference had to be dealt with within the next twenty-four hours, or Superintendent Payne would be shouting down a phone at Haddock and his sergeant, not a good start for someone who had just been assigned to the Homicide Squad.

Mid-afternoon, Natalie met with Victoria Adderley. She owed her an explanation. The woman had presented Justice Kline with the summons to appear for an interview with the police, received the sharp end of Superintendent Payne's tongue, and had called Natalie stupid for getting on the flight.

'You know what you've done?' Victoria said.

'Given Kline a way out.'

'Weakened the case against him. Never underestimate men like him.'

'Or women?'

'Exactly. What were you thinking? What if the pilot was in on it? Enough money splashed around; who knows? Fell out of the plane over the ocean, could have closed the seaplane base forever.'

'Sometimes a judgement call needs to be made,' Natalie answered. 'Who phoned Superintendent Payne?'

'Not sure, someone important. The old boys' club, stroke my back, I'll stroke yours.'

'Nepotism?'

'At work. I'm tough, same as you. I can deal with it.'

'I heard a voice in the background when I phoned you,' Natalie said. She didn't care but thought it was important to know.

'I have enough of men at work. At home, I choose who I let into my life. Satisfied?'

'Curious. Each to their own. Justice Kline was a perfect gentleman, implicated Maria Sidorov's friend.'

'Careful, not that I need to caution you. Different rules apply to minors, the sympathy vote, blame the police, the parents. Do you believe her capable?'

'Capable, but we hadn't considered her before. Need to tread carefully. I'll meet with the parents later tonight and get their reaction. I would have preferred evidence, but I can't find any. It explains how the murderer got into the building if she was already there, bound and gagged.'

'Not much to go on. I can't help other than give legal advice, but you have a job. I don't envy you. I had a brother who used to get into trouble, hooliganism in his teens, a police car at the door on several occasions. Our parents went ballistic.'

'Where is he now?'

'Preaching from a pulpit in the Northern Territory. Found religion in his twenties; he got it bad. Strange what we do in our youth. Anything you regret?'

'I was Maria in my teens,' Natalie said. 'It seemed fun at the time, but now, nothing.'

'I was married at twenty-one,' Victoria said. 'I thought he was the one for me, but realised I wasn't wired that way, divorced at twenty-six, meet up every couple of weeks for a chat, a friend now.'

'Did he remarry?'

'Playing the field, got a season ticket to Tinder.'

***

Sidorov's mansion was empty of furniture; their voices echoed off the walls, and their footsteps reverberated as they walked across the wood-panelled floor.

Natalie was meeting Rebecca's parents that night. There was one thing she needed to check, something that had not been considered before.

One of the crime scene investigators was present. His evidence might be needed later, proof of entry into the house and filming the event.

'Forget hitting yourself on the head,' Haddock said.

'I didn't intend to,' Natalie said.

They were in the bathroom where Rebecca Griffith had been found bound and gagged. Natalie intended to restage how Haddock and Maria's father had found the woman and see if she could have gagged and bound herself.

The CSI had set up two cameras on tripods, and another tripod had a light beaming down on Natalie. It was hot and unpleasant.

Whatever happened, no one was to help. Standing up, Natalie taped her mouth with ducting tape. She then cable-tied her ankles; easy enough. Cable ties around her wrists at her back required forethought. She had them loosely around her wrists; the trick was to tighten them. After five minutes of considering the situation, she moved towards the bathroom door, and by forcing her hands close to the door hinge and pushing it shut, she managed to jam the loose end of the cable. The cable ties tightened with her weight against the door and her pulling away. She then slumped on the floor where Rebecca Griffith had been found.

Haddock removed the tape from her mouth and cut the ties. There was proof that it was possible but difficult. If Rebecca Griffith had bound and gagged herself, she was a resourceful and determined woman. Ruth Stein could have offered a professional evaluation, but there wasn't time. Natalie had to go home, shower, change her clothes, and drive to the Griffiths' home. She was elated on the one hand, despondent on the other.

'No,' Griffith said. It wasn't an unexpected reaction from the father. The mother was in another room.

Natalie explained the situation and emphasised that it was a process of elimination. There was no evidence pointing to his daughter, but the police had to follow up on every lead, and there had been a comment that possibly his daughter knew more. She had said the right words and had expected the reaction but thought the mother would be present.

'Your wife?' Natalie asked.

'Multiple personality issues. Here would be difficult.'

'Even here at this time?'

'Yes. Rebecca is not affected.'

A history of mental illness in the family, a child who had grown up in such circumstances, affected by it, possibly inherited it. Natalie could see that Kline might have been correct.

'We've always seen your family as stable and loving, an ideal environment for an impressionable young woman going through a difficult period.'

'It is. My wife's condition is manageable. Rebecca is fine. Your presence in our house represents disruption, and with the death of Maria, she feels vulnerable. We all do.'

Natalie could understand that. She had felt disturbed since the fifteen-year-old female had died. It affected those in the police, Haddock included. Mary Otway's death had almost been forgotten, an aged woman in her final years of life, Old Joe was rarely spoken about, and Miriam Levine might not have happened.

It was unsatisfactory in that people move on with their lives, but the death of a child, even a child who was flirtatious and promiscuous and pushing the boundaries, remained with those who had loved and known her, with those tasked with solving her murder.

To force psychiatric evaluation would have required a court order, which would have needed evidence, proof of possible involvement in her friend's death. Natalie knew it would be impossible to satisfy a judge to issue the order. The only way was if the young woman and her father agreed.

Outside, in another room, the raised voices of two women. Griffith rushed out, leaving Natalie to look around the room, a picture of Rebecca as an infant on one wall, a bookshelf along another, a cat asleep in a chair. It was homely and loving. She could not imagine Rebecca killing her friend.

The door flung open. Rebecca Griffith stood there. 'I'll do it. Mum's worried, I can't blame her, but I didn't kill Maria. She was my friend.'

It still needed parental consent, which her father gave. Ruth Stein would have the permission required. Even so, if Rebecca was mentally capable of murder, it was impossible to prove. It was a step forward in the increasingly complex set of circumstances that led to the deaths of four people. It wasn't over yet, and the investigation had once again slowed to a crawl.

Chapter 17

Haddock spent more time out of the office with intensive marriage counselling. He was struggling, desperate to keep his marriage afloat, despairing of the relentless barrage of solving murders and family disputes. All he wanted to do was to tell his wife to be quiet, to give him space to breathe, to get off his back, and to let him hotfoot it off to State Crime Command and the arms of a woman who did not confront him with problems.

Natalie continued to receive phone calls from Jimmy Rogers, who she would admit, apart from his hygiene, was charming. If he cleaned up, she might consider a date; it wouldn't be love, but she was desperate for the touch of a man. Kline and Barry Birch, the friend of Joe Coster, would have been available, but both were older than her by more than a few years. One she couldn't trust, the other she could, even though she preferred someone younger. Regardless, for now, she would regard celibacy with the reverence it deserved, hopeful she didn't end up like Mary Otway.

Moshe Levine had been on the phone, a suspicious person hanging around. A police car had been sent, and it drove up the street twice a day, which to Haddock and Natalie wasn't sufficient, and a marked patrol car would inform the loiterer to be careful but not to desist. Levine's synagogue had been targeted in the past, and he had been interviewed by several newspapers at the time and had appeared on television.

The times they had spoken to the man, Haddock and Natalie had found him civil and polite, if a little distant, but that they put down to devotion. The man's children were with his sister. His only solace was his religion.

Justice Kline was in the news. The trial of a career gangster, a family to the west of Sydney, who regarded crime as a vocation, the same as a nurse would with saving lives, but the

Murphys didn't save lives: they took them. Big Ben Murphy, the patriarch, a fight in a pub, a bottle breaking against the head of a rival, a knife to the stomach, and the defence was arguing that it was self-defence, and the man should be acquitted. Natalie had scanned the police reports, knew the man was guilty and that the judge might end up sharing a cell with the man he would sentence. She didn't hold with Rebecca being guilty, something to do with instinct, a trait Haddock believed was an integral part of an investigating officer's tool kit. Although his instinct had believed that all four murders were connected, and that hadn't been proven.

Superintendent Payne summoned Haddock and Natalie into his office; Victoria Adderley and two colleagues were already there. It was the end of the month, when senior officers worried about key performance indicators, budgets, and personnel.

Haddock didn't like the office and didn't like Payne either. But the man was in charge, and even if he was blustering and crass at times, he had a good track record. Admired for his organisational ability, feared for his cutting through personnel like a knife through butter, those in his office prepared for the worst.

'It's a cock up,' Payne said. He was standing, a bad sign for those who had seen him in action before. The previous month, a Friday, end of the month, it had been the Fraud Squad; two detectives transferred immediately to the boonies, so far out west there were kangaroos outside the police station at the rear. The man didn't mince words, came straight to the point, took action, and didn't broker verbiage. To him, a spade was a spade, not an excuse, not an operational issue or a budgetary restraint.

Haddock wanted to speak, but Natalie nudged him. He took the hint and bit his tongue. Victoria Adderley had been screamed at once; she wasn't speaking yet. Answers to questions from the man, not defending her position until challenged.

'Four murders. I've got Kline's cohorts on my back, a representation of Sydney's Jewry writing to me, asking what we're doing about the Jewish woman's death, a retirement home that reckons they're struggling to attract new residents due to the negative publicity. What can I say to them? We're working on it, making headway? A bunch of lies, and I'm not the one to tell them. Why have you placed me in this position? And then there's Sergeant Campbell flying around the country with Kline. Questions have been asked about that. Regrettable, but the damage has been done. Is he still under suspicion? Sergeant, you can answer. Keep it brief.'

'We have no evidence, but yes. His statement of association with Alexey Sidorov is contrary to what the security guard told us.'

'The night you went paddling with Haddock?'

'Yes, sir.'

'And now, the friend is getting her head examined. Any progress?'

'Not yet. According to Dr Stein, it takes time.'

'To run up her bill. This lack of progress is disturbing. Holding to the one murderer for all four, Inspector Haddock?'

'We're not focussing on that aspect, looking to solve them individually, but I hold there is an association between some of them.'

'Hold to it. The Eastern Suburbs, an incestuous pit of vipers, wouldn't trust one of them in Point Piper, all the way up to Vaucluse.'

Strong socialist tendencies, Natalie thought. Working-class background, father a cloth-capped union leader. She didn't know if it was true, but you learnt indicators by spending time with Ruth Stein. She would check on Superintendent Payne later – if she got out of the meeting intact.

'Excludes Kings Cross,' Haddock said.

Natalie thought he was pushing his luck with the quip; Payne didn't.

'Well said, Inspector. Correlation with three of the murders, although Miriam Levine's death doesn't gel. Joe Coster, homeless, an attempt at his indigenous heritage, doesn't make sense.'

'It wasn't an issue to him, Superintendent,' Natalie said.

'It could be to someone else. I would have thought homelessness was a reason to be murdered. There are a few out there who begrudge their right to sleep on the pavement. No nutcases over there?'

'No one with a reason. Also, we might link him to Mary Otway, not that he killed her.'

'Stating the bleedin' obvious,' Payne said. The dropped 'g' when he swore. The man was working class, Natalie was sure.

'Miriam Levine is an anomaly, the most violent murder,' Haddock said. 'Apart from their religion, there seems no reason to kill her.'

'Agreed. A terrorist wouldn't have killed her and kept quiet. He'd be bragging to his friends, dreaming of the seventy-two virgins if ever we catch him. Hassidic Jews, capable of murder?'

'No, but her husband said he would if he found out who had killed her. His wife wasn't as devout as him but went along with her husband. It might have been an arranged marriage, can't be sure, and there are two children. Not sure he would kill, but I reckon it's unlikely. That would be contrary to his faith, ostracised or excommunicated, not sure what they would call it.'

'Herem,' Victoria Adderley said. 'A friend at school told me, an uncle who left the faith.'

'Thanks for the lesson,' Payne said. 'Doesn't solve our problem, does it? Inspector Haddock, what's the agenda? Which murder first?'

'Stalled with Maria Sidorov until Dr Stein gives us an update. We've proved that Rebecca Griffith could have faked the gag and the cable ties; kudos to Sergeant Campbell. We've got an expert working to identify Mary Otway's toy boy. We believe it's Joe Coster, although that's fraught with problems; she gave her money to charity, a small amount to her brother, not long for this world, none to her cousin in Melbourne, an embittered woman after Otway absconded with her husband a long time ago.

'We'll spend a couple of days with Miriam Levine, revisit the case, see if we can find anything, put it on the back burner if we must.'

'Inspector, no back burner. Find the murderer in one week, maximum, or you and your sergeant and that floozy one floor down, back of beyond. Get my drift?'

One thing was for sure, Superintendent Payne didn't miss a trick. He knew what was going on. He had spies throughout State Crime Command, sycophants looking for the big chance.

***

'At his most magnanimous,' Victoria said. Out on the street, a small café down an alley. There were three: Haddock, Natalie and Victoria. The others she had brought to the meeting with Payne had returned to where they had come from.

'I'd hate to see him on a bad day,' Natalie said.

'The man is on the ball, knows what's going on, understands that crimes are not instantly solved, and I'm not Rumpole of the Bailey, and you two aren't Sherlock Holmes and Dr Watson.'

Natalie knew of the last two, unsure of the first. She wasn't about to stop the woman when she was on a roll.

'Payne's got your number, Inspector,' Victoria continued.

'Unfortunately. Common knowledge?'

'It's a police station, bigger than most. What do you think? Bush telegraph, everyone knows, not that it matters. More than a few are playing footsy with someone or another. Too many hours in close proximity, unable to unload their troubles on the loved one at the end of the day. Same with you, Inspector?'

'It's difficult, can't give up policing, can't be the ideal husband.'

'I've not been out there, but I've seen photos of the dead, gruesome, churns the stomach. Can't go home and talk about it, can you?'

It was a conversation Haddock didn't want, and he could see his sergeant looking at him sideways. She had saved his marriage twice now, but would she the next time? He was sure she would, but he knew he wasn't about to give up the floozy, as Payne had called her. Derogatory on his part, but Haddock knew it was for effect.

At Kings Cross Police Station, Moshe Levine waited. He had received a phone call from Superintendent Payne, in that focus was to be given to his wife's death.

Upon their arrival, Haddock and Natalie met the man. Levine shook Haddock's hand but declined Natalie's. 'My apologies,' he said. 'I hope you understand.'

Natalie didn't but replied, 'I do.'

All three drove to Levine's house. Melanie Chin embraced Natalie in the kitchen, said hello to Haddock and ignored Levine.

'You're back?'

'Helping out. Mr Levine's sister asked for me to come back. I like her, the same as Mrs Levine. She makes sure I get paid more. Takes no nonsense from Mr Levine.'

In the other room, Haddock and Natalie sat with Levine. 'It's understandable, your concern about the investigation,' Haddock said.

'It's not only me but our community. You know that we are despised by some and misunderstood by others. If Miriam's death resulted from religious intolerance, someone with a vendetta against Jews, we need to know. Even now, the women are more careful within the community, only going together or with their menfolk. Until someone is arrested, we cannot relax.'

Chapter 18

Ruth Stein continued with Rebecca Griffith. 'Need an extra week,' she had said the last time Natalie had spoken to her. Maybe Payne was right, and the woman was padding the bill. She would have asked for a preliminary report if the focus was still on Maria Sidorov.

Superintendent Martin at Kings Cross reinforced Payne's directive that the focus was on the death of Miriam Levine. 'One week, pressure's been applied, Payne's sweating on a result,' he said.

A police superintendent sweating meant someone more senior was pressuring, possibly political. For a minority grouping in the city, the Jewish community had significant influence, and the fear of terrorism against a marginalised offshoot caused alarm.

Haddock realised the seriousness but that Miriam Levine's murder, while tragic, was one of four, and there were more leads to follow into the death of a fifteen-year-old. He accepted the reality, cognisant of the need to solve one in preference to the other, hopeful that they were interconnected, not as confident as he had been that they were. His life was a mess, professionally and personally, and he was at the age when the past looked wasted and the future looked bleak.

There was no option; he had to continue, to put on a brave face, realising that he would have preferred to close the door and remove himself from the world for a few days, a few weeks, forever.

Natalie was in the kitchen with Melanie, and Haddock sat with Levine.

'Melanie, the day Mrs Levine died. You were here?'

'I was, although I didn't see her. I do my job, sometimes talk to her, sometimes not, and then go home.'

'Arguments in the house?'

'No. Mr Levine rarely spoke to me, but he and Mrs Levine would speak to each other. I never saw them happy, never saw them sad. I told you, I'm here for the money.'

'Did their religion concern you?'

'At first, but I got used to it, ignored it after a while, but I've told you this before. Three months, maybe four, and I'm out, anyway.'

The options as to who had killed Miriam Levine were limited. It had to be either Melanie Chin, the cleaners, Petar and Iliana Parvanov, or Rebecca Griffith. Moshe Levine's alibi was cast-iron, not open to dispute, although the stability of the marriage was uncertain.

Levine had admitted that his wife struggled with the more severe aspects of Hassidism but had been coping. There were the two children she was devoted to, although that came with a proviso, as her husband had been in Melbourne and her children were not with her.

Natalie didn't want to think ill of the Levines, not that she understood them. But Hassidism was pacifist, and Moshe Levine was polite even though he would not shake her hand.

Outside of the house, Haddock and Levine walked around the garden at the rear. There was a substantial brick wall on all sides, high enough to ensure privacy and prevent children from climbing over, but insufficient to prevent someone determined.

'Why here?' Haddock asked. 'Wouldn't you have preferred to live closer to your synagogue, to others of your faith?'

'The house was given by Miriam's parents. I would prefer to live elsewhere, but this is Sydney, and we feel safe here. Our neighbours don't bother us. We don't bother them.'

'But they don't live as you do. Alcohol, licentious behaviour, drug taking. You're in the thick of it. How can you not see and hear it?'

'We can't. It is an imperfect world; we can't expect everyone to believe as us.'

'And I can't believe that your presence and that of your wife in the area doesn't raise suspicion, overt and covert actions against you. No offence, but a police officer sees a lot over the years, and out west of Sydney there's feuding, ethnic strife, family against family, religion against religion.'

'There has been some condemnation, but it has not been severe. Nobody has threatened physical harm or thrown a pig over the wall.'

Haddock realised that Levine did have a humorous side to him, only he kept it concealed.

'Your wife, did it upset her? Her family, did they approve of your marriage?'

'Not totally. Her parents are in Israel. They have not returned.'

'That serious?'

'Miriam was moderate in her belief and impure when we married.'

'Yet you married her.'

'For love,' Levine said. 'The concept is not unknown to us.'

'We're placing special focus on your wife's death. I must ask penetrating questions to find out if we've missed something. We suspect Maria's friend, based on advice from another. It doesn't seem likely, and we'd prefer it wasn't her. Did you know her?'

'We knew Maria, and she did bring a friend once to meet my wife.'

'Her name?'

'I don't know. I wasn't here, but Miriam said she was sensible, and I would have liked her.'

'Would you?'

'I would have been polite. I am committed to my wife; finding favour in another, lusting after her, would be against my faith. I would have taken steps if that occurred.'

'Retreated into your religion?'

'I would have sought guidance. Maria was a child, and so was her friend. Not only would it have been wrong, but it would also have been against the law. We might not always agree with the law of this country, but we will always obey it.'

Natalie had told Haddock that the age of marriage for a Hassidic female was between eighteen and twenty and for a male, from twenty to twenty-five. Moshe Levine did not need Australian law to understand that Maria Sidorov and Rebecca Griffith were underage.

'We've spoken to your neighbours. On one side, Jewish, but moderate. A rebellious daughter in her twenties; a studious son at university. Alcohol in the house, and the daughter's boyfriend spending the night with her. Her brother is gay. It must be intolerable to be that close to sin.'

'We pray more than we should. Inspector, I understand you're looking for flaws and hidden aspects of this investigation that you've missed. But I have been open with you, and as for the daughter and the son next door, we offered special prayers. Unfortunately, the wall is too high; they didn't receive them. We cannot remove ourselves from wickedness, only try to lead better lives, to show by example that there is another way.'

'Muslims?'

'A difficult question. I work with such people, and there is no difficulty, but not all feel as I do. I would not agree for one of my children to marry one. Nor would a Muslim allow one of their children to marry a Jew. It sometimes happens in Israel, but it presents problems.'

'If they did?'

'Herem, forbidden. I would not want to be in their presence, but these are not questions that advance your investigation. Do not attempt to find a reason for my wife's death with me. '

'I'm not. Either your wife's death was a random act or there is a motive, and your religion is the most likely. Yet we have no knowledge of terrorist activity in Sydney at this time, and if there was, they would want maximum exposure, not secrecy.'

'It's not our faith. If it was, why the other murders?'

Another person who thought there was a connection, but Haddock couldn't make it, nor could Natalie, who was in the house with Melanie, getting under her feet, slowing the woman's work, starting to irritate her.

'Sergeant, I can't help you. I've told you all I can. I found her on her bed, nothing more. I didn't sleep for a week, kept waking up with nightmares. I wouldn't be here apart from the money.'

'Let's go over it quickly,' Natalie said. 'You came to work, got on with your chores. The cleaners waved at you; Petar or Iliana?'

'Petar, I could hear a vacuum somewhere in the house. I assumed it was him. I didn't see them leave; nothing unusual in that. They had tried to enter Mrs Levine's bedroom, but there were clear instructions not to if it was locked, but I did, later that day. I had to change the sheets, and Mr Levine would have been upset if I hadn't, although he would have agreed with me leaving her all day to rest.'

'Did she do that often?' How about food and drink?'

'I never thought about it. Their life was unusual, and I thought she had taken some with her; no reason to be suspicious.'

'You used a key to enter the bedroom?'

'I did. There's a set of keys in the kitchen, hidden in the pantry.'

'Which means Mrs Levine's key wasn't in the lock in her bedroom. Otherwise, you wouldn't have been able to use yours.'

'I suppose so.'

'Unusual, taking out the key?'

'It wasn't my concern. I wanted to finish, to get home to my family; nothing wrong with that.'

There wasn't, Natalie knew, but no key in the lock meant that whoever had been in the room with Mrs Levine had taken it. It was an error in the investigation that she and Inspector Haddock hadn't considered.

'Did you try the room before?'

'No.'

'On other occasions, have you found someone in the room?'

'Once, five, six months ago. Mrs Levine suffered from migraines. She would take a strong sedative and sleep for hours.'

'Was the key in the lock when you tried the door?'

'I tried it, couldn't get my key in. Mrs Levine opened it for me.'

'Which means that normally she would lock the door from the inside, leave the key inside.'

'I suppose so, didn't think much about it.'

An inquest would confirm what Natalie suspected. Miriam Levine, a woman who struggled with her faith, had, while in a depressive state, alone and in her house, without the comfort of her children, suffering from migraine, her mind disturbed, committed suicide, ensured that no fingerprints were on the knife as she was wearing gloves, a point overlooked by Haddock and Natalie when they first looked at the body. On reflection, they realised that they had regarded the family as unusual inhabitants in Point Piper, and had not given due credence to what the woman had been wearing.

Moshe Levine would dispute. His religious leaders would debate and attempt political influence to remove the negative press detrimental to their small group of believers.

Superintendent Payne congratulated the two police officers on their prompt solving of the woman's death, although not without criticism that they hadn't explored the possibility before.

Melanie Chin was sacked the day after Natalie solved the case. The reason given was unsatisfactory performance. Unofficially it was because she had spoken to Sergeant Natalie Campbell.

The day's events would remain with Natalie for a long time, a severe sadness that Miriam Levine had felt the need to resort to drastic action.

***

Haddock's theory that all four murders were interconnected was down the drain, as was his marriage. Two weeks after his last encounter with her one floor down, he had been evicted from the family home and was renting a one-bed apartment in Parramatta.

'Couldn't do it, move in with her,' he confided to Natalie. 'She's a drug I could do without. Moving in with the woman would only confirm my wife's worst suspicions; need to go cold turkey.'

'You've only got yourself to blame. Besides, you'll not keep away from her.'

'Ruth Stein?' Haddock said. He didn't want to talk about his failed marriage, hopeful of a reconciliation, but knew it would not occur. 'Has she determined whether Rebecca Griffith is crazy, off the planet, or harmless?'

'Still padding the bill. I reckon Superintendent Payne was right about her.'

'Rogers? Any luck with the photos? Do we know who the toy boy is?'

'I'll check later. He's becoming a pest, keeps asking me out.'

'Reportable?'

'I can look after myself.'

'We're back to Maria Sidorov, then. Where do we go if Stein's playing hard to get, unwilling to give us more? Another flight with Justice Kline, thumbscrews with Russell Harding?'

'Neither. I survived Kline once; not sure I'd risk another meeting with him. The man's a lecher, and I'm fair game. We can be certain he's taken action to protect himself, willing to take us down at the first opportunity, throw us to the wolves or the sharks, depending on which you prefer.'

'Neither. We're dealing with persons with influence. Not sure I trust Payne any more than Kline. Sidorov's still back in the homeland, and Dima Ivanov's unemployed and probably getting drunk.'

Natalie took a day to catch up on paperwork and to set her desk up in Parramatta. She had enjoyed the small police station in Kings Cross; found State Crime Command intimidating.

'How are you fitting in?' A woman sat down beside her in the building's canteen. Natalie knew who she was.

'Fine, and you?'

The woman had come between Haddock and his wife, but there was no reason to blame her. In her late thirties, she looked like a person who had experienced life, three children by two men, looked after by their grandparents, a farm one hundred and fifty kilometres from Sydney.

'You know who I am?'

'Theresa. Yes, I know. Hard not to know around here. Still on with Inspector Haddock?'

'Not sure. It was casual but fun, and I'm not seeing anyone else.'

'Do you see many?'

'Laissez-faire approach to life. I preferred him married. Makes me sound cheap, but I'm not. Just not concerned about pretending to be something I'm not. How about you?'

It was Natalie's first friend in the building. She wanted to think badly of the woman but couldn't.

'Not even a cat, let alone a man. Not sure I approve of you and Haddock. I met his wife and got him out of trouble a couple of times, couldn't do it forever.'

'You did what you had to, but the marriage was doomed. The curse of the Homicide Squad. Enough in State Crime Command, broken marriages, a stray on the side, but Homicide's got the record. Hope you don't mind getting hit on by every stray male.'

'Do you?'

'Love it. As I said, laissez-faire. Who knows what comes tomorrow. How are the murders? Gory, plenty of blood, or do you get used to it?'

'Not sure it's entertainment. I take it you don't get out much.'

'Never. I'm with Fraud, identify the criminal online, make a case for the prosecution, send out a couple of uniforms to escort the hapless individual to the police station, listen while he or she, can't be sexist, protests their innocence.'

'And then?'

'PowerPoint, video, bank records, internet usage; show them the lot. No way back after we've brought them in.'

'Sounds a cushy number,' Natalie said as she ate lunch. The food was not as good as the restaurant in Kings Cross, but it would suffice.

'It depends if you like sitting in front of a computer all day. Personally, I do. Haddock, not much use with a computer?'

'He's a field man, old-style, works on instinct. It works well for him, good track record, although you could stuff it up.'

'How? Even Payne's got a bit on the side. I heard you went out with Justice Kline; old for you, isn't he?'

'Official business, sanctioned at the highest level. A perfect gentleman, and how do you know? Privileged information.'

'Fraud, sweeping powers. Anticorruption is one of the buzzwords around here. Added responsibility, check on who's who, who's sleeping with who, if you get my drift.'

'Are you spying on Haddock, even while sleeping with him? Hardly a romance based on trust.'

'Not Haddock, but everyone. It's my job. He knows, now you do.'

Sergeant Natalie Campbell was confused. She hadn't signed up for the vindictiveness of a woman who appeared serious.

'On whose authority?'

'Mine, who else? I thought you'd understand.'

'I don't.'

Natalie pushed her plate to one side, stood up and left. She needed to talk to Haddock.

Chapter 19

Despite Haddock's assurances that it was sour grapes on his former lover's part, it left Natalie unsettled.

She had expected State Crime Command to have more than a few male chauvinists; she hadn't expected a vindictive woman. Whatever ailed the woman was unhealthy, unprofessional, and demanding of censure. Due to the seriousness of the encounter, she filed a report with Human Resources. Whether they would act on it was open to question.

Those in authority looked to the key performance indicators: arrests, convictions, murder and other crimes solved, safety and cohesive workplace, and adherence to defined behaviour. One rotten apple and the cart would be upended. Natalie realised her stay in Parramatta might be short-lived.

Regardless of her disquiet, there were still three murders to solve. She had received notification from Mary Otway's cousin in Melbourne that Mary's brother had passed away in Queensland, and she was going to his funeral. Also, Mary Otway's will was to be contested.

It was a significant development. The claim had been filed with the Department of Communities and Justice. Natalie handled the paperwork to obtain a copy, and Haddock informed Superintendent Payne, who endorsed the action. Natalie thought Haddock should not have sought Payne's approval. The inspector oversaw the murder investigation, not the superintendent.

'Play the game, butter up the man. No harm done; it makes him feel important. He's an action man, stuck in an office. He doesn't like it, can't blame him.'

'You sound as though you like him.'

'He's not stopping us from doing our job, and he could have given you a rollicking over meeting with Kline and me for Theresa, but he didn't.'

'I've filed a report with Human Resources; it goes in her file,' Natalie said.

'And yours. Troublemakers don't last long.'

Haddock had changed; it worried her. Before, he had been encouraging and open, but now he was reticent and guarded. She hoped it was due to his marriage breakdown and a daughter forced to choose either her mother or father, a conflict that a teenager doesn't need. Plus, Theresa, the loud-mouthed former lover, although judging by the man's condition that morning, the romance wasn't over. If she was as scheming as Natalie thought and spying, officially or not, she was not a woman for him to associate with.

'If the cousin told you the will was being contested, it's not her, and the brother's dead. They're the only two we know of.'

'Which means there is a third.'

'Old Joe's dead. It can't be him.'

'We're speculating, trying to come up with a name. Give me time, and we'll know,' Natalie said. She wasn't in good humour. She had arrived at State Crime Command full of optimism and joie de vivre, but now she felt like she had made a wrong decision. It was a mood that would linger all day.

While waiting at the Department of Communities and Justice, she received an irate phone call.

'You bitch, filed a complaint after I tried to be friendly. Screwing Haddock, I know that now.' It was Theresa, and she was angry.

'With Human Resources, my prerogative,' Natalie replied. 'If you have an issue, follow up with them, and let them set up a meeting between us.'

Not the most auspicious start to joining Homicide Squad. The woman hung up.

'Here you are, a copy of the claim,' as Natalie was handed the document. She could have stayed at Parramatta and received it by email, but she was glad to be out of the office.

Two hours later, she met with Haddock at the café in Kings Cross, where the manager always ensured their mugs of coffee were full.

'The name?' Haddock asked.

'Theresa blasted me out, called me a bitch,' Natalie said.

'What did you expect? She's fiery, full of passion, full of hate. Human Resources have been on to me, asked me what I reckon.'

'Your comment.'

'An impossible position that you've placed me in. I've had to acknowledge that I know Theresa.'

'Everyone knew.'

'Not officially, and nothing in the regulations against it. However, Theresa's supposed to be professional, and she doesn't have the authority to hack computers; not sure if that's possible.'

'It wouldn't be. And if they were conducting surveillance of certain persons in the building, they would use an independent firm accredited to the police, not someone who works in Fraud. She shouldn't be there,' Natalie said. 'And you've given your wife away for her? Not a great decision, is it?'

'I've made my bed, now I've got to lie in it, and it's uncomfortable.'

'And lonely. We're a right pair, make a good team, but our private lives are a shambles.'

'Not that good, still have three murders to solve. What does the report say?'

'Bruce Gooding, an address in England.'

'What do we know about him?'

'The question is, how did Mary Otway's cousin know? She denied any knowledge of the man. He's in his seventies and claims he's still married to Mary.'

'Divorced from the cousin, married to Mary Otway? Marriage certificate?'

'There is one. It'll need to be checked, but we assume it is. Which means one thing.'

'A motive. Has the man been in Australia?'

'I'm checking, but probably not, which means the cousin needs further investigation.'

'One hour flight from Melbourne, taxi to the retirement home, a gentle push and back to Melbourne. Four hours maximum, leave after breakfast, home for lunch.'

'I'm checking passengers on flights around that time, but she could have travelled on a false name, probably did if she's that devious.'

'And in contact with her former husband. Why keep in contact? I thought the hatred was intense.'

'It probably was, can't be certain that it still is, as time dulls the anger. And the cousin could have agreed if she got her share of the money. Who knows what hatred Mary's husband has.'

***

Natalie sensed hostility when she entered Homicide Squad. She had been there for less than a week and was already creating waves. Haddock had warned her it would happen, and she had never filed a claim for sexual harassment, although one had been guilty, pinning her up against the wall in a police station. He had been drunk, and it was late at night, burning the midnight oil, and she had been young and keen. Naïve as a teenager growing up in a country town, able to fend off the amorous locals, but the sergeant who had cornered the young constable had been large and overweight, reeking of beer and curry.

Unable to reason with him and not strong enough to fend him off, she screamed at the top of her lungs. Another officer came into the room, grabbed hold of the drunk and hurled him to the floor, putting a boot into his groin and the man screaming in pain.

'Are you okay?' her rescuer asked.

'What about him?' Natalie asked.

'I'll file a report, have him out of the station within the week. He's a good officer, but alcohol is his downfall. Happens to a lot of them. You put up a good fight.'

'I've not seen you before.'

'Came back earlier today, took a bullet to the leg, off for six weeks. Inspector Hammond at your service.'

They had been an item for six months, moving in together for the last four months, only for him to be transferred on his promotion to chief inspector, her unwillingness to commit to a man twelve years older than her.

Now, in Homicide Squad, she regretted the decision.

'Ruffling feathers,' Superintendent Payne said. She had been summoned into his office, expected to receive her marching orders and set a new record, the shortest time in the Homicide Squad.

'Snitching, not recommended,' Natalie replied.

'Definitely not. Did you expect the reaction outside?'

'Inspector Haddock warned me. She seemed to know too much and thinks I'm the guilty party.'

'Hell hath no fury like a woman scorned.'

'Not scorned yet, should be. Is there any truth in what she was saying?'

'Checking on people in the building, no way. Strange behaviour, unsure what to do about it.'

'Are you suggesting I should withdraw the complaint?'

'Never show weakness. Haddock, good officer?'

'He is. Confused at present. Maybe I shouldn't be telling you that.'

'Off the record. He's kept off the grog, demon destroyer of many a police officer. Are you a drinker?'

'The occasional wine.'

'Unattached?'

Natalie hoped Payne wasn't about to put the hard word on her.

'I am.'

'No report of sexual harassment on your record. Must have happened.'

'It has.'

'Not in here. If I see it happen once, an inappropriate remark, staring too long, or wandering hands, they're out of here. Haddock, any truth in what the woman said, that he knew of her hacking the database?'

'None.'

'Keep it that way. Mary Otway? The husband?'

'We're following through, off to Melbourne to interview the cousin. A strong possibility that she murdered the woman. She claimed she hadn't heard of her former husband for a long time but must have been in contact.'

'Or he made the trip to Australia and flew back. No doubt you've considered the possibility.'

'We have, but the man would be in his late seventies. Daunting enough in your teens as a backpacker.'

'But doable.'

'The cousin knew of the claim on Mary Otway's assets. No reason to contact her if the man's married to Mary Otway.'

'True. Have a good flight. Bring her back in cuffs if you can.'

'If she's guilty,' Natalie said. 'Her, downstairs?'

'I've spoken to HR and the head of Fraud. Leave it to them, ignore the woman, and take no notice of them outside. Noses out of joint, realise that you're no pushover.'

***

Natalie wasn't convinced by Payne's assurance that the hostility towards her would abate. However, there was a more pressing issue, a flight to Melbourne.

The cousin, Sheila Cross, had been informed and would be at Prahran Police Station on Malvern Road, six kilometres from Melbourne City Centre, at eleven o'clock the following morning.

Modern, red brick, it was functional, if austere. The flight had been delayed out of Sydney due to fog, and Haddock and Natalie entered the police station at 11.35 a.m. to find Mary Otway's cousin sitting quietly, a cup of tea in her hand.

'They made me very welcome,' she said.

They had come to arrest a woman for murder; instead, they found the police serving her tea. It wasn't what they had expected.

Haddock went through the formalities at the station, presented his warrant card, met the senior officers, and made the introductions. It was friendlier than Homicide Squad but not as friendly as Kings Cross.

'Miss Cross is a local celebrity,' a sergeant told Natalie. 'Helps with the homeless in the area.'

A murderer and a good Samaritan. It wouldn't be the first time, Natalie thought.

It was formal in the interview room; no more levity with fellow officers and no more easy conversation with the cousin.

To one side of Sheila Cross, her lawyer sat. She had formally introduced herself. A woman in her fifties, stylishly dressed, looked efficient and capable. The cousin had been advised by Natalie to have legal representation.

Sheila Cross sat calmly; she had brought in another cup of tea for herself, another for the lawyer.

'Miss Cross,' Haddock said, 'you informed Sergeant Campbell that Mary Otway's will is to be contested.'

'I did.'

'And the man contesting it is your former husband.'

'Yes, although I didn't know he was alive.'

'Then how did you know of the claim? You are a cousin, not the immediate family. There was no reason for you to be informed.'

'I didn't know where he was. However, I have lived in the same house for over forty-five years. He sent me a letter two days ago.'

'Proof?' Natalie asked.

Sheila Cross opened her handbag and placed the letter on the table. It was rare to see one; only the elderly write letters, replaced by smartphones with instant communication and emails.

'There's a phone number. Have you phoned?'

'I have.'

'Why contact him? Does he want to rekindle the past?'

'He needs my help.'

'Did he say why?'

'He is unwell and cannot travel. There are details to be dealt with here. He has asked me to be his proxy.'

'He leaves you for your cousin. You haven't heard from him in over forty years, and he asks a favour?' Haddock said. He could see a wasted trip, although he wasn't ready to admit defeat.

'I told him I wouldn't do it unless…'

'He cut you in for a share of the profit.'

'Not profit, inheritance.'

'I believe, Inspector Haddock, that you are attempting to intimidate my client,' the lawyer said.

'Not intimidate, but get to the truth. Someone murdered Mary Otway, and the most logical would be someone who would gain from her death. Now we know that Bruce Gooding is in England and Miss Cross is here.'

'You haven't asked if I agreed with Bruce,' Sheila Cross reminded Haddock.

'Did you?'

'I might. It would be good to see him again. I must, can't you see?'

Haddock couldn't, but he thought as a man, logically. Natalie could; she thought it romantic, two old people rekindling love.

They had not intended to stay the night in Melbourne, but circumstances dictated. Natalie knew the rumour mill would be working overtime at State Crime Command, but duty came first, not the gossip.

The word from HR, who had phoned during the day, was that Theresa de Klerk, born in South Africa, had arrived in

Australia in 2008 and was now under investigation. Her behaviour towards Natalie had led to others registering additional complaints against the woman.

Superintendent Payne had also messaged. Natalie hoped she wouldn't have to fend him off. She would ask for a transfer if she did, knowing it would go against her. Nobody would stand up to Payne.

Payne set up the call, spoke to a counterpart in England, the city of Bath, and obtained the cooperation of Homicide in England. Natalie remembered the Roman baths from her backpacking days, the torrential rain, and the baths were green from algae.

'Bruce Gooding, late seventies,' Haddock told Inspector Maynard in Bath. It was Zoom, and both Haddock and Natalie were on camera. At the other end, a man in his fifties with a moustache. Natalie thought it didn't suit him.

'You've got the address. We need to know, seeing that it is early morning where you are. What is the condition of the man: mobile, able to travel to Australia, any convictions, the usual.'

'You suspect him of murder?' Maynard asked.

'Initially, no,' Natalie said. 'But the situation's changed. We had money on the dead woman's cousin, but we can't be sure now. Her story is plausible, with no chance of her confessing. Just don't want to waste our time in Melbourne.'

'Three hours. We'll phone back.'

Haddock and Natalie sat in a restaurant in St Kilda, a suburb near Prahran. He ate beef; she chose fish. It had been a long day, and the two were glad of the opportunity to relax.

'Ruined my love life,' Haddock said.

'Not much love, was there?'

'None. I wish I could make it up to my wife. Not so easy.'

Natalie understood. On a murder investigation, he was happier than at home.

Chapter 20

'Old, infirm, and suffering from emphysema,' Maynard said.

It had been four in the morning when Haddock was woken from his sleep; ten minutes later when Haddock had woken Natalie.

'He's not made a trip to Australia,' Maynard added.

'Did you speak to him?'

'We did. He lives close to Royal Crescent. If your sergeant has been here, she'd know where I'm referring.'

Natalie nodded. Before joining Haddock in his room, she had slipped on a pair of jeans and a loose-fitting top. He had dressed for the occasion, a towelling dressing gown hanging on the back of the bathroom door. Natalie knew that Theresa would have a fit if she knew.

'Which means he didn't kill the woman, but he believes that after forty years, give or take a few, he's entitled to the money.'

'Depends on the law in Australia,' Maynard said.

'Wealthy or doing it tough?'

'One street away, Brook Street, not up to the class of Royal Crescent, but it's above my pay scale. He owns the place, we checked, and he's financially sound; owned a couple of pubs in the city for a long time.'

'Why bother if he's not got long?' Natalie asked.

'We asked, got a noncommittal response, something to do with past history.'

'Life blighted, or was he reminiscing?'

'We couldn't be sure. He's on a respirator, gasping for breath. Maybe it was a subterfuge while we were there, but we asked a shop over the road from him. They corroborate the story. Whoever your murderer is, it wasn't Bruce Gooding.'

'Did you confront him with the names of Sheila Cross and Mary Otway?'

'Long time ago, he said, past history, one thing to do before I go, remedy what he and the dead woman had done.'

'Destroyed his first wife. Marriage in England?'

'None on record. Bigamy if he had, but you're involved with murder, two wives concurrent would be the least of your worries.'

Both officers saw that spending the night in Melbourne hadn't been in vain. That day, Sheila Cross would feel the full weight of a police interrogation; the gloves were off, and there would be no more sparring.

***

Natalie felt sorry for the woman, wilting under a barrage of rapid-fire questioning from Haddock. He was not in a good mood. His wife was on the phone at six in the morning, his paramour at seven. One accuses him of neglecting his parental duties, the other of sleeping with his sergeant and saying what a bitch she was.

'Too much to deal with,' Haddock had confided to Natalie on the drive to Prahran Police Station.

Natalie could sympathise; she had only had a philandering live-in, which had seriously affected her for months. Haddock had a worse deal, complicated by a teenage daughter. Theresa de Klerk was under investigation, a possible suspension, and involuntary leave on full pay.

Natalie had stirred a hornet's nest, and State Crime Command would view her as a disruptive element, causing an inevitable reworking of the ethics code that police officers had to adhere to. She should have been concerned but felt ambivalent. To her, policing was about policing, not internal politics, male chauvinism, and accusing bitches. She would reconsider her position, ask for a transfer or consider another occupation if she had to.

Superintendent Payne appeared to be on her side, keeping her updated about the situation. She suspected his motives, and besides, he was married, twenty years older than her a least. She was looking for love, not to become a notch on a policeman's truncheon, even if his was bigger than most.

'He told me he wasn't well,' Sheila Cross reiterated.

Her lawyer had been conspicuous by not interfering. She had been presented with the facts before the first interview and spent two hours in conversation with her client before the second. Haddock rightly assumed that Sheila Cross had been advised to hold steady, not to say too much and keep calm, nor to blurt out in an unguarded moment, 'I did it. I killed Mary Otway.'

It was what Haddock wanted, although he would spend longer in Melbourne if he could. He was off the leash, the chance to put his feet up for a night in the hotel, to watch a good movie, risqué if available. Even Natalie enjoyed the relative ambience of Melbourne, conscious of what was happening in Parramatta. Pressured to present her findings, Ruth Stein revealed a fifteen-year-old female with anger issues, above average intelligence, a Grade A student, a father she loved, and a mother she loathed. Regardless of the father's statement, the Griffith house was not a bed of roses but thorns.

No evidence, no admission of guilt, and no reason for Rebecca to have murdered her friend, and interviewing minors was difficult: no bright lights, standing close by or frightening the person, and no rapid-fire questioning.

Even Jimmy Rogers had been active, no longer trying to proposition Natalie, not after the last time she told him to back off.

'It's Joe Coster,' he had said two days earlier. 'Took a lot of work.'

The toy boy had been identified. The man had been involved with Mary Otway, but it made no sense to either Haddock or Natalie. The man was out of the picture, not interested in the money, most times incapable of registering what would have been required of him, even if he had intended to contest the woman's will. Coupled with the fact that he was the first to die and had no claim on her money. There was a correlation between Mary Otway and Old Joe, but it was so weak and tenuous that it should have been rejected. A verdict of death by misadventure, persons unknown. Haddock knew that would be the outcome, but he still reckoned something was amiss – he wasn't about to let it go.

Natalie wasn't either; after all, she had been friendly with the man and knew him to have been a good person, down on his luck, with a ruined life, an addiction he couldn't shake.

'Miss Cross,' Haddock said. 'We've gone over this half a dozen times, but you're still not answering.'

'My client does not have to answer your questions,' Sheila Cross's lawyer said. The woman hadn't said much before, a sign that she doubted her client's continuing denial.

It shouldn't have made any difference, as the lawyer was there for her client, guilty or innocent. Haddock had seen it before, the disconsolate lawyer when they realised that all was lost, but this woman wore it like a badge.

'Your client has questions to answer.' Natalie took over from Haddock. 'We've spoken to the police in England. They've met with your former husband and confirmed he cannot make the trip to Australia and that his health is poor. He has no more than a few months to live.'

'I would like to see him,' a timid voice said.

'Not if you're charged with Mary Otway's murder. There is only you. When did you learn that Bruce Gooding was alive? You said you received a letter, but how did he know that Mary Otway was dead.'

'He read it on the internet, I suppose.'

'Suppose is not good enough. Besides, we know he doesn't have a computer, nor a smartphone, and he's not been seen on the street for weeks.'

Natalie didn't know if what she said was correct; she thought it was worth trying, to see the response.

'He must have found out somehow.'

'Miss Cross, let's be honest with ourselves in this room. You had contact with him before the letter. Let's get that correct. It could help you.'

Haddock couldn't see how, but he would let his sergeant continue. He wasn't in the mood to pressure the woman. So far, that morning, a roasting from his wife and the sharp tongue of another.

'My client has said that the first she heard from Bruce Gooding was a letter.'

'Let's come back to when you came to the funeral. You were there, I saw you, but you left without a chance for us to speak,' Natalie said.

'A plane to catch, things to do in Sydney. I went to the funeral, not for Mary, but for the past. We had grown up together, friends, shared an apartment, and she had been at my wedding but stole him from me later. It might seem macabre, but memories are not always good, but they remain significant.'

'Bittersweet. What did you think at the funeral? Sorrow that you hadn't made up, or glad she was dead?'

'Sorrow for both of us and for Bruce.'

'Who you knew was in England. Have you visited him over there?'

'Yes.'

It wasn't the first time in an interrogation, when everyone was tired and winding towards a close, that there was a revelation. Haddock sat up straight, the lawyer cast an eye over at her client, and Natalie suppressed a smile.

'When? Why?' Haddock seized the momentum.

'And why have you not told us this before?' Natalie asked.

'One at a time, allow my client the opportunity to respond,' the lawyer said.

The one person not speaking sat quietly, tears rolling down her cheeks.

Haddock knew a compassionate person would have halted proceedings to allow the woman to compose herself. He also knew it was not a luxury he could afford.

The lawyer put an arm around the tearful woman and looked over to the other side of the table. She knew she should insist that there had to be a break in the interview, but knew it would not happen.'

'Miss Cross,' Haddock said, 'you have consistently told us one story, knowing there was another. I believe we are entitled to the truth.'

Natalie could empathise with the woman, but not a murderer, which increasingly appeared to be the situation.

'Twice in the last twenty years. We met in England once, in France another.'

'Rekindled romance?'

'It wasn't possible. He was part of my life; I was part of his. Too much had happened, and we could be friends, a shared hatred of the woman who had blighted our lives.'

'You both wished her dead?'

'More than that. Others might have been fooled, but we knew her for what she was.'

'You said you forgave Bruce Gooding.'

'Emotionally, I was empty. The hate had turned to nothingness. Besides, he was in his sixties the first time we met in England, closer to seventy the second. Our time had passed.'

'Why?' Natalie asked.

'No reason other than he was lonely, and so was I. He asked me to move in with him, but I couldn't. Too much to do in Melbourne, and I'm set in my ways.'

'You phoned him to tell him that Mary Otway was dead.'

'I did, and he wanted to contest the will, thought she owed us for what she had done.'

'Even if the claim, after so many years since they had lived together as man and wife, would almost certainly fail.'

'Bruce understands such things; I do not. I filled out the form and sent it to Bruce, which he signed. I suppose it will be a waste of time now, seeing that you intend to charge me with Mary's murder.'

'Is that a confession?'

Haddock thought it premature. A confession was one thing, but where was the evidence? The police didn't have any, other than the word of a disappointed woman. A defence lawyer would make mincemeat of the police if the woman changed her confession and said it was made in a moment of remorse and sadness. And for those she had loved, either cheating her or dying, she had filled out a form she now regretted.

'I suppose it is,' Sheila Cross said. Words, not spoken with firmness, but an exasperated sigh.

'Thirty minutes,' Natalie said to Haddock. He understood she had something urgent to do.

***

It was early for Jimmy Rogers, who usually woke late and worked through the night. Even so, he was pleased to hear Natalie's voice.

'Rethinking my offer, a night on the town?' he said.

'No, thanks. This is professional and urgent, two hours max.'

'I'm not in the office.'

'It doesn't matter. You've access to face recognition software on your computer?'

'I do, irregular if you're asking me to do you a favour. There are procedures: sensitive subject, personal privacy.'

'Jimmy, don't quote the rule book at me. You circumvent it when it suits you.'

Rogers knew Natalie was correct, but he was stalling for time. The chance to speak to her was rare, and he liked to hear her voice.

'Here's the deal,' Natalie said. 'We've got a woman about to confess to murder, but there's no proof she committed the crime.'

'Your word against hers?'

'Her word against her. It might be bogus, an attempt to deflect us. We don't want egg on our faces.'

'Okay, fire away.'

Jimmy Rogers opened his laptop and logged into State High Command. It was a good connection and fast. He opened up the face recognition software.

'Sheila Cross, the retirement home, the day Mary Otway died. Assume the woman was there for the day but could have hidden away somewhere, so expand out one day on either side.'

'There's an image of Sheila Cross on the database. Use that?'

'For now. You've got the CCTV footage from the retirement home?'

'I do. Need more than two hours, could take most of the day. Not up to me; put it on auto and let it run.'

'Fine. Do whatever is necessary. Get priority if you have to.'

'No need. It's to do with bandwidth, not permission.'

Haddock stood alongside Natalie, a cup of coffee in his hand. 'You're not convinced? It'll make Superintendent Payne's day if we arrest the woman.'

'Not yours if we have to release her later. A confession without any proof could make us look like fools. I'm not convinced she pushed Mary Otway.'

'Nor am I. But she met Bruce Gooding twice, told us she hadn't.'

'Easy to say, but where's the proof?'

'Check with the Department of Immigration. See how far their records go back. Sheila Cross or Sheila Gooding; she could have used more than one name.'

Inside the interview room, Natalie asked the woman, 'Passport, what name?'

'Sheila Cross.' The woman handed over her passport. 'You're uncertain if I'm telling you the truth.'

'For someone about to confess to murder, you're remarkably calm.'

'My client stated that she expected you to charge her with murder,' the lawyer said. 'That is a subtle difference to what you've just said.'

'Correct,' Haddock said. 'We will accept a confession, but we need a motive and proof, neither of which is apparent.'

'My client is only responsible for stating her position, something she has not done yet.'

The lawyer was negligent in her duty, as if she had resigned herself to her client confessing.

Natalie realised she and Haddock were being pedantic, but the four deaths had taken twists and turns. They had erred over Miriam Levine's death, not wanting to believe ill of the pious woman and her husband. Old Joe's death still made no sense, and why murder Mary Otway when any claim on her money after her death was so weak as to make it inconsequential.

The only murder with substance was that of Maria Sidorov, a fifteen-year-old schoolgirl on the cusp of adulthood, experimenting with Brett Kline, discovering love and sex in a boat shed, hopeful of meeting him at her house. But she had been thwarted, dead and floating in the harbour, her body seen by Kline's father after his night of debauchery. Too many coincidences, too many reasons for the woman to have died. She had not been sexually violated, which raised concern, as though the murderer had been disturbed, or it had been Rebecca Griffith, regarded by Ruth Stein, criminal psychologist, as having anger issues, and the Griffiths were dysfunctional, a mother with agoraphobia, a stern father. Rebecca loved one and loathed the other, but was the love for the father a conditioned response to avoid his wrath?

Yet two police officers sat in an austere red-brick police station, attempting to obtain a confession and proof, probably returning to Sydney empty-handed, a rollicking from Superintendent Payne, a confrontation with Theresa, who had been seen loitering in the street outside State High Command.

Haddock realised there was more to do in Melbourne, and another day was needed, which suited him fine. Natalie understood the rationale, not wanting to arrest a woman who had consistently lied, changed her story several times, and could still feed them a pack of lies.

'Miss Cross, before we conclude for today,' Haddock said. 'Are you willing to confess to the murder of Mary Otway?'

'It took you long enough to ask a direct question,' Sheila Cross replied sarcastically. 'Her death didn't concern me, but I did not kill her. I would have once, but she was old and dying, as Bruce and I are.'

'Yet Bruce Gooding submits paperwork at your instigation.'

'He did. Good for him.'

'Did you visit her in the retirement home?'

'Once, four years ago. I wanted to gloat, to see how far she had fallen.'

'And?'

'I felt sorry for her. She didn't know who I was. Strangely, there are times when the past seems irrelevant. Sitting with her, I remembered our childhood and the friendship we had once shared. I spoke of the good times, omitted the bad. She smiled once or twice, but I don't think she understood much of what I said. She might have known me, but it had been a long time, and I was aged, the same as her. But I was cognisant of my surroundings. She wasn't.'

The woman contradicted herself with virtually every sentence. Neither Haddock nor Natalie could separate fact from fiction. It was for others to resolve the impasse.

Chapter 21

Sheila Cross was evasive, Ruth Stein procrastinated, and Superintendent Payne became increasingly impatient. Haddock had to agree that it had been a long haul, and time had marched on with little result.

The proof Haddock and Natalie looked for would only come from Jimmy Rogers, checking CCTV footage, and the Department of Immigration.

The dates put forward by Sheila Cross for her trips to Europe to meet her former husband had been confirmed. Checks with Australian domestic airlines were not easy due to the number of people travelling, and no proof of identity was required, only a valid ticket. A false name could have been given, or Sheila Cross could have visited Sydney by private car, train, or bus.

So far, no charge could be laid against the woman, no proof that she was guilty, and a vain attempt to garner Mary Otway's wealth had a poor chance of succeeding. The disputed claim on the woman's estate smacked of malignancy, not substantive, but why? It made no sense; Sheila Cross was not unintelligent, and Bruce Gooding had run successful businesses in England.

Jimmy Rogers phoned at three in the morning. Natalie should have been annoyed to be woken, but not this time.

'Sheila Cross was there on the day that Mary Otway died. Outside the building, a car registered in her name. Lucky I picked it up, worthy of a night out.'

The man was relentless.

'A meal on me, a few drinks, and don't try it on, trained in unarmed combat.' Natalie could no longer deny him.

'Not that you mean it,' Rogers replied.

Natalie did. He wasn't her type, even if he was a decent man, but her live-in had been, and he had disappointed her.

'Is there any more?'

'Not really. She arrived at eight in the morning and left at 1 p.m. Not so easy to spot: heavy coat, a hat, large sunglasses. Facial recognition struggles without a clear frontal of the face.'

'She would have used a different name, or she could have just snuck in; not difficult.'

'Why bother? Cheaper to fly.'

'More CCTV. If she had murder on her mind, she might have thought about recognition, which means premeditated.'

'Best of luck.' Rogers hung up.

Natalie messaged Haddock; he was pleased with the news, not excited that he had been woken.

At 9 a.m. the following day, Sheila Cross sat in the interview room. This time, the mood was chilly. Specific facts and printouts from the retirement home had to be presented.

The lawyer had been told of the development and spent thirty minutes with her client before the interview commenced.

'It was an accident,' Sheila Cross said. An eloquent argument that she had driven to Sydney on a whim, that she sometimes went for long drives in the country, staying in guest houses and motels. And that she had ended up in Sydney, had visited coastal resorts on the way up, and could provide proof of where she had stayed.

Driving and staying in various places was not the issue, which may prove true. It was that she had been in the retirement home on the day Mary Otway died.

'My client will admit to meeting with Mary Otway. She will not admit to more,' the lawyer said.

'You've consistently lied to us,' Haddock said. 'Why should we believe anything you tell us now.'

'It's the truth. I met Mary, saw that she was worse than the last time I saw her, and realised that my hatred served no purpose.'

'You said you forgave her years ago,' Natalie reminded the woman.

'Hate and forgiveness are not the same. I was not angry because she could not understand what she had done to Bruce and me. The hate remained and must. She destroyed our lives.'

The explanation was plausible but could not be believed.

'You were there when Mary Otway plunged to her death?'

'It was an accident. She was not steady on her feet. I tried to hold her, but I couldn't.'

Haddock looked over at the lawyer. 'I would suggest you advise your client of the seriousness of the last three days and the lies and half-truths she told us.'

Looking at Sheila Cross, Haddock summed up the situation. 'You told us you weren't in Sydney on the day Mary Otway died, but now we have proof. No jury will be sympathetic if you hold to your story that it was an accident. If charged with first-degree murder, premeditated, you will probably be found guilty. The most you can hope for is diminished responsibility and second-degree murder. Do you want to plead guilty to the murder of Mary Otway?'

'It was an accident,' Sheila Cross said. The wronged wife and tireless charity worker maintained her story.

She would be charged with murder and transferred to Sydney to stand trial. She would never be a free woman again.

'That's what comes of hate,' Haddock said.

Natalie agreed.

***

Sheila Cross was fervent in her denial of the murder of Old Joe in Kings Cross. Although there had to be a correlation. Old Joe, when younger, had been in a relationship with Mary Otway. That was confirmed by Jimmy Rogers, who held Natalie to the agreement. He was optimistic of a good night out; she was not.

The focus was back on the murder of Maria Sidorov, which to Haddock and Natalie was the most important. Mary

Otway had been old and senile, her life ebbing, and Old Joe was unhealthy due to his lifestyle and cooking sherry. But Maria had been in the prime of life, young and healthy, a fulfilling future ahead of her.

On the first day back in Sydney, there was a warm welcome by Superintendent Payne and acceptance of Natalie. She knew that she and Haddock made a good team, even if his private life was in tatters, and now his daughter was not talking to him, siding with her mother in what was to be an acrimonious battle.

Natalie wanted to wish him well, offer moral support, and say it would work out in the end, but she knew they were worthless words and would have been said without conviction.

By the afternoon of the first day, the two were out at the Sidorov mansion. Two things had changed: the sale sign was gone and Alexey Sidorov was in residence.

'I couldn't take it,' Sidorov said.

Haddock understood. He had only come from out west of Sydney, not more than forty minutes' drive, and after his separation from his wife and revisited the area. He soon realised that nostalgia was best if not faced with reality.

Where his parents' house had stood there was now a white-brick monolith of no charm, an example of southern European crassness, and the local store, where he bought chocolate bars on his way home from school, his first cigarette at fifteen, and the park where he had lost his virginity, now residential, full of people up to their ears in mortgages and children.

Sidorov had gone from Point Piper and Sydney Harbour to a small village in the Russian countryside, freezing in winter, biting insects in the short summer.

'I was told you suspected Maria's friend,' Sidorov said.

'It has logic,' Natalie said.

'Logic is not proof.'

'We didn't expect to see you here,' Haddock said.

'Nor did I. What were you looking for?'

'Fresh eyes, distanced by time. Rebecca ticks all the boxes. She was in the building, able to fake her restraints, and has anger issues.'

Neither officer was convinced, and as with Mary Otway, too much was circumstantial, a process of elimination instead of fact. Sheila Cross's guilt would stand, as the evidence that placed her at the crime scene was too strong.

However, Rebecca Griffith's guilt was predicated on nothing more solid than they had no one else to focus on.

'Business acquaintances, persons you've had dealings with?' Natalie asked.

'In Russia, revenge, but never against a child.'

'Hardly a child,' Haddock said. 'She acted adult, your successor. Maybe someone taking a long-term view: kill the daughter, destroy the man. What would have happened if you had died and Maria was still alive? You must have had a contingency plan.'

'What is your business, Mr Sidorov?' Natalie asked. 'We know of your reputation, some of your more impressive financial successes, but you came from a part of the world known for violent gangsters.'

'My heritage is Russian; my actions are Australian. I do not deal in drugs or protection rackets, or whores. Sometimes, corporate law is vague. Lawsuits will result from me and those I'm up against.'

'Justice Kline.'

'Exactly. He adjudicated twice on matters before him. Once, it went in my favour; the other did not.'

'Any residual animosity towards the man?'

'None. He acted according to the law. It does not change the situation if I thought his interpretation was incorrect or the law was an arse. I trusted his son with my daughter, even though he is immature and arrogant, but he's smart, knew which line not to cross, instructed by his father.'

'Who, you once said before, you respected.'

'I do.'

'But who would be interested in your empire, and what will happen to it now?'

'I will progressively liquidate, possibly live here or elsewhere. My plans are unclear, and I'm still in mourning. I refuse to believe that Rebecca is involved.'

'Then who? Dima Ivanov? Not bright enough to continue what you've created, but he doesn't want for much.'

'He won't get much, either. He was meant to be on duty that night to check the doors and to ensure the girls were safe.'

'Why? Why that night? Did you suspect something? A person you couldn't trust, debtors hammering down the door. Mr Sidorov, frank and open honesty works for you and me if you want Maria's murderer to be arrested.'

'I do.'

'Yet some guilt on your part. You've played hard in business, won some, lost others, created friends and enemies.'

'More enemies than friends, but my daughter, that was different.'

'How?'

'None would harm a child, not for financial gain or a payback for an action against their person.'

But now, Alexey Sidorov was liquidating, the fire in his belly smouldering ashes. Opportunities loomed for astute and ruthless persons to take advantage, and Haddock had seen others killed for much less.

***

State Crime Command was in an uproar. Questions were being asked in parliament, the judicial hand of Kline, the Supreme Court of New South Wales, and possibly even the Premier. All rallying to support a beleaguered colleague.

Sidorov had financial clout. Levine had religion, and whereas he had accepted that his wife had committed suicide, it had taken weeks before that was established, with disruption to his family and concern within the synagogue as to why she had taken such drastic action. Was he a wife-beater? Why hadn't the elders been consulted? Why had the woman not embraced the tenets of Hassidism? Levine was under pressure and determined that others should answer questions and take the blame from him.

As for Sidorov, that remained unclear, although Superintendent Payne knew of his involvement in pressuring those in power to act, aware that more than a few would possibly be indebted to the man, a whisper in the ear as to which share to buy, a favourable loan given to purchase real estate, a probable gift, under the table or in a brown paper bag. That had happened in the past, a corrupt Premier in the seventies.

But the current Premier was above such shenanigans, elected on a promise of openness, financial accountability, and competent management. Natalie had voted for the man; Haddock had not. And Haddock knew that if Sidorov and Levine were stirring the pot, others were not far behind.

Sheila Cross was in Sydney, remanded and awaiting trial. She held that it had been an accident, but with the evidence on the balcony, plus her repeated lying, she would be convicted of Mary Otway's death.

Natalie regretted having to charge the woman but, sworn to uphold the law, there was no option. That she had been wronged by the dead woman, and had become a tireless charity worker in Melbourne, would go in her favour, and the sentence would be the minimum allowable. The most she could look forward to was an early release in the last few months of life.

'Haddock, Campbell,' Payne said as he paced around his office,' it's a fine mess you've got us into. How am I to defend against the accusations?'

'Formal?' Haddock asked. He was blustering, unsure what to say. The investigation was progressing, one murder solved, another proven as suicide, another soon to conclude, and yet he and his sergeant were in the firing line, scapegoats to be thrown out of the investigation and the police force, transferred to God knows where, careers dashed, a marriage unretrievable.

If asked, he would have said he felt depressed about the futility of it all, but he was not to have the opportunity. Payne was on the warpath.

'Why now?' Natalie asked.

'Why is not the issue,' Payne said. 'What we're going to do about it is.'

Haddock was encouraged by the 'we'.

'Why Justice Kline?' Natalie asked. 'He's got reason to keep quiet, maintain a low profile, and hope we don't pin the murder of Maria Sidorov on him.'

'Likely?'

'Not likely,' Haddock admitted. 'He was on the boat when she died, the perfect alibi. Or it would be if it was not for the women.'

'It's perfect,' Payne said. 'A Justice of the Supreme Court of New South Wales, protected by the old boys' network that does not want disrepute brought on their distinguished group. And if Kline is willing to risk his reputation cavorting with whores on the high seas, that means others could be involved, politicians, judges, even police.'

'Are you serious?' Haddock asked.

'One law for the majority; another for the rest of us. Haddock, you're from the Western Suburbs, working-class background, no doubt a socialist.'

'I am.'

'Injustice of man, those with influence or money get away with literal murder, rort the system, offshore tax havens, steal millions.'

'They do.'

'Exactly. Whether Kline's been a bloody fool or part of a network of high-powered, influential lechers, he's played us for fools. And then we have Sergeant Campbell, footsy under the table with him that day up at Cabbage Tree Point.'

'I resent that accusation,' Natalie said. 'That is a reportable offence.' She was angry, not concerned if he was her superior or not.

'You took the bait; good to see it,' Payne said. 'In my office, the cuffs are off, no political correctness or harassment. Sergeant, you've been a police officer long enough to know how it works. We all believed, even you at the time, that Kline wasn't Mr Charming that day just because he liked the look of you or thought you'd be a pushover. He was angling for something, formulating a plan, and he's got it now.'

'But why? Are you saying he's protected?'

'He is.'

'Would they be willing to conceal a crime, even murder, to preserve their reputations?' Natalie asked.

'Why not? It wouldn't be the first time. History's full of it, even in the early days of Australia, transported for stealing a loaf of bread or resisting the local magistrate's advances in England, while he and the landed gentry, the aristocrats, steal everything they can lay their hands on.'

'Are we considering the possibility that Kline might have made an error and that we should refocus on him and his son?' Haddock said.

'What about Sidorov? Any possibility he could be involved?'

'Devoted to his daughter,' Natalie said. She found the idea abhorrent.

'It wouldn't be the first time,' Payne said. 'Devoted, they might have been, but if she disappointed him, who knows? Kline's son was having sex with her, and she was underage. Not a crime we're pursuing, but at the time, most would have disapproved, and then he's got Russell Harding with a pair of binoculars trained on them. This friend of the young Kline, innocent of all crimes?'

'We believe so,' Natalie said, 'but we thought that about Rebecca Griffith, and she's under investigation – dysfunctional family, anger issues.'

'Then what are you two doing in my office?' Payne said as he sat down behind his desk.

'We're here because you wanted us here,' Haddock said.

'I did; not now. I'll deflect for another couple of weeks and give you a chance to find out who killed the young woman. Third degree the young Kline's friend, pressure Russell Harding, or, Sergeant, sweet talk him, meet with him again.'

'And for me?' Haddock asked.

'Sidorov. See if the man's got hidden depths. Not that I know about Russian heritage or beliefs, vendetta, family honour, that sort of thing. You dealt with warring Italian families some years back. You must have picked up an idea or two.'

'I did, but Alexey Sidorov, a long bow to stretch, and we still have Rebecca Griffith.'

'What about those on the boat with Kline?'

'We've not contacted them since. Justice Kline didn't kill Maria Sidorov, nor did the others.'

'You said that Kline thought he had seen something from the boat, a couple at the back of Sidorov's mansion.'

'We discounted it, thought the man was making out that he was helping us, throwing us a bone, deflecting blame from his son and Sidorov, intimating that Rebecca could have been guilty.'

'Conduct a cursory check of the others on the boat in case they saw something.'

Chapter 22

Peter Regan sat quietly in the interview room at State Crime Command. For him, it was a day to wag school, a chance to see the building, stating that he was considering joining the police force after he left school.

'My father's keen on medicine,' Regan said. 'He's a doctor, reckons I've got what it takes to be a surgeon.'

Natalie could have said follow your father's advice, but she did not. Regan's visit was official, not social. There were questions to answer, and Natalie knew neither she nor Haddock had pressured the young man, believing him to be an innocent bystander.

'We're under pressure to solve Maria's murder,' Haddock said.

A lawyer hired by his father sat alongside the young man.

Harry Rabin, in his forties, had an office in Bondi Junction, the furthest point east on the regional suburban train network – all change for the bus to Bondi Beach, a three-minute walk to the shopping centre. Natalie had encountered the man before, defending an elderly woman on a charge of hit and run, a small child hit; thankfully, his injuries had been minor. That time, Rabin had got the woman off with a stiff fine, loss of licence, and a severe reprimand by the judge. Natalie had thought it fair, as the weather had been foul, and the child had run out between two cars, his mother obsessed more with her phone than her son. In that case, a Range Rover, once known sarcastically as an Eastern Suburbs Taxi, loved by wives taking their children to school, arguing that safety was paramount, although it was for status more than safety. But now Range Rovers, once everywhere, were being supplanted by Bentleys, Lamborghinis, and Maserati SUVs.

'Are you aware that Rebecca Griffith has consented to psychiatric evaluation?' Natalie asked.

'She phoned me, worried that you suspected her,' Regan said.

'And why would she believe that?' Haddock asked. He wanted to go in hard but still struggled with the concept that the polite neatly-dressed young man could be guilty of a heinous crime, but ruthlessly aware that clothes do not define the man.

Haddock ditched his easy manner with young Peter Regan.

'Mr Regan, some anomalies pertain to Maria Sidorov's death. How did her murderer know how to enter the house and that you and Brett Kline wouldn't be there? Also, Brett's father reckons he saw a disturbance. Is that possible? You're of a similar height to Brett, to Rebecca. He thought it might be Rebecca, but it could have been you or Brett.'

'It wasn't us.'

'Is this evidence supported by fact?' Rabin asked. 'I would remind you that my client is a youth from a good family, academically gifted, with no previous involvement with the police. I believe that requires that you act in a manner befitting.'

'Mr Rabin, we are not disrespecting your client, but this is the murder of a fifteen-year-old female. Emotions are heightened due to the nature of her death and her age. Your client, we are certain, has been economical with the truth. There are possibilities to consider. Firstly, Rebecca killed her. That seems illogical, but then the murder is. She was not violated, only strangled. Secondly, Brett Kline killed her, although that also seems illogical. She was having underage sex with him, corroborated by a third party. There appears to be no reason for him to kill her, but your client has no reason to want her alive or dead.'

'I didn't do it!' Regan shouted.

It was an understandable reaction when accused of a crime.

'Then level with us,' Haddock said.

Rabin was about to step in, but Haddock was not having a bar of it. He was getting riled, the pressure of the investigation, the political and legal intrigue in the back of his mind, Payne's instruction to get on with it, broker no dissent, leave no door unopened, no scenario unchecked.

Haddock continued. 'You and Brett Kline, on the make. A dead cert for Kline, a possible conquest for you, and don't give me that you weren't interested in Rebecca Griffith. An eighteen-year-old youth, desperate for sex, not too fussy where either, and Rebecca's attractive. You must have been interested, certain that with a few drinks, maybe drugs, and Brett and Maria in another room, you and Rebecca would have given way, heavy petting at the least. Is that how it was? Were you having sex with Rebecca? Was she a virgin? We know she has issues. Lying would not be too far of a stretch.'

Natalie remembered when she had been younger, Maria's and Rebecca's age, although she had hung onto her virginity for another year, her sixteenth birthday, a party at a friend's house, Vic Pritchard, the son of the local butcher, on the back lawn. It had been a significant moment in her life. And now, Rebecca Griffith and Peter Regan. Rebecca with anger management issues, and Regan denying his intent with Rebecca. But he was young and inexperienced, and Haddock was determined, needing something to report to Payne, to get him off his back, to give the superintendent fuel to fight his masters, aware that they had an agenda, and solving a crime was not it, but self-preservation and damn the truth.

'It wasn't like that with Rebecca, but yes, who knows?' Regan said.

'And yet, the two of you decided not to go. Why? And don't give me that baloney that Brett had another woman, and you weren't fussed. Two young women; two rampant males. Nobody could refuse, not Brett, not you, not unless you're gay. Are you, Peter? Not too late to admit the truth, frightened that you'd be compromised, the butt of jokes at the school. No doubt acceptance hasn't reached the schoolyard yet, and Brett, the all-male sporting star, academically gifted, the right credentials, his future assured, the son of a Supreme Court judge, even though he's been caught with his trousers down, cavorting with whores on the sea. Did you know about that?'

'We all knew. Brett wore his father like a badge, and yes, it wasn't Brett that was gay, bisexual, or whatever else you want to call it. It was me, no interest in women, only in men, and it was Brett I wanted, and he promised me, and there he is with Maria, and I'm expected to take Rebecca. I knew she would have come across, but I couldn't, don't you get it? Impossible, couldn't maintain an erection if I wanted to.'

'Still a virgin?' Natalie asked.

'Depends on your definition.'

'Gay or hetero, either.'

'Then, no.'

The reason Peter Regan had not gone to Sidorov's mansion was revealed, although whether Rebecca knew of his homosexuality wasn't sure. It was a question to ask the young woman.

'According to our previous conversations you decided not to go, the reason Brett didn't go, according to him. But why? Surely Maria would have let him in, slept with him, Rebecca in the other room. A rampant male's not likely to be deterred just because his friend's not keen.'

'Brett had someone else, not far away, older than Maria, more experienced, he reckoned. But with Brett, you can't be sure. He's an arrogant prick, always has been, gets away with it, something to brag about.'

'And you like him?'

'You don't understand,' Peter Regan said.

'But I do,' Natalie said. 'You were in love with him.'

'Never.'

'And Maria stood between you and your one true love.'

'Conjecture,' Rabin said. 'You're using standard interrogation tactics to confuse my client, getting him to admit to a crime that he was incapable of committing, with no proof other than infatuation for one, dislike of the other, a rival for his love.'

'Not dislike,' Regan said. 'I hated her because of Brett. I realised it was not her fault that she was attractive and desirable, and her father was Alexey Sidorov, and Brett's father was Justice Kline. It was just that I couldn't compete.'

'Are you saying that the relationship between them was something else?' Haddock asked.

'Sidorov craved respectability, never truly accepted by the social set, a latter-day interloper due to his money. Justice Kline, influential and well respected, had money, but not enough, and he couldn't make more, determined that Brett would.'

'An arranged marriage?' Natalie asked.

'Maria and Brett agreed to an arrangement to get married. They liked each other, and the fathers approved. Maria would have control of the money and easy entry into the highest echelons of society. Brett could pursue a legal career, which interested him, or work with Maria to maintain the empire, enough wealth to indulge in whatever he fancied.'

'Women?'

'According to Brett.'

'Told in confidence?'

'He knew I wouldn't talk.'

'Why and how?'

'Ambition for Brett; love for Maria. She was a sensible woman, and Brett was firm in agreeing to the arrangement, the reason her father looked the other way. If Brett hadn't followed through, he would have destroyed the father.'

'All for a place in Eastern Suburbs society?' Haddock asked.

'Insidious, incestuous, all-important to some,' Regan said.

'Will Brett concur with you?'

'Under pressure, he might. But be careful, his father is ruthless, do whatever to protect his position.'

'We've already seen that,' Haddock said. He had no intention of elaborating.

***

It had been a long time since Haddock and Natalie had mentioned the death of Old Joe, the homeless man of Kings Cross, and even now the tenuous link to Mary Otway had yielded no further insights, apart from the clandestine affair years before between the two, one of them wealthy, the other, Joe Coster, young and virile.

Haddock had tried reconciling with his wife, desperate to do so, conscious that the sacrifices he would have to make were too strict. Theresa had not been seen for several weeks, for which Natalie was glad, knowing full well that the man was weak in spirit and would have slept with her again, further damaging the relationship between inspector and sergeant. Haddock admitted the woman had been a complication but that his disconnect from her had not resolved the issues with his marriage.

Natalie had seen it before. Policing was a vocation, not only a way to make a living to look after the family; it was in the blood, and personal relationships often suffered.

Natalie had the opportunity to relieve herself of a similar tension, a night out with Jimmy Rogers. They had met at nine in the evening, down by Circular Quay, no longer a semi-circle, which it had been in earlier colonial days when the harbour had been filled with ships of the line, sailing boats moving up and down the harbour, out through Sydney Heads, and then north or south, carrying goods and people.

The restaurant was packed. Rogers, no longer with dank hair and scruffy clothes, had taken a shower, cut his hair, washed behind the ears, and brushed his teeth. Natalie had to admit to being impressed, although the man was still determined, innuendos, let us make a night of it.

With another, she might have been tempted, and whereas the touch of a man would have excited, Jimmy Rogers didn't move her, not in the way she wanted. She was sad that she would have to push him away at the end of the evening, aware he

185

regarded a meal in a good restaurant as the main course and the female as dessert.

It was a common belief of many young men out on the town, of more than a few women, but not her. Those days were behind her, and her former lover was phoning every month, regretting cheating on her, hopeful of reconciliation. Natalie firm in that she wasn't interested. For her, love was eternal, not fickle or transient.

Entrée, a main course of sea bass, tiramisu for dessert, after which Natalie had been adamant, a disconsolate look from Rogers who accepted the inevitable, a goodnight kiss as he dropped her off at her place; one last try, a gentle rebuff.

'Tomorrow, Old Joe,' he said as he drove off.

An agreement over the table, unable not to talk shop, that he would see if there was CCTV in Kings Cross that might give a clue as to who had killed Old Joe. Homicide had its own CCTV officers, but they were not up to the standard of Jimmy Rogers, who worked freelance for the police.

Payne had been advised of what she and Haddock intended to do, and the man knew of Rogers' expertise in identifying Sheila Cross.

***

Justice Kline was lurking in the background. Both officers were unsure of his actions. Payne explained that those in senior positions protected the backs of others, even if one had committed an error of judgement or an indiscretion.

Natalie thought that cavorting with loose women could be construed as both.

She met with the blonde from the marina, a park bench in Redfern. Forty years previous it had been a down-at-heels suburb, but now it was gentrified and expensive.

'You were on the boat,' Natalie said. 'Did you know who the men were?'

'Christian names only, assumed them to be wealthy.'

'Due to your cost?'

'Precisely, money up front, and we weren't drinking cheap alcohol, Dom Perignon. Not that I drank much, but one or two of the other girls did.'

'To handle the situation?'

'Depends. Have you drunk Dom Perignon Champagne, three hundred dollars a bottle, and they had a couple of crates on the boat?'

'Are you saying it was because of the quality that some drank more than they should?'

'No. Two women are lesbians, and another had been mistreated as a child, next-door neighbour and family friend. Don't need to paint you a picture, do I?'

'But you're neither.'

It was a warm day, and the park had been the woman's idea, her attempt at normality, unrecognised by those in the area. That was how the woman had explained it, but a tight-fitting top over enlarged breasts wasn't easy to hide. The woman had admitted on the night at Rose Bay Marina that she was there for the money, not into drugs or alcohol, investing her money wisely. Natalie could see the woman was an exhibitionist, not averse to showing the wares in public, gyrating on a pole in a strip club or turning tricks on a boat. Natalie wouldn't have been surprised if she didn't have an online presence, provocatively dressed or not, private viewing for more debased acts.

'Not me. What do you want?'

'The men, not officially introduced, but did you recognise any?'

'I knew one was a real estate agent. There I am, giving him a blowjob, and he's handing me a business card. Typical real estate, business before pleasure, or maybe he was there for the men, pressing the flesh, a freemason, one of the club.'

'Were they?'

'Freemasons? No idea, not sure what they do.'

Natalie didn't know much more either, although she thought it unimportant. However, a real estate agent who might not have been as enamoured of women as Justice Kline clearly was would be a person to talk to.

'How about you? On the night, in between blowjobs, putting on shows, and whatever else, did you see anything on the shore?'

'Such as?'

'One of the men reckoned he saw a scuffle at the water's edge, back of one of the houses in Point Piper.'

'I had enough scuffles on the boat. A couple of the women were drunk, almost out of it, and one man had found the alcohol and thought the pleasures of the grape were preferable to me and others.'

'Offended?'

'Should I be? No, is the answer. They come on, thinking they're studs, doped up on Viagra, but they're finished after an hour, ninety minutes at most. Hyenas with a dead carcass in Africa, fighting over the spoils, and once they're sated, they are into the food and drink, occasionally grabbing one of us, not willing to let what's on offer go to waste.'

'You saw nothing?'

'Not after the over-zealous real estate agent. His eyes were big enough, can't say much about the rest of him.'

Natalie didn't need the woman to elaborate.

***

Haddock left Natalie to deal with those on the boat. He had another visit with Dima Ivanov, cousin of Alexey Sidorov, the former security guard at the man's mansion, and now unemployed and hopeless drunk.

Ivanov's squalid and cramped apartment looked as though it had been hit by a bomb when Haddock entered. In the kitchen sink, empty bottles of vodka, a woman in the bedroom, naked, lying on her back, dead.

Ivanov had been reticent to open the door when Haddock had knocked, opening it slightly, attempting to close it, but couldn't due to Haddock's brogues, size ten, black leather.

'Did you kill her?' Haddock asked.

'Not me. Heroin addict, cheap as chips, all I can afford,' Ivanov replied.

Haddock reappraised the apartment's condition, looked past the kitchen sink, over at the lounge room, at what a real estate agent would describe as a cosy space to sit and read a book, but anyone else would describe as no better than a broom cupboard. He was pleased that his sergeant was talking to the real estate agent, hostile as he was to them. Divorce proceedings had been instigated by his wife, division of assets, and the house to be sold, as he could not afford to maintain the payments. There was no point in garnering his salary. And callously, he knew his daughter was close to sixteen, a few more years and he would not have the financial responsibility, determined not to, not after what she had called him the last time they had met. He knew she was at a difficult age, with exams at school, and a venomous mother, when he, the father, was out solving crime, attempting to feed and clothe the family, no thanks to his wife, her mother, who refused to get a job. Not qualified, too old, too many years out of the workforce, and I don't know computers, no typing skills, had been her defence.

He had defended her in the past, believed that one parent should be home when the child arrived from school, but in his anger and bitterness, he realised she was bone lazy. He would fight the division of assets, selling the house, his half liquidated due to maintenance of their daughter, and even though he was angered by his wife's action, he knew he had caused the rift. If only he had not become involved with another woman. But now, and there was a dead woman to deal with. He phoned the crime scene investigators and the local police station. He informed Natalie of the situation and that he'd deal with it.

In one corner of the lounge room, when Haddock looked over, Ivanov had passed out in a drunken stupor. The woman was dead due to a heroin overdose; drug paraphernalia on the bed. If it was accidental, Pathology would confirm, but due to the seriousness of Maria Sidorov's murder, Ivanov's apartment would be a murder scene until confirmed otherwise.

When informed of the situation, Sidorov arrived at the apartment twenty minutes later. 'Can't do it,' he said. 'He's worthless, but he's still my cousin. I'll get him cleaned up at my place. You can interview him there.'

'Not so fast,' Haddock said. 'I've got Forensics on the way. Also, the pathologist is coming. It could be several hours before we can release him into your custody, and the woman's death is unconfirmed.'

'Overdose, you said.'

'I've seen a few, almost certain it is, but the circumstances dictate that we act cautiously. If he could kill this woman, induce her to shoot up more than she should and make out that it was an accident, that would be murder. And if Ivanov can kill one person, he can kill another.'

'I don't believe it,' Sidorov said.

As others had said, it always came down to Alexey Sidorov's ill-founded belief in family. Even though he had little time for the cousin, paid him a pittance to guard the mansion, and did not socialise with the man, blood was still thicker than water.

On the street, crime scene tape, a crowd gathering, and a coffee shop on the opposite side of the street doing sterling business.

Four hours later, Ivanov was free to go. He drove away in his cousin's Mercedes.

Haddock had a statement, confirmation that the woman had injected herself, her fingerprints on a police database, as were Ivanov's. Recent sexual activity had been confirmed, and the woman had drunk vodka, clear evidence of the couple wrestling or fighting or making fierce love in the lounge room and the bedroom. The thought of the two, amorous, drunk, and drugged, was not pleasant, and he preferred not to think about it, but

Ivanov was in the clear. Although the man had shown drunkenness and violence, Haddock did not believe he had killed Maria but realised that additional focus would come to bear on the man, as it would on his wealthy cousin.

Chapter 23

An incurable romantic, Sergeant Natalie Campbell regarded love as pure, not commercial and crass, shows for the boys, all-in orgies. But work with the police for a few years, and a good officer becomes pragmatic about such matters, understanding that life is difficult for the majority, and one person's pleasure is another's poison. Clearly, the blonde at the marina had no issues with what she did, although the real estate agent might when the heavy hand of the law descended on him in his agency in Double Bay, disparagingly once also known as 'Double Pay', but now that title belonged to every suburb in Sydney, from the west to the east, from the north to the south. Natalie was feeling the pinch; the rent on her apartment had gone up more than the rate of inflation, so a possible move to Parramatta, which she did not want, but to remain in cosmopolitan Sydney and the Eastern Suburbs, where she felt at home, would mean a further tightening of the belt or somewhere cheaper.

Russell Harding, an enigma who knew everyone, was pleasant when Natalie phoned and invited her to his office. She hoped it would not be the three-course meal and the bottle of expensive wine. It was answers she wanted to questions she wasn't sure of.

'A fortune,' Harding said when Natalie asked the first: how much he knew about people and how much they would pay for his discretion.

He was dressed smartly, unlike the state of the small but drab office. Outside, to the rear, a gentle ripple on the small beach caused by a motorboat passing by. On the street, at the front of the building, pedestrians: shopping, gossiping, eating and drinking at myriad coffee shops and restaurants. Some takeaway, others sit down and expensive. This was the area of the wealthy, the upwardly mobile, children in fifty-thousand-dollars-a-year schools, both parents working horrendous hours to keep the family afloat, driving expensive cars they didn't need, wearing designer clothes they didn't want, pretending that life was great, but the expressions on their faces indicated another reality. Trapped on a treadmill, the same as a rat, unable to maintain momentum, unwilling to get off, to go and live elsewhere, to enjoy a quality of life untainted by greed and boasting.

Natalie realised Alexey Sidorov's life was similar, the veneer of everything people aspired to, 'if I win the lottery.' Money didn't buy happiness, but it had given Russell Harding what he wanted, the ability to live life on his terms, the satisfaction of no financial and emotional servitude, beholden to no one, a free agent.

'You've heard about Mary Otway?' Natalie said, realising it was an inane question. This was the man who knew everything about everyone.

'Her cousin. Provable?'

'Yes, convictable, manslaughter, possibly diminished responsibility due to her age and Mary Otway's provocation. Did you know?'

'Before?'

'Yes, you seem to know more than us. Gave us a story about the woman and Old Joe, dead in Kings Cross, proven to be true.'

'I gave you nothing, Sergeant, only a story.'

'Alexey Sidorov is back in Australia,' Natalie said. 'Have you met with him?'

'You don't want another story, do you?'

'Not a story, assistance. His cousin is with Sidorov in Point Piper. He got drunk, a prostitute dead in his apartment. Alexey's weakness, you once said.'

'I did. Ivanov is a thoroughly bad lot, not fit to guard a chicken coop, let alone Alexey. Not criminal, just a low performer, not too bright, had a chance with the golden egg but blew it.'

'The golden egg? Alexey or Maria?'

'Alexey.'

'Celebrities? I heard it mentioned.'

So far, no meal, no wine, for which Natalie was pleased. She wanted the man to talk but knew wine would not loosen his tongue.

'Not often, but I am asked from time to time to sweep their rooms and check no stalkers or uninvited paparazzi can get in. The beefy bodyguards are for show, but most are on steroids, not as strong as they look.'

'Either Rebecca Griffith, Brett Kline, or his father killed Maria. What do you reckon to the boys' club, Justine Kline exerting pressure on the police to get him off the leash?'

'I've no answer. I don't believe any are involved. What about the son's friend? Possible?'

'Not sure. He's gay. Why he didn't want to be forced onto Rebecca, probably incapable of rising to the challenge, if you get my drift.'

Harding did and smiled.

'In love with Brett, who we know had some arrangement through the fathers to the woman.'

'Love is a powerful force.'

'We've not made a connection between Joe Coster and Mary Otway other than their relationship in the past. Although it makes no sense. He had no claim on her wealth, and even Sheila Cross and her former husband, even though they lodged the necessary paperwork, would not have succeeded.'

A knock on the door, this time a light snack – no alcohol, no three-course meal. Natalie was thankful, neither in the mood for a heavy meal nor hungry enough to eat it. Besides, Haddock was impatient to get a confession from someone, not sure who, and the pressure for a resolution was intensifying. Kline was continuing to rattle chains through his associates.

Sitting there with Harding, thinking about Haddock and Kline and the murders, eating a sandwich, and drinking coffee, Natalie realised she was sitting with the man who could burst open the investigation. A man who had looked in windows at copulating couples, seen Maria and Brett, young lovers in the boat shed, plighting their troth, discussing the future mapped out by their fathers, cognisant that they would not say no, both sensible, both aware of the responsibility and the privilege, but was it love between the two? Young as they were, adolescents, too young to marry, too wise to refuse the offer.

'Justice Kline, using his skills and influence to divert from his indiscretion,' Natalie said.

Harding was sitting back, an afternoon nap for him. She could see that he wasn't the man he had once been, and that age was taking its toll. No more late-night stakeouts of young lovers or even older lovers, ready to hang up his cape and retire to his house, more comfortable in his office, a second home for him, a couch in one corner, a blanket strewn across it.

'Protected by a veil of invisibility. If you bring him down, it will reflect across the entire sphere of our legal system. There is a need for the public to believe in the impartiality, the incorruptibility of our institutions.'

'When they're not.'

'They are, most of the time, but one rotten apple in the cart. Well, you know the consequences. It's happened with the police, one bad egg, corruptible, taking backhanders, committing a crime of violence, and then every police officer under suspicion, evidence thrown out of the court, police officers given the third degree.'

'Are you saying not all approve?'

'Most don't. A few would be glad to see the back of Kline, a Justice of the Supreme Court. But there are others, moral and religious, who understand how politics work and are forced to compromise on legislation and toe the line. They disapprove of Kline's behaviour and are personally offended, morally indignant, and aware they will be tarred with the same brush. Thankfully, in Australia, corruption and coverup are not endemic. A government teetering, and mud sticks, not only with the legal but across the board, drag the police with it, you and Haddock, thrown to the wolves, scapegoats, hung out to dry. Are you shocked? Young, idealistic, believe that ability and competence are the only criteria for you to shimmy up the greasy pole, to sit where Payne is.'

'Once, I might have, but I've seen too much now. It's jarring, demoralising, realising that forces are rallied against us. What's Sidorov got to do with it? Is Mary Otway involved? How about Joe Coster?'

Natalie was pushing her luck, aware that Russell Harding had told a story the last time, but she could see that he had taken a shine to her, not sexually, but more as a father for a child. He had spent a lifetime unburdened by a wife and family, and she thought he might regret it, not that he would admit it. This time, she hoped for facts, not a story, aware that taking direct involvement instead of being circumspect, observing from the sideline and maintaining a low profile, would change his modus operandi, behaviour that had kept him free from censure, prosecution, and denouncement. The power behind the throne, if he had been in politics, but she suspected he was apolitical.

Harding sat straight, rested his arms on his desk, and looked at Natalie. 'Sergeant, Kline's not a murderer, nor is his son; no percentage in it for either of them. The father can't control himself, believes he's invincible, and his position ensures he will be protected. He is correct in this, and the son has been well-trained. He's young, impressionable, can be stupid, the prerogative of the young, but he knew the lie of the land, the keys to the castle, his for the taking.'

'But why would the son want Sidorov's wealth? He's young, believes he can make it himself, the age of invincibility.'

'As you were at that age. Got around, did stupid things, slept with a few boys you wish you hadn't?'

'Personal questions,' Natalie said, uncomfortable with Harding's question, unsure where they were leading.

'Observational. You're similar to Maria in some respects: tall, slim, attractive, and naïve. She had the naivety of youth, not fully cognisant of her father, his ruthless drive, and some of his actions. You're naïve due to a sheltered upbringing. Good family environment? Loving parents?'

'Yes, they are.'

'And so it should be, but now, exposed to the reality, you've become disillusioned, unsure if you are cut out for policing, aware that it's not good against bad. More criminals walk the street than are in prison. And with enough money and influence, you can get away with murder. Kline would know that, gave you a trip in a plane, a fancy meal, more drink than you wanted.'

'Why did he do that? I've never fully understood. It would be me for censure and a disciplinary, no skin off his nose.'

'His motives would have been ulterior, sounding you out, a possible liaison, romance even. Although I doubt the second, too visible, you and him, an idealistic police officer, hopeful of promotion, now aware that promotion can be slow or fast. What about Superintendent Payne? Tried it on with you?'

'Not yet.'

'He will, in time.'

'Are you saying I should be realistic, accept whatever, look for the opportunity, sleep with a man to gain it?'

'Would you?'

'Never,' Natalie said firmly.

'Then remember what you've said here today. You're a good person, better than the police deserve, but you're outnumbered. Haddock's a plodder, a good investigating officer, hopeless at office politics, and too outspoken. But you, Natalie, are wise before the event, see the grubbiness of society, the depravity that some will sink to, and the diligence they will apply to remove themselves from criticism. Kline played you for a sucker, weakened your resolve.'

'I don't think he did.'

'No, of course you don't. But you came back, full of it, proclaiming he had been a perfect gentleman.'

'Which he was.'

'He is, but not a perfect person. He took a backhander from Sidorov: scratch my back, I'll scratch yours; let your son marry my daughter.'

'Can it be proved?'

'Never. A judge presiding, a decision in Sidorov's favour, a point of law. Don't bother; deal with the reality. Kline was desperate for his son to stay with Maria, as was Sidorov. Forget the Klines; focus elsewhere.'

'Rebecca Griffith?'

'Good father, erratic mother. The daughter's been affected, but she didn't do it.'

'Then who?'

'Grill Ivanov. Dig deep, the hatred for the cousin, living in a slum, enough money to afford a drug-addicted streetwalker worn ragged by countless men, pawed, beaten, and abused, no doubt raped, possibly with AIDS.'

'Full-blown. No condom with Ivanov. But why kill Maria if he hated the father?'

'Supposition, not sure if I'm right, but hate's powerful, and without a daughter, who's next in the line of succession?'

'Ivanov. But he wouldn't have known what to do, run the business into the ground.'

'With that much money, not aware that Sidorov is going through a lean period, overstretched with those who lent him money, not a bank that you and I would use. Mafia-type characters who would bury you up to your neck in a termite nest if they have to. Sidorov knows this; the reason he didn't stay in Russia, the reason he came back, can't avoid them, not when others back in the home country are willing to strike a deal with the Australian criminal element. How's security at Sidorov's?'

'You must know, seem to know everything else.'

'Tight, not tight enough.'

'And you know who these people are. Is that why you are telling me?'

'In part.

'Joe Coster?'

'No idea, not yet. Have you checked out Mary Otway's business empire? Does her wealth align with her businesses?'

'We believe it does. We've had accountants check the figures, and even though the woman was forgetful, she still had control, proxy to a lawyer who had worked with her for years.'

'You've interviewed him?'

Natalie felt it was a course in police investigative techniques. She was exhilarated that a master tactician was giving her ideas that neither Haddock nor the police academy had. She had to admit to enjoying herself.

'We have; sent an accountant from the Fraud Squad. They would be thorough, used to villains.'

'Her money? Local dog's home? Charity?'

'No one to inherit, charities of her choice, a small amount to her brother. Doesn't seem an ideal way to end a life, no one to care for or assist.'

'No different to me, intend to spend the last few years indulging myself,' Harding said.

Natalie knew he wouldn't; stuck in his ways, the desire to splash out, to travel the world, to buy expensive cars and trinkets was more for the young. Her parents were of a similar age to Harding, a few years younger possibly, as Harding's age was indeterminate, and now, after a lifetime of work, they yearned for a quieter life, devoid of possessions that had once given them joy, but now were an encumbrance. The vintage car her father had cherished, a 1950s Rover, English and solid, full of character, leather upholstery – gone. Her mother's Lladro figurines, sold on eBay. Time has moved on, and Harding, more agile than most and quick-minded, was heading that way, albeit slower than them, but they had lived in the country all their lives, not in fast-moving Sydney.

'Ivanov? Criminal? Running with a gang? Sufficient clout to take on Sidorov? Need more brains than him,' Natalie said.

The day was still young, four in the afternoon, but keeping up with Russell Harding was taxing on the brain. Later, she would not return to Parramatta but to her apartment, possibly a stroll around the area, allowing the mind to coalesce all that had been said, attempting to compartmentalise, and formulate a plan of action.

She knew that Haddock would understand; after all, he believed in walking around the area, taking in hidden places of interest to get into the mind of a killer. But Ivanov was not calculating or intelligent, not even devious, a low performer, and if he was directly or indirectly involved in the death of Maria, others were behind him.

'Can't help you there,' Harding said. 'Not that I would not, but I'm hidden in the bushes. Stick my head up and ask questions, likely to get it knocked off.'

'These people frighten you?'

'If I don't know who they are, what they are, then yes. And you, Sergeant Natalie Campbell, should also be. *Into the valley of death, rode the six hundred*, from a poem by Alfred, Lord Tennyson. You might remember it from school.'

Natalie didn't.

'You're not six hundred, just one. I don't want you to end up where they did.'

'Dead.'

'The charge of the Light Brigade, 1854. The Crimean War. Not the British Army's greatest moment, but immortalised in history. Just make sure you're not also.'

'Is that a warning?'

'A caution. I don't know more, or I would tell you, but Kline's actions are understandable from his point of view. Stir the hornet's nest, attempt to solve murders, and some will take any action to protect themselves, and you will not know until it's too late.'

Chapter 24

Confusion, intrigue, reds under the bed, mafia goons. Harding's openness had once again left more questions than answers. Haddock wasn't afraid to admit he was out of his depth and that he was a humble policeman, dedicated to his profession, arresting wrongdoers, not competent with political machinations and legal eagles who used their profession as an opportunity for getting up to mischief and their eminence to protect them.

Superintendent Payne's office, eight thirty in the evening. Payne was effusive; believed he had the bull by the horns.

Haddock sat with a beer in his hand, Natalie kept to orange juice, and Victoria Adderley, State Crime Command's legal expert, drank water. Adderley admitted she did not have Kline's skill or the legal clout.

'Can you prove it?' Payne asked.

'Prove what, Superintendent?' Natalie asked. She thought meeting with Payne was premature. She had reported on the meeting with Harding, conscious he had opened up with her more than anyone else. The first time she and Haddock met the man, he was careful in what he said, ensuring he did not offend or raise a concern about his discretion.

But the second time, when Natalie had met him without Haddock, he had been more effusive, and even verbose the third time. She could have said that the man had grown tired of snooping and knew more secrets than he could retain. His reputation was his protection. And now, admitting that Kline was playing a strategic game, not sure where it was heading and that some were protecting him, forcing others into an untenable position: political affiliations, the old boys' network, and reputations dashed if Kline went down, not without a fight, taking some with him, putting focus onto others.

'No,' Natalie said. 'None of it, not yet. Ivanov's still at Sidorov's and might be involved in Maria's death.'

'He's confident that he isn't,' Haddock said. 'I phoned him before the meeting, put some of the finer points to him, argued that he should be careful and that, cousin or no cousin, Ivanov was a person of concern.'

'The prostitute in his apartment?' Victoria Adderley asked.

'He might have seen her shoot up,' Haddock said. 'He denies it. No history of drug use, only gut-rot vodka if he's paying, the best quality if he can pilfer from his cousin. It's not murder, but Harding states that Ivanov might be involved with others more dangerous.'

'Sidorov's confidence in the man ill-founded?' Payne asked.

'Totally,' Natalie agreed. 'He's been warned, but Sidorov's a sentimentalist, not that he was born in Russia, no experience of his parents' village five hundred kilometres northeast of Moscow. You can find it on Google Street view. Holds on to this belief that family loyalty is all-important to a Russian. Russia's no longer Tsarist or Communist, or whatever he believed, but the worst excesses of capitalism.'

'Why's Harding talking?'

'He's taking a shine to Natalie,' Victoria joked.

Natalie would have preferred it not to have been said. She felt she had to defend herself. 'He's a lonely man who feels at ease with me and tends to unburden himself. Can any of us imagine what secrets he must hold?'

'Out of order, Victoria,' Payne said. 'Keep it professional.'

'Yes, Superintendent, apologies to Natalie.'

'Not needed. Another time, we can joke about it, but this is serious. Harding's revealing hitherto hidden facets of those in power, concern that he's placing himself in harm's way, concern for us that we'll be nobbled, a closed case, personae non gratae, Sidorov dead, along with Ivanov and anyone else who gets in the way.'

'Are you saying, Superintendent, that you take what Russell Harding said as serious?' Natalie asked.

'I am. Rebecca Griffith, could she have killed her friend?'

'Still to be determined,' Haddock said. 'No evidence, only circumstantial. She could have faked her restraints; Natalie's proved that. We're inclined not to believe that she did, although it could be that we're prejudiced, not neutral as we should be. Peter Regan, the young Kline's friend, is in love with Brett and has an intense hatred of Maria. He had the motive, but he's mild-mannered, slightly effeminate, couldn't blow the skin off a rice pudding, and Maria had meat on her, some strength in her, and Rebecca's no pushover.

'Statistically, you're right. Men murder significantly more than women, but we're dealing with star-crossed lovers here, mere children. Remember when you were their age, the schoolyard crush, the drunken parties, musical beds, copulating when you could, knockbacks most of the time, and there's Regan desperate for Maria's boyfriend, the woman in the way, and what about this Rebecca? I've read the reports. She is a sensible woman, mature beyond her years, or could she be introverted? Who knows what she could do? Stein, our resident psychologist, odd herself, could she be wrong or right? How would you know? Instinct, what do you reckon, Haddock, Sergeant Campbell? Another drink before you answer?'

Natalie could see an astute man. After hours, the camaraderie of his office, a few drinks, kind and encouraging words, and then, straight for the jugular, put his people under pressure, let the ideas flow, bizarre or otherwise.

Haddock helped himself to another beer, which was not a problem. The place he was renting was only two blocks away, leaving his car at State Crime Command and walking, and Theresa was in the other direction, three blocks away.

He had been firm when questioned by Natalie, a gentle ribbing earlier in the day, that it was over and he hadn't heard from her, assumed her to have taken administrative leave pending the enquiry and gone overseas, a trip back to South Africa, to

Fish Hoek, the small town where she had grown up, before they had destroyed the country, according to the woman. Natalie had been there when younger, loved the country, but was not so keen on the crime, acknowledging that Sydney wasn't as safe as it was, but you could still drive down a darkened street at night, even walk, without fear of mugging or worse.

But in the Eastern Suburbs, murders, three in a row, another proven as suicide. Was it one person or two, even three? Was Haddock back with the woman? He'd admitted that the marriage was over, impossible to reconcile, too much water under the bridge or over it, and jokingly he had said footloose, fancy-free, but she had not believed him.

He was a lovable bear of a man, flawed, but who wasn't? Everyone carried baggage they wished they didn't, even her. Jimmy Rogers was coming on strong, and in her teens, she would have said yes, and slept with him; but now, in her late twenties, she looked for love and realised she was becoming more like her mother. Which she had to admit was a heavy cross to bear, as she couldn't see herself giving up the police force, although incompatible with the demands on a wife and mother. On the shelf, past her use-by date, only attractive to men like Jimmy Rogers, on the make, not professing love, only lust and a quick roll in the hay.

'What's his game? Payne posed a rhetorical question, not expecting anyone to reply. But Natalie was keen to answer, unsure if she should, as was Victoria but not Haddock. The man was exhausted, with too many late nights, too much worry, murders to solve, and a marriage in the past tense. Not a fit man, physically strong, but snatched meals, McDonald's too often, cheeseburger and fries, washed down with a chocolate milkshake. Sustenance food: full of calories, an energy-burst, high in fat, low in nutrients. It wasn't balanced, no different to the man's health, a candidate for a heart attack, hardening of the arteries, and his breath was short.

'Kline?' Victoria Adderley asked. Natalie had observed it, Haddock had not, and maybe the lawyer hadn't known it, but

Adderley had a tendency to be obsequious, pandering to her superiors, her voice affecting the requisite tone, stern if needed, sweet and fluffy if needed, subservient if responding to a superior's rhetorical question.

The man had phrased the question correctly, with a hand on his chin, a quizzical look, as though thinking out loud helped his thought process.

'Precisely, Victoria.' The response was friendly, almost agreeable. Natalie, perceptive where Haddock wasn't, thought she could see the hidden signals, possible lovers of a night, flirtatious at least, snatched kisses in the printer room when no one was looking.

Maybe seeing something when it wasn't there, Natalie couldn't be sure, but she had reflected on that day in Rose Bay; Justice Kline, gentlemanly, not a word said out of place, no attempt to brush against her at the restaurant, both over the legal limit to drive, not that it mattered, private plane to whisk them back to Sydney Harbour. Was it as innocent as it appeared? Had she been party to what Kline was attempting to do now? Would the man cover up the murder of Maria if it was his son? Or even the friend? Or Rebecca Griffith?

She rejected the folly of what she was thinking, too ridiculous to contemplate, a man in his fifties, a young woman in her teens. But was it? What if he was enamoured, secretly lusting after Maria, knowing that his son was sleeping with the woman? Male school teachers and their female students, it had happened. In her teens, one of her friends, not as attractive as her, was teased because of it. Not mocked when Mr Bennett, the history teacher, forty-one, was arrested, convicted, and thrown in prison, his marriage in tatters, his career over. Chubby had been the temptress, Mr Bennett, the devoured. She had felt sorry for the man. But not for Kline.

'Old boys' network,' Natalie eventually said. 'Protect their own, one rule for our rulers, another for the riff-raff, the poor and impoverished.'

'Harding? Wised you up?' Payne asked.

Natalie gave Haddock a nudge, causing the man to open his eyes. 'Yes, that's it, on the button.' It was an automated response, unsure of what had just been said.

'Inspector, have a good night's sleep; leave this enquiry and your easy woman outside. Can't burn the candle at both ends. Puts more pressure on your sergeant. She's got Harding on her side, Kline wining and dining her. Any luck with Sidorov, Sergeant?'

'Inspector Haddock talks to him more than me.'

'Reverse the roles, just a suggestion. Haddock, you're not too keen on Ruth Stein, but go with her, meet with this Rebecca. Take it easy; no complaints of intimidation or browbeating a minor, even if she knows as much about young men as Maria Sidorov did. Don't want complaints. What about Regan? Could he be guilty?'

Natalie thought Payne was all over the place, throwing out suggestions and seeing where they fell. She admitted that it had relevance, though his suggestion about her inspector meeting with Rebecca Griffith seemed ill-founded. After all, she had met Rebecca along with Brett Kline and Peter Regan early in the investigation, spoken to them as a friend, not as a police officer, enticing them with coffee and cake, unsure of what had been achieved.

A school teacher at Cranbrook called into the headmaster's office to explain why he had pornography on his school-issued laptop, receiving a warning, a verbal six of the best, and the next time it would be immediate dismissal. Another at Maria and Rebecca's school, Kincoppal-Rose Bay, had an unhealthy obsession with the male form, a degree from a university, impressive and gold-embossed, two hundred and fifty dollars on the internet. There was no warning for her, out the door that day, instant dismissal, a letter drafted and sent by the school's legal representative to the agency that had supplied the woman, a refund of their commission, the equivalent of three months' salary of the disgraced teacher. Another teacher with no chance of another teacher's position in Australia.

'Sergeant Campbell, stay with Russell Harding. He knows more, a lot more than we do. Could he identify the murderer? Not willing to do so, bad for business. Who knows what goes on over where he lives, where the murders are. Turn a blind eye, nothing to do with me, that sort of attitude. It wouldn't be the first time. Could I be onto something?'

'Russell Harding is a closed book,' Natalie said, 'the same as Justice Kline. Harding has survived too long in the area, respected by those who know him. If he had been involved in inappropriate actions, it would have arisen before now, and there are no black marks against his name. I can keep in contact; not sure it will do us any good.'

'And Kline? Any idea what's going on? Victoria, what's the word with the legal fraternity, must leak like a sieve, just like the police department? Salacious gossip must be going around about Kline. They might be trying to protect him, but they would be laughing behind his back, and a Justice of the Supreme Court, a privileged position, not handed out with packets of cornflakes. How did he get the job, anyone with his nose out of joint because of him? Anyone Natalie can talk to?'

'Not much we hear at State Crime Command,' Victoria Adderley said.

'Is there any way to find out?'

'For what purpose?' Haddock asked. Payne was open, almost friendly, and both men had drunk more than a few beers. Instead of his usual reticence with the superintendent, Haddock felt he could ask questions. He did not appreciate Payne's intervention in the murder investigation but understood the man was probably receiving flak from his superiors.

'What the grapevine is saying,' Payne replied, possibly a little perturbed at Haddock's querying, Natalie thought. 'What about those who disapprove of Kline and his behaviour? There must be more than a few. Not all are into whores, young boys, and whatever else. Those with strong moral ethics; any you know of, Victoria?'

'A lecturer at law school, a former judge, came in part time, spoke to us about ethics and innocent before guilt, jurisprudence.'

'Did he believe it?' Natalie asked.

'I hope so, pillar of his church, on the local council.'

Haddock didn't think evoking the man's religious belief or civic responsibility were recommendations, having met enough rogues with similar qualifications on many occasions.

'Talk to him within the next two days. See what the word is on Kline,' Payne said. 'Anymore for tonight?'

'Justice Kline, my trip out with him,' Natalie said.

'Meet with him again, but be careful. The man was a gentleman the first time, but now, he's got the backing of the majority and might feel invincible; might try it on with you. No more flying around the countryside. Keep it local, open setting, a couple of plainclothes to keep watch on you.'

Natalie had no issue meeting Kline again; after all, he was a person of interest, although she was afeared on several counts. Justice Kline was smarter than her, smarter than anyone in Payne's office, and the man had a way about him, able to defuse the situation, ease her concern, and take advantage. She had met smooth talkers before and had been able to handle them, but they had been her age; with Kline, she wasn't so sure. She had deflected Jimmy Rogers, but he was not strong-willed. Justice Kline apparently had immunity, unconcerned about his behaviour with prostitutes, impervious to criticism. Able to deflect with ease, rationalise, and sweet talk a young female police officer, if not into committing an indiscretion, at least into convincing her of his innocence, one more person on his side, when she should remain impartial.

Chapter 25

Why Alexey Sidorov supported his cousin remained unclear to Haddock, who had not travelled outside of Australia since arriving at age ten, apart from a cruise up to New Caledonia in his teens, where he had drunk more alcohol than water in the ocean.

Natalie had spent six months with friends backpacking around Europe and understood Sidorov's loyalty but not the excess. She understood that family was important in continental Europe, more so in the countries skirting the Mediterranean. She had taken a discount flight to Moscow, saw the sights, and gained a minimal understanding of Russia, but did not come away with the idea that family was critical, not as much as in countries further to the south.

Regardless, with the reversal of roles outlined by Payne, although not totally endorsed by either Haddock or Natalie, they were willing to go along with his suggestion. Natalie felt unsure about meeting with Ivanov, a man who had mentally undressed her that first time they had met on the jetty at the back of Sidorov's house. It didn't help that the man was sunning himself on a recliner close to the water's edge, his host not present in the mansion.

'We're still confused,' Natalie said, perturbed by the man wearing speedos and a string vest, making no attempt to make himself decent for her. An arrogance she did not like, and she didn't want to be there on her own but needed the man to open up. And as with Harding, and possibly with Kline, a third party, even if female, would have dampened the meeting.

She could see the man was excited, forgetting that it was a murder investigation of one of his relatives, and that he was visibly animated, an obvious sign below his belt. She knew she should run, but anger and arousal were mighty forces, and

Ivanov, even though he acted as a security guard, was not in good physical condition, flabby around the waist, a four-day stubble on his face and his breath smelling of garlic.

Natalie kept her distance, not acceding to his request to take a seat or share a drink with him, which she was sure was his inarticulate and crude way of saying he was available and there were numerous bedrooms in the mansion.

She had prepared in case, the reason she ensured a patrol car fifty yards up the road and, in her pocket, a panic button. Even though she hadn't known that Sidorov wasn't in the mansion, she thought it was an appropriate response from her.

'A woman dies in your apartment from a drug overdose. You don't seem concerned,' Natalie said.

'I didn't kill her, hardly knew her.'

'First time?'

'With her, probably. Drunk, I feel the need; sober, I don't bother.

'And you're drunk now, drinking vodka neat.'

'The only drink for a Russian,' Ivanov said.

'The night you were not here, the night Maria died. Let's go back over it.'

'Not much to say. Maria didn't deserve to die, and Alexey doted on her and could see no wrong. He had infinite patience and believed she was the future. But then, I knew his hardworking, faithful, honourable wife, and there's Alexey off with other women.'

'As befitted his position, isn't that what you said once before?'

'I might have, can't remember. She understood but didn't like it. I knew her better than him, time together as children, although she was older than me, more like an older sister. I loved her, not in that way, but as a brother. She helped me through difficult times, then met Alexey and transferred her affection to him.'

'You saw her as more than a sister?'

'There was an age difference. I've told you that, and I was poor, whereas Alexey was not.'

'But she was there initially when he had no money.'

'He had a car; I had a bicycle. And then, when I had a car, he had a Mercedes, always one step ahead. She wasn't stupid. She knew what the future held and told me once, "Dima, you will always be a nobody, don't have what it takes. But Alexey will be rich and ensure our children have the best of everything."'

'You told her you loved her?'

'Maybe I wanted more, foolish, I suppose. She was right; I can't blame her for Alexey.'

'Dima, you're a disreputable character with few redeeming features,' Natalie said. She moved back from him, unsure of his reaction, but didn't expect him to laugh.

'I am. Lazy, unambitious, and want for nothing. Alexey will always ensure I'm safe and secure, even if he doesn't like me. Blood stronger than water.'

'Disdain for Alexey, love for his wife, infatuation for Maria?'

'Yes. Life is complicated, so I've read.'

Natalie couldn't imagine Dima Ivanov ever reading. The saying must have come from Alexey, fond of witticisms and literary quips.

'We've got three possibilities for Maria's murderer: one of the two Klines, Rebecca Griffith, and Peter Regan. We've not included you or her father, believe it illogical, but the elder Kline is causing trouble, and we need to put the boot in to get to the truth. You see plenty, not as stupid as you make out and might know something, no matter how minuscule.'

'Why would Alexey kill her? He worshipped her, could do no wrong in his eyes.'

'Alexey could have killed her unintentionally, in anger, if she had disappointed him. But how would he remain calm and act as the suffering parent?'

'Whereas I haven't been any other than a disreputable fool,' Ivanov said as he downed another shot of vodka.

The man's speech was slurring, the eyes were glazing, but his eyes continued to wander. Natalie moved further away, picked up her phone, and sent a message: 'Position your vehicle outside the house.'

She intended to raise the heat on the man. Drunk, lecherous, and angry, a lethal combination for the man to do or say something he would not have when sober. Her actions were not out of the police handbook and would be reprimandable if Payne found out. But the case had dragged, and her and Haddock's time was running out. Another four or five days, and there would be reinforcements imposed on them, or else a transfer to where she didn't want to go. Not since a particular inspector in the Cybercrime Squad had taken her fancy. She thought it could be a romance, keenly aware that Ivanov hoped to beat the man to a seduction.

'Have a drink. Take the weight off your feet,' Ivanov said.

'No thanks. Not with you, never. You are a despicable piece of humanity, ogling Maria, ogling me. Did you try it on with her? And why is Alexey looking out for you? Did you see him misbehave with Maria, not sexual, not accusing him of that, or maybe he hit her the day she died, threatened her with violence if she kept seeing Brett Kline?'

'Alexey would never have hurt her.'

''Not hurt, but the truth? The idea that he approved of his fifteen-year-old daughter having sex with Brett Kline goes against all we hold dear in Australia. She was a minor, a child, even if she thought she wasn't. And if Alexey was forced to go along with it, it has to do with the elder Kline. What hold did the man have over Alexey? Sure, you weren't involved. He wouldn't have taken you into his confidence, but you observe, hear, see things, and we need to know.'

'I wouldn't dishonour Alexey by telling you.'

'There is something?'

'Sure, Alexey didn't like Maria with Brett Kline, but he couldn't say anything.'

'Why?'

'What's it worth? A drink? Maybe a little affection?'

The man was drunk, almost paralytically. He had been drinking steadily since Natalie had arrived, and on the ground was a discarded bottle of Sidorov's premium vodka, a second bottle on the table alongside the man, close to empty. A red face, a bulbous nose, slurring of speech, and in another five minutes he would be incapable of speech.

'The truth, or I'll record in my report that you were withholding evidence due to a demand for sexual favours. The dead woman, did you see her inject? Don't answer. I know you did. Aiding and abetting her death would not look good if you're withholding evidence, charged with perjury.'

Natalie knew what she was saying had some truth, but mostly it was verbiage, an attempt to make the man react.

He came at her, a drunken anger. She stepped back from where she had been standing, close to the harbour wall, and he fell backwards into Sydney Harbour.

Onshore, after she had fished him out, he was back on the recliner, not sober but awake for the moment.

'The truth, Dima,' Natalie said, barely repressing a laugh at the sight of the man lying across the recliner, hair across his face, seaweed across his chest, and a small crustacean clambering up his left leg.

'Baragkhan versus Murray, four years back. That's when it started, Kline and Alexey.'

'Baragkhan?'

'One of Alexey's companies. Murray was an adversary. Don't ask me for the details, don't have them and wouldn't understand. Something about it gave Kline a hold over Alexey.'

'Acrimonious?'

'Not necessarily. You see, Alexey is Australian, couldn't survive in Russia. Over there, if someone threatens, you remove the threat.'

'You would if you were placed in a similar position?'

'Illegal in this country, debatable elsewhere.'

Natalie could see the need to further examine Ivanov's history in Australia.

***

Victoria Adderley had two challenges: meet with a former lecturer and investigate Baragkhan Pty Ltd versus Murray Financial Services. One company hid behind the veil of an offshore company, the other was a well-established and credentialed mortgage lender with impressive offices set high in a building in the central business district, a panoramic harbour vista.

Both women were present at a meeting with the senior financial officer. Victoria had given Natalie a briefing that the case had run for three weeks, a dispute due to the dissolution of the partnership between Baragkhan and Murray Financial Services. An agreement to dissolve had been reached, but there was a disagreement over the amount of money on settlement. Accountants on either side had presented their figures, and the debate had become animated in the corporate board rooms. Baragkhan claimed three hundred and two million dollars owing to them as repayment on initial investment plus further funds deposited to bolster Murray when interest rates were rising and real estate prices were deflated.

Murray argued they owed the principal plus interest and a twenty-million-dollar bonus as goodwill: one hundred and sixty-six million dollars.

Baragkhan's take was that consultancy fees, especially the value-added input of Alexey Sidorov during the transition from loss to viability, were to be costed at the difference in what Baragkhan wanted and Murray thought appropriate.

'You denied this amount,' Victoria said.

'Totally. The initial agreement when the partnership was agreed was that Sidorov's involvement would come at no cost and that he was available for consultation at any time.' The senior financial officer was in his late forties, one of a breed that had come up through university, had a sharp mind, and had worked as a futures trader for four years. Made himself twenty million dollars and made others even richer until exhaustion had got the better of him. With financial stability came burnout, no longer capable of taking the quantum risks that either gave the wealth of Midas or the empty pockets of the homeless.

'And the court case was protracted?'

'Both sides with senior counsel and highly-capable financial advisers. Not unusual, and certainly no personal animosity. We knew Alexey Sidorov, no issues with the man, but our issue was not with him but with the money involved. Ultimately, we lost, costs against us.'

'How much did you lose?' Natalie asked.

A wry smile. 'Two hundred million dollars plus costs. Another twelve million for them, give or take a few hundred thousand.'

Natalie was struggling to get another fifteen thousand to put a deposit down on a one-bedroom apartment, and the man referred to a few hundred thousand as no more than loose change.

Victoria realised the significance of the wry smile. She assumed that Natalie had. Murray Financial Services had been pushing their luck, arguing points of law, disputing the contractual agreement, aiming to set a precedent or to sow enough doubt for judgement to go in their favour.

'You lost the case. What then?' Natalie asked.

'We licked our wounds. One of our sister companies is in bed with another of Alexey Sidorov's companies. It's business, unemotional, and certainly not personal. Important distinctions. Is this related to Maria?'

'It is. Did you know her?'

'I met her a few times, came along to board meetings sometimes. Impressive.'

'She was the heir apparent, or more correctly, the heiress apparent. Would she have been capable?'

'No doubt. She had the best teacher and was a sensible woman, asked a few questions at the meetings, supplied a few answers sometimes.'

'She had a boyfriend?' Victoria said.

'Kline's son. Yes, we know.'

'Why would you know that?'

'A complete dossier on how Alexey structured his empire, his family and their history. Necessary when a lot of money is at stake.'

'What else do you know?' Natalie asked. 'The two Klines, elder and younger.'

'Five minutes while I consult our lawyers.'

Natalie and Victoria took the time to look around the room. On one wall, a Picasso; on another, a Monet. Neither woman was in any doubt that they were genuine. This was big business at the sharp edge, where decisions were not made regarding a few million but in the hundreds of millions. Billions moved through Murray Financial Services in a year, and Sidorov's money was significant in that it would have affected the bottom line but not destroyed it.

Deals were made, and money moved electronically one way or the other, legitimately in most cases, sometimes skirting around the law or else in the grey areas of government legislation, debating a point, aiming to get it changed.

Victoria understood how it worked. Owe the bank a million, the individual is in trouble; owe the bank, Murray Financial Services, or Alexey Sidorov a hundred million, and they're in trouble.

After fifteen minutes, the senior financial officer returned. 'Okay, this is what I can reveal,' he said.

Natalie wanted the whole story, not a truncated version, but realised it would need more than two women, one a police officer, the other a lawyer employed by State Crime Command. And even in a trial, would the truth be revealed?

'There were concerns about the legality and truthfulness of the evidence presented by Alexey Sidorov and his people,' the man said.

He was standing up in one corner of the room, adopting a pose that to Natalie looked like a lecturer talking down to his students. She did not like his attitude, thinking it came from a hefty salary and a superiority complex. She was not inclined to take him to task, aware that a rebuke or slighting his character could make him withdraw. She was also aware that the man could distort the truth, emphasise what he wanted to, and negate what he did not.

'We believe that Alexey Sidorov was honest,' Natalie said.

'He is, but there were financial irregularities in the figures presented in the court.'

'Which you might have been guilty of in another circumstance,' Victoria said.

'It's a fine line. This is complex, arguing a point. The country's best legal and financial minds working for one side or the other. However, it was clearly established that Alexey Sidorov, through one of his companies, was in error.'

'But?' Natalie said, sensing a hesitancy in the man's speech.

'Dismissed by the judge, disputed by our people, ignored by Sidorov's.'

'You believe that the judge was biased?'

'If he had managed to sway the judge by foul means or other, there wasn't much we could do about it. Before the trial commenced, there had been an agreement that the judge, Kline, as you know, was to be the final arbiter, and there was to be no avenue of appeal.'

'Unusual,' Victoria said.

'Highly unusual, but the case had dragged on for a long time, and we were still doing business with the man. Time to move on, and we were involved in an even bigger deal with Sidorov. We didn't want this case hanging over us, the sword of Damocles, bad blood likely to spill at any time.'

'You accepted Kline's decision, conscious of the man's bias?'

'We didn't appeal, never raised it at the time. We had been beaten, even if not fair and square. We licked our wounds, shook hands with the opposition, and forged another deal.'

'That deal?' Natalie asked.

'Still in place.'

'Then why tell us about Kline?'

'Someone killed the young woman. At some stage, the police will make an arrest, and then there'll be an unravelling, the media looking for the dirt, the police asking questions, and our concerns about the trial might become known. Possible condemnation of us, bad publicity, at least.'

It seemed weak reasoning to Natalie, as Murray Financial Services had an unassailable position as one of the country's major lending organisations. 'Why?' she asked. 'Why tell us? Do you believe Kline committed a major crime?'

'His decision could be debated by others, who might come up with a different conclusion. I'm saying that we continue to believe that Kline acted inappropriately. We weren't sure at the time whether of his own volition or with Sidorov's urging. But now, Sidorov's daughter is dead, and Kline's son was involved with her. And Sidorov and Kline in bed together, discussing the empire's future, their children as the glue that would hold them together.'

'Are you saying Kline might have wanted out?'

'I'm saying nothing. You asked about Justice Kline, Murray Financial Services, and Alexey Sidorov. I've given you what this company believes is the probable truth. I'm not giving you a murderer, nor a crime, purely information.'

Chapter 26

Ruth Stein gave her findings to Haddock and Natalie, stating that the young woman, Rebecca, was troubled and had anger management issues, balancing good common sense with the hormonal imbalance of youth, and that she had envied Maria for her easy life, a tolerant and indulgent father, a boyfriend. However, she admitted that she didn't like Brett Kline who she felt was too arrogant and full of himself.

As previously stated, she respected her father but not her mother, although some of the woman's troubles had affected the daughter, and Rebecca suffered from mild agoraphobia.

'If she murdered Maria,' Ruth Stein continued, 'she might have repressed it, no longer conscious of committing the act and unable to confess.'

Natalie knew that would be a problem, as no jury would convict a fifteen-year-old female based on circumstantial evidence, and Rebecca would be a credible witness. She had impressed Haddock and Natalie with her maturity and would do so with a judge and jury.

The interview at Kings Cross Police Station, planned for some time, was delayed due to other lines of enquiry and other persons to interview. It was three thirty on a Friday afternoon, the weekend for the young woman to recover.

Haddock and Natalie were in the interview room, and this time Rebecca was not only with her father but also with a barrister employed by the father. Natalie thought it appropriate.

A young woman in school uniform was disarming, and the fifteen-year-old looked much younger than when Natalie had met her, Brett Kline, and Peter Regan in a restaurant some weeks before.

Haddock dealt with the formalities. Rebecca appeared calm, her father agitated, and the barrister focussed. Not known to either of the police officers, he was an imperious-looking man, smartly dressed in a suit and tie, whose countenance was that of someone who rarely smiled. Natalie thought he had a comical look with his dated haircut, more pudding than style, although Stuart Forsyth was only in his forties. He had an office in Cronulla, a beachside suburb south of Bondi, a popular destination for those from the Western Suburbs, as the train terminated close to the beach. In the past, there had been racial disturbance with ogling men from the Middle East eyeing the scantily-clad women on the beach.

Haddock went through the investigation so far, outlining the events of the night that Maria Sidorov had died, and that Sergeant Natalie Campbell had proven it was possible to use cable ties on her ankles and to tighten them on her wrist with her hands behind her back.

Natalie thought it would have been best not to mention that so early in the interview, but the barrister had full visibility of the investigation and would be cognisant of that detail.

'She was my friend,' Rebecca said. 'I didn't see who tied me up, honest.'

The young woman remained calm, although Natalie was sure that wouldn't continue. The truth was often revealed in an unguarded moment, and it was important not to use interrogation tactics that would have been acceptable for an adult. Rebecca Griffith was a minor, and aggressive, rapid-fire questioning, browbeating, and intimidation, even if she finally admitted to the murder, would not be appreciated in a trial. Concern for the welfare of a minor, and sympathy for the trauma that had forced her to commit a heinous act, would result in a reduced sentence, release within a few years after psychiatric counselling and for good behaviour, and reintegration into her community.

Natalie knew the statistic and that once a person had killed, they would be capable of another, and Rebecca Griffith was fifteen, not five or six. If she was guilty, it was a psychiatric or psychopathic reason that had caused her to kill.

220

'Let's go over the events again,' Haddock said. He was holding back as if he was talking to his daughter, who was communicating again after a troubled few weeks when his marriage had ended. A short phone conversation and then two days later, a meal in Manly, close to the ocean, where he had tried to explain that it wasn't either parent's fault. Only for the daughter to remind the father that he was sleeping with another woman, and she couldn't forgive him.

'You're probably right,' he had said in a conciliatory tone, confident she did not believe him any more than he did. Dealing with a villain was one thing; dealing with a teenage daughter was another. And now, in front of him, Rebecca, the same age as his daughter: unsure of herself, subject to peer pressure, young men who only wanted one thing, young women who had social media and were bitchy.

In his day, growing up had been less complicated. Back then, frustrations were taken out on the rugby or the soccer field or out on the ocean with a surfboard if you lived close enough.

'It was Maria and me. We knew Brett and Peter weren't coming, which upset Maria more than me,' Rebecca said.

'Did you know that Peter Regan was gay? Or that he believed he was in love with Brett?'

'Everyone knew, no reason to hide it away. There is no stigma, and some of our teachers are lesbians.'

'And that Peter Regan wouldn't have been interested in you?'

'He would have. He couldn't have Brett but would have me if I had agreed. Any port in a storm, isn't that the saying?'

It was, Haddock had to admit, although where it came from, he didn't know. Only that the young woman was probably right. In your teens, peer acceptance was all-important; no stigma in being gay or whatever else, although refusing the offer of a willing female would have opened the young man to ribbing from his peers.

'Are you saying he would have been capable? We saw no proof of it,' Natalie said.

'What we want, we don't always get. Peter knew that, and Brett was bisexual. I've known that for a long time.'

'Did Maria?'

'She did, but thought he wouldn't look elsewhere if he had her.'

'Was she right?'

'Probably, although I wouldn't know. It was none of my business. I had my own issues to deal with.'

'Such as?'

'Another boy I fancied.'

'Did he fancy you, ask you out, want more than you were willing to give?'

'Not yet, but he will.'

'You'll target him?'

Rebecca's father said nothing. The barrister had explained that an emotive parent served no purpose and that the police were within their rights to question, push, and cause embarrassment.

'I'll be sixteen in three weeks. My father might disapprove, but I will make my own decisions. I am not oversexed like Maria, although you couldn't be sure about her. She's her father, over the top, always taking, not always wanting. It was a game with her, tease the male lecturers, get Brett excited, another if she could.'

'Were you aware of this arrangement between them? That the fathers had arranged.'

'Maria was okay with it, and Brett had no problem. It gave both of them the security they wanted, but Brett would gain the most, the son-in-law of Alexey, the consort to the head of the empire within ten years. He is ambitious but knows there is more than one way to skin a cat. Why work if you can marry?'

'And you at sixteen? A similar strategy?' Natalie asked.

'Not me. He's middle class, well-mannered, smart enough, low achiever. Love is not quantifiable, isn't it.'

'No,' Natalie said. She had been in love, and he had cheated on her, similar to the boy Rebecca described. 'I proved that you could have tied yourself up. And even if you deny it, how can we be sure? Neither you nor Maria acted wisely that night, allowing two boys to visit, her father at the front and you at the rear. And there was meant to be security, a cousin of Alexey.'

'Dima. Yes, we knew him, not that he would have bothered us, too busy drinking or perving in a window if Maria and Brett were going hard at it.'

'Did he do that?'

'Maria knew, gave him the occasional flash, not that I saw it. But she told me she did. I thought she was foolish, but she reckoned the man was so closely tied to her father, beholden to him, something to do with the old country and that she was safe. I wasn't so sure.'

'She wasn't,' Natalie said. 'Damn stupid. May as well wave a flag at a shark if it's targeting you. Both are centred on the target, oblivious of distractions and moral and social responsibilities, and Dima Ivanov is a man of few scruples. You heard about the woman in his apartment?'

'Not her name. Is that the heroin addict?'

'It is. Maria was wrong to assume Ivanov would back off. He could have hit you on the head and tied you up. Anything you remember?'

'Not me. I came around, unable to move, and shouted for Maria, but she wasn't there. Not sure it was him; he smelled of garlic most of the time, even from two metres – disgusting.'

Without heavy pressure, Haddock knew the interview would ultimately be inconclusive. As long as the young woman remained calm and didn't show the anger issues she apparently had, it would be impossible to break her story, which had remained consistent since that first day when Maria died. Apart from the revelation of another young man she was interested in, and that in three weeks, at the age of sixteen, she was at the age of consent, and if the new boyfriend worked out, she would sleep with him, regardless of her mother, conspicuous by her absence, and her father. A determined woman who would go far in a life lived on her terms, coupled with innate wisdom.

The similarities paled in comparison with his daughter, who showed traits like Maria, but without the financial support and her devotion to her father. Haddock knew his daughter tolerated him and that her mother was continuing to distance each from the other; hell hath no fury like a woman scorned. And he had scorned her badly, and all for a woman of insignificance, but then he considered that it was a policeman's lot to walk alone; long-term relationships always suffered.

'Was the door at the rear open for Brett Kline and Peter Regan?' Natalie asked. She understood Haddock's frustration. They may be sitting in a room with a murderer, yet tiptoeing around the woman.

'Maria would have gone down to open it, but we knew they weren't coming. She wasn't happy about the situation but wouldn't admit it.'

'Not happy because of Brett or because he would have had sex with her?'

'Both. It wasn't the great love of their lives; how could it be at that age? Do you intend to charge Brett?'

'Sexual intercourse with a person under the age of sixteen. It's a crime but not our main focus. It's unlikely it will proceed. Maria's death is more important.'

'If the door was locked, who could have opened it? Who would have had a key?'

'I don't know. It was the first time I had stayed the night. Dad's not keen, reckons I'm too young.'

'And we know your father is strong on discipline,' Haddock said.

'Firm,' Rebecca's father said. 'Too much temptation these days.'

The man had been remarkably calm during the interview, and the barrister hadn't interjected once. For an interview attempting to solve a murder, it was lame, and Haddock regretted calling it. However, Natalie wasn't so sure. For her, Rebecca Griffith had revealed one crucial fact. She wasn't the goody two shoes they had believed, and at sixteen she intended to give her virginity to the new boyfriend, whoever he was. The question was, who was he? Where was he? Did he know of the arrangement? A friend of the young Kline or Peter Regan? They were questions to be answered, but they wouldn't be that day.

***

Joe Coster, or as he was commonly known, Old Joe, had not been forgotten, only pushed to one side as the more pressing issue of Maria Sidorov's death took precedence.

That was the way it would have remained – until Sunday. Grace Iles was an old woman, homeless like Old Joe, but her history was even more unique. In the late fifties and early sixties, until her youthful appearance had deserted her, she had performed in one of the clubs on Darlinghurst Road in Kings Cross. A stripper by profession, she had turned tricks for those who paid, a room around the back, a proprietor who turned a blind eye if he received a percentage of what she received in payment. To the visiting louts from out west, and for American soldiers on R & R, someone to shout lewd remarks at and to have sex with. She had had a Christian upbringing, her youth sullied by a sour-faced mother and a drunken father, apart from Sundays, where one had gone from sour to cheerful and the other from drunk to upstanding and sober.

However, it didn't stop his abuse of her as a teen, the conflict she felt as she aged, the inability to love, and the unwillingness to trust another man, the reason she left university after one year and progressed up to the Cross. Never addicted to anything more than bad men, she had avoided the excesses of drugs, never overdosed or woken up in a strange bed, bruised and battered. In her late twenties, with the Vietnam War ending and the visiting American soldiers not throwing their money around, she began work in a gentlemen's club on Victoria Road, a two-minute walk from where she had stripped and whored.

For twelve years, she had worked in the club until fresher faces, most out of Asia, in their twenties, had replaced her. And then, she had nothing, no discernible skills, no ability to find a job or a man to look after her. That was when she found alcohol, the day she was doomed.

No longer in her prime, she moved slowly around Kings Cross, up as far as Oxford Street, Paddington, down as far as Challis Street, Potts Point, sleeping on the street or a park bench if she could. Natalie knew who she was, but the woman was uncommunicative, scowling at a police officer, even if kindness was offered. For over forty years, she was a fixture in the area. Waste bins were her food source, as were the backs of restaurants where they placed their leftovers. Passers-by who knew the woman would give her a bottle of water, food to eat, receiving a scowl in return, but never a thank you. A charity had tried to help but was rejected. Although most regarded the woman disdainfully, she hadn't deserved to die that morning.

It had been cold the night before, unusually so for the time of year, and there had been heavy rain for two days; the woman's clothing and bedding were sodden. The crime scene investigators found that her death had not been natural but intentional. It was murder, which made no sense. There could not be a motive for a woman whose history was known.

It proved to Haddock that a serial killer was in the area, although he had been wrong in assuming that the previous four deaths had been one person. But now, unequivocal proof, his instinct proved correct.

'A foot on the throat, crushing the larynx,' the pathologist said.

'Conscious of it?' Natalie asked. She had attended the autopsy, not that she ever enjoyed them, too much blood and unpleasant smells for her, enough to turn the stomach if not used to them.

'She was old, in her early eighties. Surprised she lived that long, considering her physical condition: signs of malnutrition, emaciated, probable worms. A fractured arm in her youth, a broken leg in her thirties, possibly her forties, can't be certain.

Also, rheumatism, inflamed gums, abscess in her mouth, painful, could have been treated.'

'She was unapproachable, accepted her burden.'

'Tragic,' the pathologist said. 'All too common. The other homeless individual was younger and in much better condition. As I said, at her age on the street she had a strong will to live or a remarkable constitution.'

'You've read her case history?'

'I have. Not much to recommend it. Any clues as to who killed her?'

Natalie was confident that with two murders in Kings Cross, it wouldn't take long to make the connection, formulate a pattern, and find the person. Haddock was jubilant, a vindication of what he had believed all along. Natalie thought a dead person deserved sympathy, not joy.

'Similar modus operandi to the other homeless individual, only this time not asphyxiation by applying pressure and closing the air passages, but by a boot to the throat.'

'Whose boot? Any idea?'

'Talk to Forensics. Small, I'd say, might even be able to give you a pattern from the sole. Pressure applied might indicate the person as big and strong or small and weak, but this was an elderly woman in poor physical condition.'

Haddock was tied down at State Crime Command, preparing a report, answering to Payne about the investigation's progress into Maria's death, but unable to respond positively other than, 'We're working on it, making progress.'

Payne would have admitted to being sympathetic, but he had his own issues. His seniors were giving him hell, and then there was the budgetary constraints, staff to let go, push those remaining, tighten the KPIs, and get results. Some restrictions were political, others financial, and all were an annoyance. Before, out in the bush, a long way inland from the sandy beaches and the ocean, it had been dry and dusty, and nobody had wanted his job nor wanted to visit, acquiescing to his demands. But in the metropolis, it was impossible to avoid interference, most times relevant, sometimes downright stupid. And this was one such time.

Kline was pushing his weight around, questions from the Supreme Justice of New South Wales and Alexey Sidorov.

Natalie made the trip to Forensics, spoke to the person in charge, received a lecture about the time required, and standing at the door like a lemon, asking when was counterproductive, and just got everyone's back up. Natalie laid on the charm and empathised. How she understood, and wouldn't it be great if we could all have more staff, but could Forensics grant a special favour?

Ninety minutes later, she walked out with a provisional report: pressure applied, size of boot and pattern of the sole, dirt marks on the dead woman, and on the ground nearby. All she had to do was correlate the size of the boot and where it was bought, hopeful that it was sold in Kings Cross, although probably Bondi Junction. Who it was sold to and when, and then an arrest within a few days.

Payne took the news well and even complimented Haddock for his choice of offsider. 'Couldn't do better than her,' he said, although Haddock wasn't sure whether that meant professionally or personally. He preferred the first, and besides, his sergeant wasn't his type, too thin and definitely too young. Theresa de Klerk carried more than a few kilos, and even though he had sworn off her, as an alcoholic swears off the drink, the occasional relapse wouldn't cause his conscience to grieve, and besides, his wife's demands were too much to handle, and financially he was done for. A distraction was what he required and intended to have that night, even though the woman was still on administrative leave and causing a headache for Human Resources, who would have preferred that Sergeant Natalie Campbell had left well alone.

Natalie called Haddock and found the man ebullient, although why she didn't know and he didn't intend to tell. She told him about the boot, the size and the pattern of the sole. She gave the make of boot and a list of shops to check; Forensics had done that for her. Haddock, for his part, walked into Homicide, grabbed four constables lounging around a water cooler, and gave them each a file and a list of what they needed to find out.

Nine o'clock the next morning they were to check all shops selling shoes and boots, centred on Kings Cross, extending out to Bondi Junction and the centre of Sydney, increasingly wider concentric circles until they had a result. One of the constables looked pleased to be given the task, another two said the right words, and the fourth gave cheek and said she wasn't a drudge but a degree-educated police officer and that investigations could be conducted in the office, with phone calls and the internet.

Haddock might have agreed, but her attitude got his back up. He'd watch out for her and remember to give her dirty jobs in future. Police service was cohesive, not divisive, and if she thought she was superior to others due to her father being a chief superintendent, she had another think coming.

Chapter 27

Victoria Adderley met with her former lecturer as she had agreed.

'Yes, I remember him. We were at law school together,' the lecturer said.

Kline, Victoria knew, having met with the man, was in his fifties, but a good fifties, still with colour in his hair, a youthful, mischievous look, and whippet smart. However, Geoffrey Fotherington was not. He was a distant relative of an aristocratic family in England, which he had no connection with and did not want, an ardent republican who regarded the monarchy as outdated and unsuited to a country on the other side of the world, more aligned to Asia than a previous colonial master. There was a dusty look about the man, too much time studying weighty tomes of legalese, barely conscious of the world outside of the cloistered halls of academia.

However, Victoria fondly remembered her days as a student and there was something reassuring about a crusty academic, even if he looked much older than his contemporary, Justice Kline.

Natalie had come along too. She had time to spare while the constables pounded the pavement with a photo of a similar boot to the one they were looking for. Haddock had not responded kindly to the one who had stood her ground, adamant she would remain in the office, a phone in one hand, a computer keyboard in the other. Natalie had to admire the woman, believed she was right, and the days of pounding pavements were long gone, even though she had been guilty of it, and it had yielded results. She was increasingly confident that the deaths of Joe Coster and a woman in her eighties would be solved, and the murderer would soon be in custody.

'What can you tell us?' Natalie asked.

'Good man, brilliant student, top of the class.'

'You're aware of our interest,' Victoria said.

It was remarkable, Natalie thought, that Victoria had adopted the persona of a detective. The two were becoming friends, and they had shared a night out a week before, Victoria bringing her current lover, a beautician in Parramatta, slim and tall, attractive if inclined; not, if you were Natalie, who thought the woman severe and lacking in humour. Natalie had come alone, and even though Jimmy Rogers would have been keen and would have made for a good evening, she knew she couldn't trust him not to get the wrong idea.

The evening had ended well, although it had not been an unqualified success. On reflection, Natalie wondered if Victoria's lover had got the wrong idea – assumed she was interested in Victoria, which she wasn't. She knew what her lovers would be, male and unashamedly so.

'I have read a preliminary report that you sent me. His son was involved with a precocious underage female, the daughter of a wealthy and influential man. And there is concern that either of the Klines could be responsible for her death. I assume your visit here is not to lend weight to the case, as I have not seen the man for over thirty years, but to give you an insight into him and whether he is capable of murder, and if his son, by default, could be equally capable.'

'That's a fair summation,' Natalie said.

'Then I'm not sure I can help you to any extent. Other than the man was aggressively ambitious, hard-working, did not cheat or lie, and had an eidetic memory.'

'We don't believe he murdered the young woman.'

'Although the son could have. The elder Kline was attractive as a student and always had one woman or another, but his behaviour in recent years has become suspect. Not that I'm offering a comment, just an observation. High office requires a certain standard of behaviour, and he has overstepped it.'

'He is protected.'

'Of course. Would you expect the Supreme Court to open themselves to censure and ridicule?'

'We wouldn't. But why? What makes Justice Kline tick? To believe he can get away with it? To show indifference that others know? Why isn't he open to ridicule?'

'Too important, a tactical advantage.'

'Which means?'

'Eidetic memory, as I said. Remembers everything and knows everyone: their weaknesses, strengths, not hesitant to call in favours, or to remind people of their indiscretions.'

'Corrupt?'

'Not as you and I would define. Not as the law, either. Does he use it to his advantage? Almost certainly. Would you, if you could? Probably, and that's the truth. Human nature, don't underestimate it.'

'A boat with easy women, a son having sexual relations with a female under the age of consent, a relationship of some sort with Alexey Sidorov, not sure if it was fractious, mutually beneficial or not, or if Kline ruled in Sidorov's favour. That would be corruption.'

'Would it? The judge, the final arbiter, a point of law that couldn't be proved. Ask two accountants to prepare your tax return, and they will produce a different result. The same applies to the law; too many precedents and too much legalese; depends on the interpretation. Even if Kline corruptly ruled in favour of Sidorov, it would be unprovable.'

Entertaining as it was with Victoria's former lecturer, Natalie could not see much coming of it other than Kline's peers would rally around one of their own, which they already were, and that if Kline had ruled in favour of Sidorov in his dispute with Murray Financial Services, it would not be regarded as criminal, fraud or otherwise.

Natalie was ready to make her and Victoria's farewells and leave. There was still plenty to do, and there had been progression with the boot, a message on her phone.

'Of course, I've heard some would like to bring the man down,' the lecturer said.

Natalie and Haddock had heard it referenced before, but now it seemed irrelevant. 'For what reason?' she asked.

'Ethics, morality, glad of a chance to see the man get his comeuppance.'

'But not criminal?'

'I researched when Victoria said she was coming, the lawyers' bush telegraph, better than the grapevine.'

'And?'

'Internal enquiry, Supreme Court to investigate Kline's suspect ruling. Don't expect them to release the result, even if they ever come to a conclusion or meet to discuss.'

'Any point in following up?'

'None. I'm mentioning it because it might be true. If Kline was in Sidorov's pocket or the other way around, it could explain why the son got away with sleeping with the daughter. Sidorov's a possessive man, fond of his daughter from what I've heard; a tyrant in business, soft with his daughter, and she was still a child in the eyes of the law. That is conduct unbecoming. I also found out that the son is arrogant, a chip off the old block, not to be trusted, not that he is regarded as violent, and why would he be? After all, a young woman on tap, hardly a reason to kill.'

'The young Kline might be bisexual, not sure. He's at an age where chasing and seducing willing females gives the person bravado, notches on his laptop.'

***

On reflection, Haddock and Natalie felt not much had been gained from the lecturer besides the confirmation of hearsay. It might come in handy in the future, but there was a boot and a list of four persons to check, two living in Bondi, another in Darlinghurst, and the fourth in Potts Point.

One interesting fact from Forensics was that there was wear on the heel of the left boot, indicating that the person walked with a limp, landing heavily on the left. The style was discontinued, un popular due to its angular design. The purchasers were women, except one man who had purchased them for his wife as a present, which she had subsequently returned two weeks later to be told that as they were old stock, on sale, the boots could not be returned. There had been a dispute in the shop, the manager arguing his point of view, the woman getting hot under the collar and storming out in a huff. And then wearing them solidly ever since. 'Walking the dog,' she said.

She was a shortish woman, barely up to Natalie's shoulder. Friendly, with an Irish accent. Natalie thought a fiery temperament, judging by when the woman opened the door and demanded to see her and Haddock's warrant cards. After that, agreeable when she had invited them in for a cup of tea and a sit-down, a chance to talk about the Blarney Stone, Dublin on a wet summer's evening, and leprechauns. Also, her husband had since died, and the boots reminded her of him even though they were still ugly.

Natalie hoped her husband had been more attractive than the boots. She took a photo that Forensics had supplied and held it up to the boots, saw even wear on both soles. It was not the boots that had stamped on a homeless woman's throat.

Although this woman was obviously not the murderer, Haddock and Natalie were increasingly jubilant. The boot had been an end-of-season sale, limited stock, and they had to believe that one of the four on their list was the murderer. It was an optimism coupled with a policeman's instinct. It was not infallible, but the plusses outweighed the negatives, and the resolution of Old Joe's death would be a red-letter day, the most problematic of all the deaths.

The second person lived in Darlinghurst, not far from the down-at-heel strip that ran through Kings Cross.

Darlinghurst: cosmopolitan, full of restaurants and upwardly mobile, old apartment blocks made new, maintaining their original façades, all mod cons on the inside, the towering edifice of the Horizons Building on Forbes Street. Forty-three storeys, the home of the wealthy, once the site of a carpark for the Australian Broadcasting Corporation, the national broadcaster. On the other side of the road, SCEGGS Darlinghurst, a school for the daughters of the Eastern Suburbs, fifty thousand dollars a year before books, uniforms, and excursions.

Marjorie Easterley lived on Forbes Street, close to the intersection of Liverpool Street, a two-storey terrace dating back over one hundred and forty years. When Haddock and Natalie knocked on the door, she was accommodating and invited them in. Natalie realised the woman was a gossip and that every tit-bit, the juicier, the better, would go into her arsenal of repartee to recount to her friends. She was in her sixties, straight-backed and upright, schoolmarmish in appearance, and the boots, which she proudly showed them, suited her. Even so, they were not the boots they were after, and after exchanging pleasantries, almost fighting their way out of the door, as the woman regaled them with stories of rogues and villains she had known, but were more than likely harmless individuals that the woman didn't like. Haddock could see a hater. Offend her, or call her out for gossiping, and that person would be akin to the devil.

'Where to?' Haddock said. They had walked from one woman to the next, no more than a kilometre, but his feet ached. It had been a heavy night previously, a disconsolate wife in one ear during a long phone conversation, a daughter who was asking when he was coming home and if she could live with him, and saying that her mother was becoming impossible. But his life was complicated by a lover who was demanding and critical due to his lack of ambition and disinterest in her. And when would he divorce the harridan and marry her?

He was caught between a rock and a hard place, and what he wanted was a couple of weeks to himself, to go through all that had happened, to take stock, to consider whether he should remain in the police or go walkabout, as had Old Joe done in his younger days. The latter appealed but he realised it was not feasible, and who had killed mattered little to him. Natalie would have said he was callous, and she would have been right, but there's only so much a person can take, and he had reached the limit.

'Five minutes, no more,' Natalie said, although it was closer to twenty, as far as Paddington. A car accident on New South Head Road caused the delay. There was a siren on their vehicle, but this wasn't an emergency, although it was important. Improper use of the siren to circumvent traffic would have been deemed irresponsible, a reportable offence, and Haddock had enough to deal with; he didn't need more.

Underwood Street, Paddington. Terrace houses from another century, humble abodes once, but now multi-million-dollar edifices, gutted on the inside, the outsides maintaining their architectural heritage.

The woman who opened the door was in her late forties, short and stout. Around her neck, a string of pearls. She wore a loose-fitting top and a pair of jeans which were too tight for her. In one hand, she held a cane.

Haddock went into cautionary mode, phoning for a patrol car. Natalie showed her warrant card, kept her hands free, and prepared for drama. 'Boots,' she said.

'Black and dangerous,' the woman said.

Inside the house, Haddock and Natalie sat, the woman cuffed. 'Why?' Haddock asked.

A string of complaints. Her life hadn't worked out. Her husband had left her, money was tight, and what with her leg smashed in a hit and run ten years earlier, what was there for her? The woman spoke for another ten minutes about why life had not turned out well, not once explaining why she had killed two people.

The boots had been examined by Natalie and placed in an evidence bag. Forensics would confirm, but Natalie had seen the wear on the left boot. They had their murderer, but not a reason why. It would not stop the woman's arrest, but a confession would be the pièce de résistance, the final nail in the woman's metaphorical coffin. It was clear that even though she was young, her physical condition was not, and unless incarceration agreed with her, she would age rapidly.

'You've not explained why,' Natalie repeated Haddock's initial question.

'Because I could,' the woman replied.

'We all could, but we don't. Why the homeless? Was it personal? Did you know Joe Coster? What about the old woman, Grace Iles? Did you know her?'

'My life, what it is, and there in Kings Cross, doing nothing, sponging off the government, parasites, bleeding us dry, you and me.'

Haddock had to agree the homeless were a burden but understood that was the price Australia paid for a civilised country. Natalie had travelled more and would have been more succinct, believing that life sometimes gets too much and people drop out, including the woman in cuffs, but she still had a roof over her head.

'Cancer,' the woman said. She had identified herself as Elizabeth Oatley, her previous profession a chartered accountant, her former husband a rat, and as for her daughter, a worthless piece of trash.

A troubled woman, Natalie could she had possible psychological problems, anger issues, and frustration at her lousy life. But then many people were doing it tough, with a stagnant economy and inflation heading into double digits. Most would take a deep breath, deal with and get on with their life. But this woman wouldn't: depression, complicated by sadness and ill health.

'It still doesn't explain why you killed them,' Haddock said.

'The old man, late at night. I went for a long walk, hobbling along, and there he is, drunk, asking for a handout.'

'He was not conscious when he died, a drunken stupor.'

'I carried on walking. Later, I returned past the man and saw him lying on the pavement, obviously intelligent, with a book on one side. Impulsive, I lent down and killed him.'

'How did you feel afterwards?' Natalie asked.

'A strange feeling, a sense of elation. I don't know why, but I felt no guilt and forgot my troubles for a few hours. It was an elixir, what I needed.'

The woman was mad, Haddock knew. A written and signed confession was critical, but no psychiatrist would deem her sane. A secure institution for a few years, medical treatment for her cancer, and assistance with her leg if possible.

'Elizabeth Iles?'

'I didn't know who she was, but she looked old.'

'Over eighty, on the street for close to forty,' Natalie said. 'Uncommunicative, antisocial, an incredible age considering.'

'Look at me. Forty-nine and my life is over.'

Natalie could have said it wasn't, but the woman was a murderer. Justice had to be served before any sympathy could be given to her.

'When did you choose to kill her?' Haddock asked.

'That night. I was down, emotionally, unable to function, and my leg throbbed. Strange that after I had killed her, the pain went away.'

Haddock could see scarring on the leg. There was injury, but the adrenalin rush of murder had impacted the brain's pain receptors. She would kill again if given a chance.

'A confession, duly signed?' Natalie asked.

'No reason to stay here. Yes, if you want.'

Natalie did not reply. It wasn't what she wanted, but what she must do. It was what Joe Coster and Elizabeth Iles deserved.

Chapter 28

As expected, Superintendent Payne was delighted. 'Three down, one to go,' he said.

Victoria Adderley complimented Natalie when they met at State Crime Command, and Haddock received a few choice words from his former wife after she read about the arrest and the names of the arresting officers. He thought she was mean-mouthed, but realised that he only had the phone call from his daughter, but she had had the face-to-face. A troublesome teenager going through a difficult phase in her life. Her angst was understandable, but those on the receiving end had to go through hell. And now, her school was complaining about her disruptive behaviour, and she was displaying promiscuity and using foul language.

Haddock knew he had to do something, but he wasn't sure what. He was too busy, the pressure too great, and he didn't have Sidorov's wealth, no means to pay a third party to keep a watch on her, no means to pay for counselling. Life for the man was becoming unbearable, and the accolades for the arrest paled in significance.

Apart from the paperwork, there was one murder left to solve, the most disturbing of all.

The tie-in of Mary Otway and Joe Coster seemed circumstantial until Natalie pulled Jimmy Rogers into a room at the back of Kings Cross Police Station. She laid out the arrest of a woman for the murder of two homeless people, and she had suspicions that he had misled the investigation. Under the pressure of a relentless woman and an aggressive Haddock, who had joined them, Rogers admitted that his identification of Joe as the mystery lover of Mary Otway was tenuous. And that under rigorous analysis by experts at a subsequent trial, it would have been invalidated.

'Why?' Natalie asked. She had seen the man as competent, diligent, and reliable.

'It was ninety per accurate,' Rogers said.

Natalie wanted to say it was not good enough, but she knew the truth. The man was enamoured of her and had allowed the personal to interfere with professional. She thought to register a case against him but knew she wouldn't. She had done that with Theresa de Klerk, Haddock's bit of fluff, who he continued to meet, which caused aggravation and distrust of her at Parramatta. She didn't want to go down that road again.

Rogers scurried out of the police station; his head held low.

'End of a perfect romance,' Haddock said to Natalie. His witty remark wasn't appreciated.

For two days, a sense of calm reigned. Natalie stayed close to Kings Cross, a police station she preferred to the bureaucratic jungle of State Crime Command in Parramatta.

Haddock met with his wife. An appointment with the headmistress at their daughter's school, an explanation as to why their daughter had changed, and they were hopeful that she would soon calm down. It was a tense meeting, the headmistress more experienced in such matters than the two parents. She informed them that some latitude would be given, and a counsellor would talk to their daughter.

Over coffee and cake at a café near the school, the antagonists decided that their daughter was more important, and there would be no slagging each other off in front of their daughter, although Haddock never had. However, it was a time for conciliation, to consider their child, not the emotions that raced through the parents, the mother's anger and the father's despair. Both were in the right; both were in the wrong. They could at least agree on that.

Outside the café, the sun shone, a day for a stroll, and for the first time in many years they found enjoyment in each other's company, but it was short-lived. The reality was around the corner. She had a part-time job to go to, and he had a murder to solve.

It was Natalie who broke the peace by phoning her inspector. 'Point Piper, thirty minutes,' she said.

'Sorry, luv,' Haddock said as he kissed his wife on the cheek, the first sign of affection between them for several months. His wife received it warmly, wished it could be different, but knew it couldn't. He reflected that he had warned her in their courting days that a police officer is never off duty and that holidays and days off were luxuries, not givens.

'Ivanov found him,' Natalie said.

They were in the front room of the mansion, a large room decorated with statues and oil paintings. Natalie had thought it gaudy the first time she had entered: Russian baroque, heavy on symbolism. But now it was a room of death, Alexey Sidorov's lifeless body on the floor.

'Too much for him,' Ivanov said. His face was pale and he was sweating. He had been crying. His eyes were red and puffy.

'Suicide?' Haddock asked.

'Handwritten note,' Natalie said. 'Shot himself, gun in the mouth. Can't blame him under the circumstances.'

Haddock couldn't.

Alexey Sidorov's death was the last roll of the dice, the prelude to the main event. Ivanov was overcome with grief; Justice Kline offered his condolences to Natalie, although why her? She suspected but didn't want to lay the truth to the obvious. She had just had a run-in with Jimmy Rogers; she didn't want another with Justice Kline, old enough to be her father and who should have known better. Rogers had been naïve and meaning no harm, but Kline was neither. The meeting with the man was scheduled. It would go ahead.

The crime scene investigators were all over the mansion. And even if it was obvious, due to the complexity of the investigation and the other murders, no stone was to be left unturned. This was a powerful man, rich as Midas or close enough not to quibble over the difference. Entrenched, distraught, a loved daughter murdered, a dead wife, an incompetent cousin who continued to get under the CSIs' feet until Haddock dragged him off to one side and marched him down to the jetty, the scene of a murder.

'Dima,' Haddock said, 'why? Alexey was a fighter, irrepressible, unwilling to give in, and then he goes and shoots himself, leaves a note, proof positive.'

A tap on the shoulder. Haddock turned around, unprepared but willing to go into battle with the person who had disturbed his train of thought. He realised he was testy, shouldn't be at work, and his sergeant was upset at Rogers' deception.

'The letter's a forgery.' It was his sergeant, sad in the face, pleased that one of the CSIs had identified flaws in the handwriting. A curl at the bottom of the 'G', a slant on the 'B'.

'Positive?' Haddock asked, almost apologetic, almost saying it to his sergeant, but wouldn't. Too much familiarity breeds contempt, and he appreciated the distance they kept. Even so, he had to admit that in her sadness, there was a vulnerability about her that he found endearing, a child lost in the wood, but their wood was bigger and more violent, full of wolves and phantom spirits, and to his side, one of the wolves, or maybe Ivanov was no more than a cub, answerable to another.

'Subject to Forensics, but they'll confirm. I've got one coming down, and it's a top-rate forgery; it would fool most people. The pathologist is on his way, need to be one hundred per cent on this one. Sidorov's death is big news; the media are on their way, tipped off by we know who. Prepare yourself for the hovering helicopters; better make sure we have the place sealed off tonight.'

'Ivanov,' Haddock said, turning back to the man, 'I was willing to give you the benefit of the doubt, but this is murder, and you're here. How are your writing skills? Forged a few cheques you've found lying around the place, the bonus you never got, helped yourself to it?'

'I arrived not long ago and found him there. I didn't touch anything, and believe me, I never cheated Alexey, family honour.'

Dima Ivanov and family honour were not compatible. The man was a low-life, barely able to tie his shoelace, employed by Sidorov out of misplaced family loyalty and honour. He was the person most likely, but he almost certainly did not kill the man and would not have had the expertise to forge a letter. The man's death had been thought out by others playing a strategic game, but what it was, wasn't clear at this time.

'Who's his lawyer?' Natalie asked, although she suspected the answer.

'Justice Kline, a legal office in Vaucluse, a couple of employees, trained lawyers. That's all I know.'

Haddock would stay at the mansion. She was heading east. Kline had been notified, acquiesced to her request and would meet her there in forty minutes, maybe a bite to eat afterwards. The man was incorrigible and dangerous. He was unemotional when Natalie met with him. How he knew of Sidorov's death so early was unclear. Haddock had Ivanov by the scruff of the neck, and the man was going to talk that day. Also, Russell Harding, regardless of his homilies on life in the Eastern Suburbs, rogues I've known, no names given. The gloves were off, and Superintendent Payne had made it clear. 'No soft-shoe shuffle. Forget who or what Kline is, the third degree, okay?'

'Okay by me,' Haddock said. 'What about you? The powers on high, ducking for cover. It could be your career.'

'Not at the expense of our integrity. The law applies equally, with no fear or favour, no special deals. Hit Kline hard, his son, if you have to, forget this nonsense about him being a minor.'

'He's not.'

'The young woman, her as well, and young Kline's friend. Throw the book at him, ram his homosexuality down his throat, get him angry, and see the response. Any idea who the beneficiaries are? It must be a fortune for a lucky individual. Ivanov, reckon it's him?'

'No idea, not yet. Sergeant Campbell is meeting Kline at his law office. A couple of lawyers there working for him, dealing with Alexey. She'll ask about assets and who's on the list, better than the lottery, a solid motive.'

***

Kline's ambivalence, his cavalier attitude in his subtle attempts at seduction, brought out the worst in the young sergeant. She had experienced sexual harassment before, recognised the signs, and realised the Kline was smooth, intelligent, charismatic, and a lecher. On the drive to Kline's office in Vaucluse, she decided that any exception she had given to the man was ill-founded. And that Kline, another time, another place, in the early days of settlement, would have been one of those in England, sitting high in the magistrates' court, debauching behind the scenes, stealing what he could, who would send a child in chains to Australia as a convict.

She hoped he was the murderer, but knew he wasn't. His alibi was too strong, not from the men on the boat, but from the women with no cross to bear other than remorse at being pawed by the ageing Lotharios.

However, young Brett Kline wasn't off the hook, and now somebody had murdered Alexey Sidorov, although his killing appeared professional, not amateurish, as the others had been.

'What I can tell you,' a female lawyer in Kline's office said as she smiled at her boss and scowled at a police sergeant, a dead giveaway to Natalie, 'is that Mr Sidorov had decided not to put in place a complex document outlining disposal of his assets in the event of his death.'

'Why?' Natalie asked.

Kline answered. 'Alexey was a fatalist. You come into this world with nothing and leave with nothing. His daughter was his beneficiary, the money to be placed in trust until she was twenty-five or married. He didn't change it after her death, left it as is.'

'If the money is in trust, who would have responsibility for it? I assume that must have been taken into account.'

'Complicated, exceptionally complicated. Six months to unravel, but it will be handled by this office and a group of persons that he trusted, that hold senior positions within his organisation.'

'Others will benefit from his death. Is that what you are saying?'

'I am.'

'And that you would be one of those to benefit.'

'That was already agreed to. Alexey trusted me implicitly, had no doubts, and the future was assured with my son and his daughter.'

'Except she's dead. Some might say convenient. A great deal of money would tempt even the most resolute.'

'Are you inferring that I'd be tempted?' Kline said. The man's attitude had changed; he was hostile. Natalie felt like she had been thrust into the lion's den with no more than a warrant card to protect her. She was out of her depth. She needed assistance.

A quick phone call. Victoria Adderley would be in Kline's office within the hour, but she was in Parramatta, and traffic would be heavy.

'I'm out of my depth here,' Natalie said to Kline. 'Which group of people, and how could they be trusted?'

'Complex,' Kline reiterated.

To Natalie, complex meant one thing. Multiple opportunities to cheat and steal, to argue points of law. Maria would have been mincemeat to such people, and Brett would have been the bunny who ensured she was pregnant and distracted with love. There was mischief afoot, that much she knew, but no way that even Victoria could make sense of it in the short term.

'The mansion?' Natalie asked.

'It will be sold, dependent on suitable offers.'

'We need to meet the trustees.'

'Not all are in Australia, and besides, the identity of some will not be revealed. I am one, and so is Brett, but in a junior capacity. I know you were talking to Murray Financial Services, trying to find out about an indiscretion on my part. Commendable of you to try, but pointless. The decision that I made was correct, an arguable point of law. They know this, as do I, and now do you. Sergeant, you are clutching at straws, hoping to pin Alexey's death on me and Maria's on Brett. But you won't succeed, never will, not even—'

'You are both guilty. Is that what you want to say.'

'Sergeant Campbell, this meeting is concluded. In future, we will meet in a location of my choosing. I will ensure that I have the best legal and financial advice. Unfortunately, you will have Adderley and Haddock, minnows swimming with sharks.'

The meeting had turned sour, but Natalie, who should have been appalled, even distraught, realised a corner had been turned.

The previously unflappable Kline had lost his cool, spoken from the heart, if he had one, which Natalie thought unlikely, instead of from his immense brain.

Could he have become angered when he realised his seduction of the young female sergeant was askew and she was no longer responsive to him? Natalie thought it but brushed it aside. The man couldn't be that stupid, or could he? He had spent time with whores on a boat in the company of other men, now protected by those of his ilk, some approving, others not. One more push and the man would cave in.

Even so, they had two murders to solve. Alexey's was fresh; Maria's had gone stale with time, despite no shortage of suspects.

***

246

Haddock and Kline met in Kings Cross. There was a reason for celebration, for remorse, for concern. Four deaths had been solved, two to go, although Natalie, more sensitive than Haddock, felt for the victims and their families, especially the former husband of Mary Otway, the philanderer she had stolen away from Sheila Cross, who, on being told of developments in Australia, had suffered a fatal attack. The two officers conceded that the man had probably been decent, as had Sheila Cross, proof that love, hate, and the inability to forgive were powerful emotions and they had led a charitable woman in Melbourne to kill. Both incapable of forgiving and moving on with their lives until they were too old to care either way.

Joe Coster had a stepbrother in England; Elizabeth Iles had no one. The send-off that had been given Old Joe was accorded her too, and Natalie would attend. Haddock said he would come, but Natalie couldn't be sure. The man appeared to have an aversion to funerals, probably the result of seeing what had happened to the person before death.

The homeless in Kings Cross were a dying breed as the area changed, and now the Bourbon and Beefsteak, the largest pub in Kings Cross, the one where the American GIs on rest and recreation had flocked to, was closed, as was the Empire Hotel on the corner of Darlinghurst Road and Roslyn Street, and the shops in between, and the low-cost tenement buildings. In their place would be high-cost dwellings, a multi-storey hotel, and shops for those who would pay, not for those who would attend Elizabeth Iles' send-off.

The Eastern Suburbs Railway ran under the area; its entrance was on Darlinghurst Road, two stops to Town Hall and the Queen Victoria Building, once run-down and abandoned, but now a tourist draw for locals and overseas visitors, with all the best shops and plenty of restaurants.

'If Kline's rattled, it may be to our advantage, it might not,' Haddock said.

The Chef de la Fontaine had not been in the area for more than a few years, an ice cream parlour before. But it was popular: queues outside early morning, needing their hit of caffeine, not instant, but a myriad of choices. It wasn't Haddock's preferred place to sit and talk, but Natalie felt the need that day. She had had a rousting from Kline and realised that taking a flight with that man might not have been such a good idea.

Outside the café, two chairs and a table, people passing by, traffic moving up and down the street, enough noise not to be overheard, enough life to make Natalie relax, and for Haddock to attempt to remove himself from his personal matters, which if not over, appeared to be in a precarious balance. If his sergeant asked, which he knew she would not, he would say that Theresa did not hold the allure she once had. Noncommittal sex, no discussion of family or permanency, had been fun, but now it was not, and he was willing to break it off, not sure if it would backfire, as the woman was addictive, a distraction after a day and a night of dealing with murder and its aftermath.

'Kline's vengeance could be something we don't want,' Natalie said. She was tired of the investigation, as was Haddock. He had his issues, and so did she. A live-in boyfriend had disappointed her; Jimmy Rogers had misled her to get closer, romantically involved if he could. And now, Justice Kline had shown his true colours and that his agreeable demeanour, even when suspected of wrongdoing, was a cleverly-engineered attempt at seduction.

Twenty-five minutes later, Haddock's phone rang.

'Your sergeant's visit with Kline is causing friction,' Superintendent Payne said.

Haddock replied, sensing agitation in the man's voice. 'It was logical, considering that Alexey Sidorov used a law firm of which Justice Kline is the principal. The man's dead; who are the beneficiaries? Who will gain from his death? The man had his fingers in many pies, and what was it with Maria not having control until a certain age, a group of trustees set up to monitor his wealth, make decisions, isolate Maria, and throw her on the street. And then we've got Brett Kline, tied to Maria, marry her at

248

some stage, get her pregnant, and then, if he's like the father, push her to one side.'

'You don't need to convince me. Just letting you know. I've had the Commissioner of the NSW Police in my ear. She is receptive, realises corruption in the highest echelons of politics could bring down the government. Anxious to stem the flak.'

'Will she? A whitewash?'

'Not her. Carte blanche, go in heavy, keep Adderley informed, and find out how Sidorov's estate will be carved up. There are bound to be persons hindering, Kline at the forefront, but he's received a warning from someone more senior than him, told to cooperate. Put the hard word on your sergeant?'

'She's not comfortable with the man's behaviour, shown his true colours, or he's frightened.'

'The latter. Tell her to rise above it. Forty-eight hours maximum. If he's threatened, he'll fight like a caged animal. One fallen Supreme Court judge, aspersions on the other – you can imagine the flak if that happens. They're meant to be impartial, but Kline's clearly not. He couldn't have murdered Maria, but Alexey, that's another issue.'

Payne ended the call. Haddock turned to his sergeant. 'Payne's on board, and so is the commissioner. Go in heavy, no stone unturned, and if Kline tries his tricks, be prepared.'

Three hours later, long enough for Natalie to go home, shower, and rest, she was back out at Kline's law firm. This time the man was not present.

Victoria Adderley had accompanied her, pleased to be out of the office. Also, Konstantin Szare, a Russian-speaking immigrant, a member of Fraud Squad in Parramatta, eight years in Australia, from Kharkiv in Ukraine. He could translate and, hopefully, understand if any documents were in Russian.

Chapter 29

Justice Kline had his own issues to deal with. A hastily-convened gathering of the Supreme Court Justices: a wooden-panelled room, a walnut conference table, in Phillip Street, not far from the NSW Parliament where a similar meeting was in session, presided over by the Premier of New South Wales.

Kline stood firm and gave a detailed and documented account of his relationship with Alexey Sidorov, omitting specific details such as his son's relationship with a murdered daughter, the bond that held an entrepreneur of note and a Justice of the Supreme Court entwined. It was an impassioned delivery, full of facts, provable in a court of law, but those listening were unconvinced. They were threatened; if mud stuck to one of them, they would be sullied by association.

None of the above concerned Natalie and her two compatriots. They had met twenty minutes earlier and discussed the situation and that irregularities were one issue, murder was another. Victoria was convinced they would find nothing, and Konstantin, new to the team, told them that if there were grey areas, he would spot them, maybe not that day, but in the weeks following. Except, as Natalie informed him, 'Forty-eight hours before the hell hounds descend.'

Natalie, innocent when she had first coupled with Haddock, now saw life as it was: dirty, dishonourable, and more sharks in positions of power than swimming in the harbour.

Inside the law firm's office, reams of paper, bound and indexed. It was an attempt to stifle the police. Natalie did not intend to be swayed, realising that it was a précised summation that she wanted, not an overabundance of confusion couched in legalese.

'The short version?' Natalie said.

The two lawyers opposite, one male and one female, were intelligent and well-paid, judging by the BMW and the Mercedes alongside the building. Minor functionaries, whose sole purpose was matters pertaining to the dead man. In fact, Natalie was sure there was no other client. She wondered why they hadn't visited before, although that was obvious. Kline had not proffered the information, nor had Sidorov, and even if they had, without Sidorov's death they would have received short shrift instead of an endorsement by the Premier and Chief Justice to resolve the matters urgently, to let them know before it became public knowledge, before they arrested Kline or someone else.

It was a request that she and Haddock would consider, but it would not be easy. Outside the office, a waiting chorus of reporters with cameras and microphones, some professional, others with an iPhone.

Victoria, she trusted; Konstantin, she wasn't so sure. The man was enjoying himself too much as he cast a scant look at the documents.

In town, Kline had left his office, and his son was no longer at school, the two heading west to a retreat on the other side of the Blue Mountains. Even Rebecca Griffith was out of school and at home with her parents. Dima Ivanov and Peter Regan were the only ones visible. Regan maintained that he wasn't involved.

Haddock had taken on the responsibility of checking on the other players, convinced that one of them, possibly two, was a murderer. The retreat was known due to Brett Kline's inability to keep off social media, and local police were heading there. No intent to arrest or impede but to monitor. Haddock had phoned Rebecca's father, told him he would be over at some stage and asked how the family was holding up. The reply had been negative, as his wife had taken to her bed and Rebecca was sitting in her room doing very little except looking out of her window at a reporter standing in the street. As for him, the father damned the day Rebecca had become Maria's friend. Haddock had to agree; anonymity was far better than what anyone was experiencing, even his wife, who had received a phone call. The forty-eight-hour deadline was reduced to twenty-four, work around the clock, snatched naps, no going home to bed.

Konstantin spent the next ten hours in the office, a court order to ensure he had access to the documentation but not the authority to remove it. Justice Kline had committed no provable crime, and even though he was contactable by phone, he was reticent to assist the enquiry any more than necessary. Natalie was unsure if the documents that Konstantin waded through, assisted by Victoria, were the most important. There were plenty, enough to keep a team of accountants and lawyers occupied for several weeks, but they had twenty-four hours, no more, a dictate from Haddock. He had been on similar cases before, strike while the iron is hot, enough time to make headway before the opposing forces coalesce and fight back.

Alexey's death was unimportant to those clamouring to wrest control; the breakup of his empire was. Who would get what and when? And what about those companies listed on the stock exchange, leaderless? The price was bound to drop, corporate raiders in the wings, vultures picking over the rotting carcass, hyenas nearby, but was there a lion who would see them all off?

Regan was in the hot seat. Natalie returned from Kline's office and sat with Haddock as they faced off against the young man. He'd had the opportunity to kill Maria, a motive that would hold up in court, in that he was infatuated with Brett, love, he said, and Maria was with his man. Infatuation or love, an adolescent's mind, disturbed by notions of eternal love, aware that Brett would stay with Maria, even if it wasn't love, but certainty as to his future, the ability to philander, either male or female, or both.

Haddock had slept thirty minutes in the last fifteen hours; Natalie had fared better with ninety. Even so, she was exhausted, and Victoria and Konstantin were working through, having rejected additional help. Konstantin quoted a Russian proverb from his childhood about how too many cooks spoil the broth.

He was right. There had to be a system for examining the documents, starting with the oldest and progressing to the newest. Any mention of Maria was to be copied and saved on a laptop. The two lawyers in the office slept in one corner, the occasional eye opening to observe, but otherwise impassive, answering questions when asked, saying nothing if not.

'An attractive man, Justice Kline,' Victoria had said earlier to the woman, attempting to exchange repartee with her, conscious of Natalie's asserting that the interaction between Kline and the lawyer was suspect. Although she thought Natalie was oversensitive, pleasantries in an office did not have to be automatically suspicious.

The woman had nodded but said no more, probably Kline telling those who worked for him to be polite and cooperative but not to offer assistance, which Victoria would have said made sense.

'I don't know,' Regan's standard replies to every question. There was a lawyer to one side who said little, but might say more when the tempo of the questioning was raised.

'There are four people who could have murdered Maria,' Haddock said. 'You're the one with the most significant motive. Circumstantial evidence goes against you; proof doesn't.'

'What is the point of this interview?' the lawyer asked.

Haddock chose to ignore him and continued. Outside the police station, it was a sunny day, but inside the interview room, it was distinctly chilly. The previously affable Regan was starting to stew, a reddening of the face, his fists starting to clench. Haddock had seen it, and so had Natalie.

'Brett Kline and his father are hiding out.'

'Brett phoned and advised me to get out of town. But where? I hadn't done anything wrong.'

'Except to be a friend of Brett's. Are you aware of the trouble his father might be in?'

'Not really. Brett said his father was complex, with many facets to him.'

'Which meant?'

'What you see is not what you get.'

'Succinct for an eighteen-year-old.'

'Why not? We're not all from out west. Some of us are educated, attend good schools, and have successful parents.'

Natalie noted the slur against Haddock and his Western Suburbs upbringing.

'Not all.' Haddock refused to rise to the bait. He knew that socially he would be a pariah to a young man who had everything on a plate.

'Your parents? Do they know that you're homosexual?'

'No.'

'And if they did?'

'They wouldn't like it. But they're your generation, different values.'

'I have nothing against you due to your sexual orientation, and your snobbery does you no credit.'

'Not snobbery, boredom with this constant questioning. You know what I am, my relationship with Brett.'

'Physical? We know he wasn't the macho man he portrays; he could swing both ways.'

'Not with me.'

'With others?'

'He might have, don't know. We didn't hang out together all the time, but he wanted me that night and thought I'd take Rebecca. But she's not my type. Pointless for me to go.'

'Brett was on a sure thing. He would not have stayed back. Could it be that he was straight, and you did not like it, saw a resolution, and we know you have a temper, barely concealing it now.'

Haddock left the room and called Forensics.

'How long have you had a problem with sweating?' Haddock asked on his return. 'You're nervous here, no longer full of yourself, feeling vulnerable. At eighteen, it's what we would expect, but under your arms, sweat stains, a pungent odour.'

Natalie had noticed but did not think to mention it.

'Excessive sweating, especially in the armpits, coupled with odour, indicates an underlying medical condition.' Haddock repeated what the forensic scientist had told him. It was too technical for him, but there had been a trace of a chemical on Rebecca Griffith's clothing when she had been tied up. Little credence had been given to it then, but in that small room, hotter than it should be, and with Regan feeling uncomfortable and agitated, it had reminded Haddock of the Pathology and Forensics report.

'It's called hyperhidrosis,' Haddock said. 'You will be subjected to tests, analysis of your medical condition and why you have body odour, not that we've noticed before. If what we find matches traces on Rebecca Griffith's clothing, then you, Peter Regan, murdered Maria Sidorov.'

'I didn't mean to. It was an accident. I knew Brett wasn't going, and I thought I would have it out with her, tell her to leave Brett alone. Rebecca would have supported me, or I hoped she would. She knew Maria was throwing herself at a man who would ultimately disappoint. She's an incurable romantic, believes in eternal love, although why, considering her parents, I don't know.'

Natalie did. Someone to share life with was preferable to being alone, and even if Rebecca's mother had severe problems, it paled in comparison to the alternative.

'Accident?'

'Yes, she opened the door, saw me there, and told me to leave. Rebecca's upstairs, and she couldn't see where I was, no lights, not that night. We were on the jetty, and she started hitting me, telling me to go away. I grabbed her, and then I flipped. There I was, a rope in my hands and then around her neck, sucking the life out of her. Honestly, I didn't mean to do it.'

'Rebecca?' Natalie asked.

'I wasn't sure what to do. Impulsively, I went upstairs. She was looking the other way. I hit her over the head with a piece of wood, tied her up in the bathroom and left. No idea why, but I felt nothing. Not even now.'

Lives destroyed due to adolescent passion; it seemed to Natalie a terrible waste. Another murder was solved, but at what cost?

***

What remained, and seemed to be a tragic error by the perpetrator, was Alexey Sidorov's murder, made to appear as a suicide, revealed by the crime scene investigators as murder. The man's death had the mark of Ivanov, close enough to have killed his cousin, probably degenerate enough, but Ivanov was not an intelligent man and thought by Haddock not to have the subtlety to write a faked suicide note which was good enough to fool most persons. Also, why would Dima Ivanov kill Alexey, who had always looked out for him, as had been the case at his apartment when an OD'd prostitute had died?

A re-enactment of the events leading to Sidorov's death had been conducted, a junior male police officer from Kings Cross taking the part of the man, arriving in the room, looking around, cautious, as Sidorov would have been ever since Maria's death. Why the mansion had been vacant the day he died made no sense, as Ivanov had been staying in the house, a small room downstairs, not in the central part of the building, as he was still the hired help, even if related and in trouble.

One interesting fact from recreating the events leading up to the death was that it would have been difficult to enter the room and sneak up behind someone unseen. There were mirrors on each wall, Sidorov would have been conscious of another's presence in the room. The junior sergeant had moved around the room while others looked for blind spots. It was a well-used room, and the signs of others, including Ivanov, Maria, and even Brett Kline, were apparent. However, no evidence of Peter Regan in the room, not that he had killed the father, but the daughter.

His arrest had been big news in the Eastern Suburbs, one of their cherished few, arrested for a heinous crime. Ruth Stein spent time with the man, remanded in Long Bay Prison, to the south, close to Botany Bay, where Captain Cook had arrived in 1770 on his voyage of discovery. She said the young man was immature, idealistic, and in love.

It tended to agree with Natalie's summation in that she had found Regan a polite young man, in many ways a reflection of Rebecca Griffith, who was back at school, studying for her exams. Natalie had met with the young woman, purely social, and found that the emotional stress had taken its toll, and her appearance was pallid, her skin whiter than before.

'It's Mother,' Rebecca said. 'She's not well, and the stress has affected her. We've put her in care for a couple of weeks, a place Dr Stein suggested. A chance for her to relax, a change of scenery, and my father's a changed man, morose and withdrawn.'

'It's those left who suffer. Peter Regan?'

'Maybe I should be surprised, but I don't think I am. It's one of those situations, once you're told, the indicators you have seen but disregarded become relevant. I had seen him look away whenever Brett was with Maria, not in the boat shed, but elsewhere.'

'Elsewhere?' Natalie asked. She had always liked the young woman, as she had Peter Regan, but this time she was not as likeable as before. Natalie knew the reason, as she had seen it before. Association with crime, accused of it, subjected to the bright lights and the intensive questioning, even the innocent begin to feel some guilt. And the young woman had been subjected to more than most, courtesy of Ruth Stein, whose gentle manipulation of her questioning, attempting to get the truth, to get into her psyche, had laid bare repressed emotions. Rebecca's mother had agoraphobia, and Stein believed other issues were hidden deep. And that Rebecca had ridden above the inherited trait of her mother's fear of open places, but she had admitted to Natalie before that what you see isn't necessarily what you get. And yes, virginity was not due to her age, but fear of revealing her inner demon if she opened her emotions to another. She feared the physical act would change her in a way she could not control.

'Nowhere specific. Brett was with Peter most of the time. Not sure if it was Brett who wanted him or if Peter was the fawning admirer. The same as Maria and me.'

'Was it?'

'Oh, yes. Maria was the person I wanted to be, open, extrovert, confident in herself.'

'No hangups?'

'Not Maria. But then she had Alexey, and I had my parents. What do you reckon?'

Natalie reckoned that for an impressionable teen, parents did matter. They should not hold a person back as an adult, but Rebecca wasn't there yet. A few more years, and she'd be fine.

'Not quite the same, Brett and Peter. Peter was in love with Brett, and what was it with Brett? Possible latent homosexual?'

'Possible, but not with Peter.'

'Would you know?'

'I believe I would.'

The two Klines returned to Sydney five days after they had left. Brett returned to school for his end-of-term exams. Justice Kline returned to the Supreme Court and prepared to adjudicate another case, embezzlement, the doctoring of a large engineering company's financial records, over two million dollars missing, a problem found during a tax audit.

The woman had worked for the company for eighteen years, knew the innermost workings, and in charge of finances, so she had the books. She had figured that changing the number of zeroes on a financial entry, credit or debit, was easy enough. No one checked, no independent auditor, until the tax department had stood at the door, asking for immediate access to all records.

It was the day when Kate Handley got into her car and drove off at high speed, only to end up in a ditch.

Natalie wasn't concerned about the embezzlement, but with Justice Kline, who now paraded in the area, confident in his superiority, almost giving Haddock a verbal finger-up as they passed each other in traffic.

Russell Harding had gone to ground; they were suspicious of the speed at which it had happened, but with so many things in recent weeks, it wasn't unexpected. The man had opened up to Natalie in a way he hadn't with anyone else, an old man enjoying the company of a pretty young woman. But Kline had influence, and for now he was riding high, no proof against him, no improprieties in how his firm had dealt with Alexey Sidorov's legal affairs.

That was, until Victoria Adderley, back in State High Command, after receiving emailed copies of documents in Kline's office, had seen an anomaly.

Haddock and Natalie met with her in Parramatta, in the small space she occupied, more a broom cupboard than an office.

'Kline was aware the verdict he gave was in error.'

'How?' Natalie asked.

'Murray Financial Services, we met with one of their people, they accepted it as a fait accompli.'

'Only because they would have done the same if they could have. '

'Exactly, but that's not the point. A reference in his notes showed that Kline had researched it before giving his final verdict. He had listed the precedents and points of law and taken advice from someone overseas. He had ruled in favour of Sidorov when he should not have. Murray Financial Services, not that they are any better than Sidorov, were in the right. Any bearing on your investigation?'

'It was a lever over Alexey, gives us reason to talk to Kline. Up to it again, Victoria?' Haddock asked.

'Not this time.'

'Good. We weren't asking you. Just make sure we've got bullet points of questions to ask. The man will be evasive, hide behind his veil of legal respectability, not that it'll work, not this time.'

Natalie wasn't so sure. Kline was highly intelligent and had even managed to protect himself at the Supreme Court and had explained his rapid departure to the countryside with his son as a need for reflection, to recharge the batteries, to formulate a vigorous defence against slurs and innuendos.

Chapter 30

Dima Ivanov opened the door to his apartment, much cleaner than their previous visits, the hand of a woman, Natalie realised.

'A cleaner,' Ivanov said. 'Alexey, he did me fine, left me money. I told you, blood is thicker than water.'

'How much?' Haddock asked as he sat down, the smell of eucalyptus in the room, a clean window to look out.

'One million dollars. For me, a King's ransom.'

It was also to Haddock, who was struggling to pay his commitments, anxious to keep his wife and daughter in the family home. The relationship between him and the two women had mellowed, so much so that he had been to the house, had a meal with them, discussed the situation, and explained to their daughter that things do not always work out as we would like.

'You're still in this apartment,' Natalie said.

'I don't have it yet; twenty thousand to keep me going. What do you want with me?'

'Who read the will? Do you have a copy?'

'Kline told me at his office. Got me to sign a non-disclosure agreement.'

'Non-disclosure of what? You just told us,' Haddock said.

Natalie looked around the apartment, peered into the bedroom where the dead woman had been found, and saw signs of another woman, but she wasn't present. In the second bedroom, a small unmade bed, boxes stacked on top, Ivanov having a spending spree, watches, computers, and jewellery.

'Who's the woman?' Natalie asked on her return.

'Upmarket, got the money now,' Ivanov said.

'Not until we solve the murder, that's what you said,' Haddock reminded him.

'Kline gave me some on account. I just told you that.'

Natalie sensed something was amiss. Kline did not give money out of kindness, only duly documented, and non-disclosure agreements indicated an attempt to hide something, and this was a murder investigation – no concealment of information was allowed.

Even though Kline was unaware, the noose was tightening. Superintendent Payne, updated on the current status, had contacted his superior, who had contacted the Premier's department. The Premier, a political animal, had used one of his contacts to update Kline's superior. The man's power base was crumbling, and people ducked for cover. If Kline was to go down, they did not intend to follow.

A phone call from the man for the two police officers to meet with him at his office in Vaucluse. Haddock wanted to meet at the police station but realised that Justice Kline, under pressure, was dangerous, and in the confines of an interview room would be a caged animal. Whether he was a saint or a sinner, he was a man who did not adhere to common morality and success at any cost was acceptable, even as far as giving an incorrect verdict; even committing murder.

Kline was magnanimous when they met, openly admitting that these were trying times for him. In his office, the two lawyers who worked for him, and now, even they were friendly.

Natalie was suspicious. She'd had the Kline treatment before, a flight up to the Hawkesbury River, a meal at a high-quality restaurant, and then, to rub salt into the wound, he had admitted that his admiration for her went from respectful to lecherous.

Even under immense strain, the man intended to fight, although not with the police, but with his peers. The disrepute to the legal system would have long-term repercussions.

'We're here, responded to your summons,' Haddock said sarcastically. He knew the man was on the ropes, willing to needle him to see if he would break.

'Brett's not involved,' Kline said. He had taken a seat in one corner of the room.

'Not in Maria's murder,' Natalie said. 'We know that. Is Brett bisexual?'

Two rational sentences, one an attempt to throw the man.

'Sexually liberated, a healthy appreciation of the human form, the expression through passionate physical contact. I have no issue with that.'

'Which doesn't answer the direct question. Did you have reason to believe in intimacy with Peter Regan? Did Russell Harding give you photos of your son and Maria copulating?'

'Not Harding, but Sidorov.'

'Why? Why would a father want to see such a photo?'

'Brett was weakening, allowing the carnal to override the financial. Not using his brain, thinking from below the belt. I had no issue, but Brett wanting to break the agreement with Maria's father, that I could not countenance.'

'And if Sidorov died, your fortune would have been secure. What about this board of trustees? What about Ivanov?' Haddock asked.

'He's unimportant, not needed in the new order, or is he?' Natalie asked.

'He is,' Kline said. 'Alexey used his contacts in Russia for financing. Not always, but often. A merchant bank in Australia would have wanted more robust security and a higher interest rate. In Russia, much more flexible, awash with money, some illegal, some not, but Alexey was a pragmatist. Agree to their conditions, and no loan is ever refused. Only to deal in Russia, to get money from them, you need to be Russian. Alexey could do it, and so could Maria and Ivanov.

'Are you saying he lives because he is useful?'

'To someone, he is.'

Haddock and Natalie couldn't understand where Kline was leading the conversation. With every utterance, he was digging a bigger hole for himself.

'And that someone is?' Haddock asked. 'You're the person most likely, and why are you telling us? Without names and proof, Alexey's death points back to you. Ivanov might have been given money, a fortune to him, but a mere pittance compared to Alexey and your aspirations.'

'Not to him, it isn't. You know the man and where he lives. Lazy, corruptible, debased, a million dollars in his pocket, and he'd be either drugged or drunk most nights, whores in and out of his place on rotation. Controllable, he's useful; otherwise, he's not.'

'And you could control him?' Natalie asked. She could see Kline's halo slipping. A Supreme Court judge's utterances should be circumspect, impartial, and noncommittal, although very little of what he was saying was.

'Why are we here?' Haddock asked. He knew he would be out of his depth, unable to unravel Kline as he spoke, whether he was telling the truth or indulging in an academic exercise, the highly-educated judge trifling with the peasants.

Natalie, who'd had more intimate involvement with Kline, knew he was a dangerous individual who did not need a murder to advance his cause but only the glib tongue of a master tactician, which he was, as well as the father of a young man who had inherited his traits.

It was Natalie who cut short the meeting with Kline, conscious they could not lay a hand on the man, and the longer they spent in his company, the more convinced they would become that he was the innocent, the injured party, and that the man's predilection for high-class escorts, ocean cruising, and attractive young police sergeants was not only acceptable, but a credit to the man.

***

Natalie saw it clearly, as she tried to explain it to Haddock. It was another late night, de rigueur during a murder investigation, the two in the office at State Crime Command. Payne had come in earlier in the evening, giving a speech about professionalism, the department's track record, and how he had complete faith in his star police officers before skedaddling off to a function for new inductees.

Haddock struggled with the concept that Natalie put forward, prejudiced against Justice Kline and his educated speech, aiming to belittle a police inspector, succeeding admirably.

Natalie had to explain, the first time in their short time together as a team, that she, the sergeant, with her feminine wiles, could see through the man, an advantage over her superior who was forced to deal with logic and a policeman's intuition, unable to sense the inner workings of a devious mind.

'It's obvious,' Natalie said. 'We could spend a day with Kline and be none the wiser. The man's a strategist who makes numerous plans. If one doesn't pan out, he goes forward on another, similar to a chess player. He's had a successful career as a barrister and judge. But then along comes Alexey Sidorov, who makes the man look like a pauper. Kline senses the opportunity, rules in Sidorov's favour in a contentious trial, gains the man's confidence, and sees a bright future. But he knows it needs someone of his calibre to control the situation and keep the end goal in sight. But there are, as in any complex plan, difficulties.'

'Maria's death?' Haddock said. He was sitting back, revelling in the eloquence of his softly spoken sergeant, willing to admit that hers was a more astute mind than his.

'Unexpected. Justice Kline's unsure what to do; his son is no longer a key player. He loves his son, but it is more than love with the two of them, peas from the same pod. Like father, like son, love is only one factor. Political intrigue and advantage are more relevant.'

'Are you saying that Justice Kline would throw his son to the wolves if it would be to his advantage?'

'Not throw. Let them gnaw on him. Kline's in big, a fortune in his sight, persons disposable, not family, not at first, but trap a rat in a corner and any and every option is on the table.'

'How did Kline gain so much control over Sidorov's fortune?' Haddock asked. He appreciated Natalie's analysis of the situation, unable to follow it totally, blind as to where it was heading.

'Sidorov dealt with shady oligarchs in Russia, borrowed heavily from them, no doubt skirted the law on many occasions, and then, there is Justice Kline, incorruptible supposedly, although the man's got a perversion, not the worst there is, but not good for a senior legal in the country. In Kline, the son of Russian immigrants finds a likeminded soul, someone he can trust, aware that the man will act to his advantage, and then there is Brett, the father's clone, and Maria, the clone of hers. The future is secure, the empire is safe.'

'And then Maria dies.'

'That one event changes it all. Brett is out of the picture. Alexey is distraught, but with time and distance, he moves on emotionally and starts to reengage with his business empire. Kline can see what will happen. His leverage is gone, namely son and daughter. And then, a few years pass and Sidorov will start to isolate Kline, no longer in the driving seat, but a minor functionary.'

'Kline murdered Alexey?'

'Not Kline, remember that. He's got control, but he needs Sidorov dead. Only one person could have done it, don't you see?'

Haddock could; it was impossible to contemplate, but could it be true.

'Not Ivanov, although he might have, for sufficient money, a few million dollars more. But he's Russian and a relative, blood is thicker than water, and one day, drunk on vodka or women, he would blurt it out, effusive tears, the works, might even admit it to the police, more likely to Sidorov's kin in Russia, dead within the week.'

And that was how the day ended, no more said by either police officer. Haddock returned to his modest accommodation, unsure if he should phone his occasional paramour to come over. Natalie drove to her two-bedroom apartment, opened the refrigerator, and looked at an out-of-date bottle of milk and half a bottle of wine. She chose the latter, crying herself to sleep over how lonely she was, aware that tomorrow she and Haddock would make an arrest that neither wanted to, but by her evaluation, it was clear who the murderer was.

Victoria Adderley had been advised, the legal implications discussed: the fightback, legal, verbal, antagonistic, and almost undoubtedly political influence brought to bear. Superintendent Payne, updated on Natalie's evaluation, was aware that a perceptive mind had seen through the quagmire and come to the only logical decision.

At nine thirty on a bright sunny morning in Parramatta, Brett Kline was in the interview room. Natalie outlined all factors in the investigation. The boy's father listened, wanting to speak but could not. It was his son, and it was murder, and even though the evidence was circumstantial, it was condemning.

Haddock attempted to take part, offering comment where appropriate, aware that he was minor to his sergeant and that the subordinate was now the master, that his sergeant would rise further than a sergeant, as high as chief superintendent if she wanted. Green when she had paired with him, she had learnt what she could and gained an insight into the devious mind of Justice Kline.

'Brett,' Natalie said, 'it can only be you. Your father and your future were secure with Maria alive, but with her death, Alexey Sidorov would have weakened your father's position, knowing that in time the lever he had over him would no longer hold and that the decision he made in Sidorov's dispute with Murray Financial Services would be of historical interest, but nothing more.'

'Incredible,' Justice Kline commented but said no more, which disturbed Natalie. As if the man… But that couldn't be correct, surely.

'Is it?' Natalie said. 'You maintained a firm hand over Sidorov, your son playing his part, the tie that united the families. Maria wanted Brett, and he might have wanted her or might not

267

have. It's irrelevant, only that with the jealous killing of the poor girl, you could see the future, dystopian for you, nothing more.'

'Why would a Supreme Court Justice become involved with such intrigue?'

'Only you could answer that question or maybe you couldn't. It could be love or hate, power or wealth, or a combination of all four. Maria tempted you, a predilection for young women, virtuous or not, but she wasn't for you, but your son, young for him to agree to such an arrangement, but who knows. Have you trained him well?'

'He has,' Brett said. 'Time, father?' he said as he looked at his father.

'Yes, reluctantly. Are you sure about this?' Justice Kline said.

'Father, what other option do we have? The future is well served by my sacrifice.'

In another room, Superintendent Payne sat, stunned by what he was hearing. Victoria Adderley sat nearby, enthralled.

Would the father sacrifice the son? The answer was obvious, as Brett outlined the scenario.

'I knew what I must do, the fragile relationship between my father and Maria's. I would have preferred her, but without the option, I did what I must. I killed Alexey in cold blood, emotionless, devoid of passion other than preserving the Klines, a noble family.'

At eighteen, an age to contemplate the future, Brett Kline had made his decision. Whether it was his totally or not would never be known, other than the Klines would have their wealth and influence, and damn the criticism, petty and bourgeois. The Klines and those they aspired to were not tarred by middle-class morality but by higher ideals.

Later that night, in Payne's office, the enormity of the arrest sank home, the second time in as many days that Natalie cried, Victoria putting her arm around her.

Haddock could see his sergeant retained her humility, which he did not. He should have felt sad but did not, only thanking Payne as he offered him another beer.

In a cell, father and son sat. 'Five years, low-security,' the elder said.

'Overseas after that,' Brett said.

'I'm proud of you, son. You acted decisively and, at your age, not long in prison, a cushy cell. I'll make sure of that, and in five, possibly ten, forgotten by all barring a few. Then you can take your rightful position at the head of the empire.'

'Maria's empire,' Brett reminded his father.

'Yours now, as it was always going to be. You showed great foresight and the ability to act decisively, the traits of a master. In time, people will clamour to be by your side, basking in your presence.'

Justice Kline sat back in admiration, knowing that by the time he had finished counselling a defence barrister and wielding his influence, his son would be regarded as an avenging martyr, not as an indiscriminate murderer, not like Peter Regan who would not have the advantage of Justice Kline in his corner.

Justice Kline mused as he left the cell that night, kissing his son on both cheeks and hugging him. 'If only Maria hadn't died, how much easier it would have been,' he said, almost inaudibly. He sighed, looked back at his son, and realised that the fruits of his loins were to be acknowledged, not condemned. That night, after he had visited a lady friend of his, Justice Kline would sit down and formulate another plan, its sole objective to ensure the early release of his son.

The weeks ahead would be difficult, with many challenges and tribulations, but Kline was enthusiastic. This was the man at his best.

As for the young sergeant, there were plenty of other fish in the sea. He would no longer chase her; she was wise to his deceit, more intelligent than he wanted his women.

That night, Haddock drove to the family home, not to spend the night with his wife, aware there was no way back, but to talk to her, to unburden what had happened at Parramatta, and that a young man had been charged with murder. But mostly because he wanted to see his daughter and tell her he loved her.

The End

ALSO BY THE AUTHOR

DI Tremayne Thriller Series

Death Unholy – A DI Tremayne Thriller – Book 1

All that remained were the man's two legs and a chair full of greasy and fetid ash. Little did DI Keith Tremayne know that it was the beginning of a journey into the murky world of paganism and its ancient rituals. And it was going to get very dangerous.

'Do you believe in spontaneous human combustion?' Detective Inspector Keith Tremayne asked.

'Not me. I've read about it. Who hasn't?' Sergeant Clare Yarwood answered.

'I haven't,' Tremayne replied, which did not surprise his young sergeant. In the months they had been working together, she had come to realise that he was a man who had little interest in the world. When he had a cigarette in his mouth, a beer in his hand, and a murder to solve he was about the happiest she ever saw him, but even then, he was not one of life's most sociable people. And as for reading? The occasional police report, an early-morning newspaper, turned first to the racing results.

Death and the Assassin's Blade – A DI Tremayne Thriller – Book 2

It was meant to be high drama, not murder, but someone's switched the daggers. The man's death took place in plain view of two serving police officers.

He was not meant to die; the daggers were only theatrical props, plastic and harmless. A summer's night, a production of Julius Caesar amongst the ruins of an Anglo-Saxon fort. Detective Inspector Tremayne is there with his sergeant, Clare Yarwood. In the assassination scene, Caesar collapses to the ground. Brutus defends his actions; Mark Antony rebukes him.

They're a disparate group, the amateur actors. One's an estate agent, another an accountant. And then there is the teenage school student, the gay man, the funeral director. And what about the women? They could be involved.

They've each got a secret, but which of those on the stage wanted Gordon Mason, the actor who had portrayed Caesar, dead?

Death and the Lucky Man – A DI Tremayne Thriller – Book 3

Sixty-eight million pounds and dead. Hardly the outcome expected for the luckiest man in England the day his lottery ticket was drawn out of the barrel. But then, Alan Winters' rags-to-riches story had never been conventional, and some had benefited, but others hadn't.

Death at Coombe Farm – A DI Tremayne Thriller – Book 4

A warring family. A disputed inheritance. A recipe for death.

If it hadn't been for the circumstances, Detective Inspector Keith Tremayne would have said the view was outstanding. Up high, overlooking the farmhouse in the valley below, the panoramic vista of Salisbury Plain stretching out beyond. The only problem was a body near where he stood with his sergeant, Clare Yarwood, and it wasn't a pleasant sight.

Death by a Dead Man's Hand – A DI Tremayne Thriller – Book 5

A flawed heist of forty gold bars from a security van late at night. One of the perpetrators is killed by his brother as they argue over what they have stolen.

Eighteen years later, the murderer, released after serving his sentence for his brother's murder, waits in a church for a man purporting to be the brother he killed. And then he is killed.

The threads stretch back a long way, and now more people are dying in the search for the missing gold bars.

Detective Inspector Tremayne, his health causing him concern, and Sergeant Clare Yarwood, still seeking romance, are pushed to the limit solving the murder, attempting to prevent more.

Death in the Village – A DI Tremayne Thriller – Book 6

Nobody liked Gloria Wiggins, a woman who regarded anyone who did not acquiesce to her jaundiced view of the world with disdain. James Baxter, the previous vicar, had been one of those, and her scurrilous outburst in the church one Sunday had hastened his death.

And now, years later, the woman was dead, hanging from a beam in her garage. Detective Inspector Tremayne and Sergeant Clare Yarwood had seen the body, interviewed the woman's acquaintances, and those who had hated her.

Burial Mound – A DI Tremayne Thriller – Book 7

A Bronze-Age burial mound close to Stonehenge. An archaeological excavation. What they were looking for was an ancient body and historical artefacts. They found the ancient body, but then they found another that's only been there for years, not centuries. And then the police became interested.

It's another case for Detective Inspector Tremayne and Sergeant Yarwood. The more recent body was the brother of the mayor of Salisbury.

Everything seems to point to the victim's brother, the mayor, the upright and serious-minded Clive Grantley. Tremayne's sure that it's him, but Clare Yarwood's not so sure.

But is her belief based on evidence or personal hope?

The Body in the Ditch – A DI Tremayne Thriller – Book 8

A group of children play. Not far away, in the ditch on the other side of the farmyard, lies the body of a troubled young woman.

The nearby village hides as many secrets as the community at the farm, a disparate group of people looking for an alternative to their previous torturous lives. Their leader, idealistic and benevolent, espouses love and kindness, and clearly, somebody's not following his dictate.

An old woman's death seems unrelated to the first, but is it? Is it part of the tangled web that connects the farm to the village?

Detective Inspector Tremayne and Sergeant Clare Yarwood soon discover that the village is anything but charming and picturesque. It's an incestuous hotbed of intrigue and wrongdoing. And what of the farm and those who live there. None of them can be ruled out, not yet.

The Horse's Mouth – A DI Tremayne Thriller – Book 9

A day at the races for Detective Inspector Tremayne, idyllic at the outset, soon changes. A horse is dead, the owner's daughter is found murdered, and Tremayne's there when the body is discovered.

The question is, was Tremayne set up, in the wrong place at the right time? He's the cast-iron alibi for one of the suspects, and he knows that one murder can lead to two, and more often than not to three.

The dead woman had a chequered history, though not as much as her father, and then a man commits suicide. Is he the murderer, or was his death the unfortunate consequence of a tragic love affair? And who was in the stable with the woman just before she died? More than one person could have killed her, and all of them have secrets they would rather not be known.

Tremayne's health is troubling him. Is what they are saying correct, that it is time for him to retire, to take it easy and put his feet up? But that's not his style, and he'll not give up on solving the murder.

Montfield's Madness – A DI Tremayne Thriller – Book 10

A day at the races for Detective Inspector Tremayne, idyllic at the Jacob Montfield, regarded by the majority as a homeless eccentric, a nuisance by a few, had pushed a supermarket trolley around the city for years.

However, one person regards him as a liability.

Eccentric was correct, a nuisance, for sure, mad, plenty thought that, but few knew the truth, that Montfield is a brilliant man, once a research scientist. And even less knew that detailed within a notebook hidden deep in the trolley, there is a new approach to the guidance of weapons and satellites—a radical improvement on the previous and it's worth a lot to some, power to others, accolades to another.

And for that, one cold night, he died at the hand of another. Inspector Tremayne and Sergeant Clare Yarwood are on the case, but so are others, and soon they're warned off. Only Tremayne doesn't listen, not when he's got his teeth into the investigation, and his sergeant, equally resolute, won't either. It's not only their careers on the line, but their lives.

DCI Isaac Cook Thriller Series

Murder is a Tricky Business – A DCI Cook Thriller – Book 1

A television actress is missing, and DCI Isaac Cook, the Senior Investigation Officer of the Murder Investigation Team at Challis Street Police Station in London, is searching for her.

Why has he been taken away from more important crimes to search for the woman? It's not the first time she's gone missing, so why does everyone assume she's been murdered?

There's a secret; that much is certain, but who knows it? The missing woman? The executive producer? His eavesdropping assistant? Or the actor who portrayed her fictional brother in the TV soap opera?

Murder House – A DCI Cook Thriller – Book 2

A corpse in the fireplace of an old house. It's been there for thirty years, but who is it?

It's murder, but who is the victim and what connection does the body have to the house's previous owners. What is the motive? And why is the body in a fireplace? It was bound to be discovered eventually but was that what the murderer wanted? The main suspects are all old and dying or already dead.

Isaac Cook and his team have their work cut out, trying to put the pieces together. Those who know are not talking because of an old-fashioned belief that a family's dirty laundry should not be aired in public and never to a policeman – even if that means the murderer is never brought to justice!

Murder is Only a Number – A DCI Cook Thriller – Book 3

Before she left, she carved a number in blood on his chest. But why the number 2 if this was her first murder?

The woman prowls the streets of London. Her targets are men who have wronged her. Or have they? And why is she keeping count?

DCI Cook and his team finally know who she is, but not before she's murdered four men. The whole team are looking for her, but the woman keeps disappearing in plain sight. The pressure's on to stop her, but she's always one step ahead.

And this time, DCS Goddard can't protect his protégé, Isaac Cook, from the wrath of the new commissioner at the Met.

Murder in Little Venice – A DCI Cook Thriller – Book 4

A dismembered corpse floats in the canal in Little Venice, an upmarket tourist haven in London. Its identity is unknown, but what is its significance?

DCI Isaac Cook is baffled about why it's there. Is it gang-related, or is it something more?

Whatever the reason, it's clearly a warning, and Isaac and his team are sure it's not the last body that they'll have to deal with.

Murder is the Only Option – A DCI Cook Thriller – Book 5

A man thought to be long dead returns to exact revenge against those who had blighted his life. His only concern is to protect his wife and daughter. He will stop at nothing to achieve his aim.

'Big Greg, I never expected to see you around here at this time of night.'

'I've told you enough times.'

'I've no idea what you're talking about,' Robertson replied. He looked up at the man, only to see a metal pole coming down at him. Robertson fell down, cracking his head against a concrete kerb.

Two vagrants, no more than twenty feet away, did not stir and did not even look in the direction of the noise. If they had, they would have seen a dead body, another man walking away.

Murder in Notting Hill – A DCI Cook Thriller – Book 6

One murderer, two bodies, two locations, and the murders have been committed within an hour of each other.

They're separated by a couple of miles, and neither woman has anything in common with the other. One is young and wealthy, the daughter of a famous man; the other is poor, hardworking and unknown.

Isaac Cook and his team at Challis Street Police Station are baffled about why they've been killed. There must be a connection, but what is it?

Murder in Room 346 – A DCI Cook Thriller – Book 7

'Coitus interruptus, that's what it is,' Detective Chief Inspector Isaac Cook said. In a downmarket hotel in Bayswater, on the bed lay the naked bodies of a man and a woman.

'Bullet in the head's not the way to go,' Larry Hill, Isaac Cook's detective inspector, said. He had not expected such a flippant comment from his senior, not when they were standing near to two people who had, apparently in the final throes of passion, succumbed to what appeared to be a professional assassination.

'You know this will be all over the media within the hour,' Isaac said.

'James Holden, moral crusader, a proponent of the sanctity of the marital bed, man and wife. It's bound to be.'

Murder of a Silent Man – A DCI Cook Thriller – Book 8

A murdered recluse. A property empire. A disinherited family. All the ingredients for murder.

No one gave much credence to the man when he was alive. In fact, most people never knew who he was, although those who had lived in the area for many years recognised the tired-looking and shabbily-dressed man as he shuffled along, regular as clockwork on a Thursday afternoon at seven in the evening to the local off-licence.

It was always the same: a bottle of whisky, premium brand, and a packet of cigarettes. He paid his money over the counter, took hold of his plastic bag containing his purchases, and then walked back down the road with the same rhythmic shuffle.

Murder has no Guilt – A DCI Cook Thriller – Book 9

No one knows who the target was or why, but there are eight dead. The men seem the most likely perpetrators, or could have it been one of the two women, the attractive Gillian Dickenson, or even the celebrity-obsessed Sal Maynard?

There's a gang war brewing, and if there are deaths, it doesn't matter to them as long as it's not their death. But to Detective Chief Inspector Isaac Cook, it's his area of London, and it does matter.

It's dirty and unpredictable. Initially, the West Indian gangs held sway, but a more vicious Romanian gangster had usurped them. And now he's being marginalised by the Russians. And the leader of the most vicious Russian mafia organisation is in London, and he's got money and influence, the ear of those in power.

Murder in Hyde Park – A DCI Cook Thriller – Book 10

An early-morning jogger is murdered in Hyde Park. It's in the centre of London, but no one saw him enter the park, no one saw him die.

He carries no identification, only a water-logged phone. As the pieces unravel, it's clear that the dead man had a history of deception.

Is the murderer one of those that loved him? Or was it someone with a vengeance?

It's proving difficult for DCI Isaac Cook and his team at Challis Street Homicide to find the guilty person – not that they'll cease to search for the truth, not even after one suspect confesses.

Six Years Too Late – A DCI Cook Thriller – Book 11

Always the same questions for Detective Chief Inspector Isaac Cook — Why was Marcus Matthews in that room? And why did he share a bottle of wine with his killer?

It wasn't as if Matthews had amounted to much, apart from the fact that he was the son-in-law of a notorious gangster, the father of the man's grandchildren.

Yet the one thing Hamish McIntyre, feared in London for his violence, rated above anything else, was his family, especially Samantha, his daughter. However, he had never cared for Marcus, her husband.

And then Marcus disappeared, only for his body to be found six years later by a couple of young boys who decide that exploring an abandoned house is preferable to school.

Grave Passion – A DCI Cook Thriller – Book 12

Two young lovers out for a night of romance. A shortcut through the cemetery. They witnessed a murder, but there was no struggle, only a knife through the heart.

It has all the hallmarks of an assassination, but who is the woman? And why was she beside a grave at night? Did she know the person who killed her?

Soon after, other deaths, seemingly unconnected, but tied to the family of one of the young lovers.

It's a case for Detective Chief Inspector Cook and his team, and they're baffled on this one.

The Slaying of Joe Foster – A DCI Cook Thriller – Book 13

No one challenged Joe Foster in life, not if they valued theirs. And then, the gangster is slain and his criminal empire up for grabs.

A power vacuum; the Foster family is fighting for control, the other gangs in the area aiming to poach the trade in illegal drugs, to carve up the empire that the father had created.

It has all the makings of a war on the streets, something nobody wants, not even the other gangs.

Terry Foster, the eldest son of Joe, the man who should take control, doesn't have his father's temperament or wisdom. His solution is slash and burn, and it's not going to work. People are going to get hurt, and some of them will die.

The Hero's Fall – A DCI Cook Thriller – Book 14

Angus Simmons had it made. A successful television program, a beautiful girlfriend, admired by many for his mountaineering exploits.

And then he fell while climbing a skyscraper in London. Initially, it was thought he had lost his grip, but that wasn't the man: a meticulous planner, his risks measured, and it wasn't a difficult climb, not for him.

It was only afterwards on examination that they found the mark of a bullet on his body. It then became a murder, and that was when Detective Chief Inspector Isaac Cook and his Homicide team at Challis Street Police Station became interested.

The Vicar's Confession – A DCI Cook Thriller – Book 15

The Reverend Charles Hepworth, good Samaritan, a friend of the downtrodden, almost a saint to those who know him, up until the day he walks into the police station, straight up to Detective Chief Inspector Isaac Cook's desk in Homicide. 'I killed the man,' he says as he places a blood-soaked knife on the desk.

The dead man, Andreas Maybury, was not a man to mourn, but why would a self-professed pacifist commit such a heinous crime. The reasons aren't clear, and then Hepworth's killed in a prison cell, and everyone's ducking for cover.

Guilty Until Proven Innocent – A DCI Cook Thriller – Book 16

Gary Harders' conviction two years previously should have been the end of the investigation. A clear-cut case of murder, and he had confessed to the crime and accepted his sentence without complaint. But now, the man's conviction was about to be overthrown, but why? And why is Harders not saying that his confession was police coercion? His prints are on the murder weapon, but Forensics has found another set.

Not only is there proof of either the Forensics department's error, incompetency or conspiracy, but Commissioner Alwyn Davies is getting tough on crime, draconian tough.

Detective Chief Inspector Isaac Cook and Chief Superintendent Richard Goddard are under pressure to take sides, aware that a positive return ensures promotion, but at the cost of their respective souls.

Davies has powerful backers, persons willing to make a deal with the devil. To allow violent putdown of those who disrupt the streets and removal of those who cause unsolicited and anti-social crime.

The plan has merits, a return to the safe society of decades past, but where will it stop. Who will say it's time to ease off, and then, what's the Russian mafia got to do with it? Too much from what DCI Cook can see, but he's powerless.

Murder Without Reason – A DCI Cook Thriller – Book 17

DCI Cook faces his greatest challenge. The Islamic State is waging war in England, and they are winning.

Not only does Isaac Cook have to contend with finding the perpetrators, but he is also being forced to commit actions contrary to his mandate as a police officer.

And then there is Anne Argento, the prime minister's deputy. The prime minister has shown himself to be a pacifist and is not up to the task. She needs to take his job if the country is to fight back against the Islamists.

Vane and Martin have provided the solution. Will DCI Cook and Anne Argento be willing to follow it through? Are they able to act for the good of England, knowing that a criminal and murderous action is about to take place? Do they have an option?

Steve Case Thriller Series

The Haberman Virus – Book 1

A remote and isolated village in the Hindu Kush Mountain range in North Eastern Afghanistan is wiped out by a virus unlike any seen before.

A mysterious visitor clad in a spacesuit checks his handiwork, a female American doctor succumbs to the disease, and the woman sent to trap the person responsible falls in love with him – the man who would cause the deaths of millions.

Hostage of Islam – Book 2

Three are to die at the Mission in Nigeria: the pastor and his wife in a blazing chapel; another gunned down while trying to defend them from the Islamist fighters.

Kate McDonald, an American, grieving over her boyfriend's death and Helen Campbell, whose life had been troubled by drugs and prostitution, are taken by the attackers.

Kate is sold to a slave trader who intends to sell her virginity to an Arab Prince. Helen, to ensure their survival, gives herself to the murderer of her friends.

Prelude to War – Book 3

Russia and America face each other across the northern border of Afghanistan. World War 3 is about to break out and no one is backing off.

And all because a team of academics in New York postulated how to extract the vast untapped mineral wealth of Afghanistan.

Steve Case is in the middle of it, and his position is looking very precarious. Will the Taliban find him before the Americans get him out? Or is he doomed, as is the rest of the world?

Standalone Novels

Malika's Revenge

Malika, a drug-addicted prostitute, waits in a smugglers' village for the next Afghan tribesman or Tajik gangster to pay her price, a few scraps of heroin.

Yusup Baroyev, a drug lord, enjoys a lifestyle many would envy. An Afghan warlord sees the resurgence of the Taliban. A Russian white-collar criminal portrays himself as a good and honest citizen in Moscow.

All of them are linked to an audacious plan to increase the quantity of heroin shipped out of Afghanistan and into Russia and ultimately the West.

Some will succeed, some will die, some will be rescued from their plight and others will rue the day they became involved.

Verrall's Nightmare

Historians may reflect on what happened, psychoanalysts may debate endlessly, and although scientists would attempt to explain, none would conclusively get the measure of all that had occurred.

Others, less knowledgeable, aficionados of social media, would say that Benedict Verrall was mad, or else the events in a small hamlet in the south of England never occurred and that it was a government conspiracy. That Samuel Whittingham was a figment of Verrall's imagination and the storms and their devastation, unprecedented in their scope and deaths, were freaks of nature, not of evil.

The truth, however, was more obscure, and that Verrall was neither mad nor was he malicious. Although he was responsible for instigating what was to happen, that hadn't been his intention.

He did not believe in the paranormal or the metaphysical, but then, he had not considered the brain tumour pressing down on his brain.

Or was it Verrall's madness, either the dream or the nightmare? That will be for the reader to decide.

ABOUT THE AUTHOR

Phillip Strang was born in the late forties, the post-war baby boom in England; his childhood years, a comfortable middle-class upbringing in a small town, a two hours' drive to the west of London.

His childhood and the formative years were a time of innocence. Relatively few rules, and as a teenager, complete mobility due to a bicycle – a three-speed Raleigh – and a more trusting community. It was the days before mobile phones, the internet, terrorism and wanton violence. An avid reader of Science Fiction in his teenage years: Isaac Asimov, and Frank Herbert, the masters of the genre. Still an avid reader, the author now mainly reads thrillers.

In his early twenties, the author, with a degree in electronics engineering and an unabated wanderlust to see the world left England's cold and damp climes for Sydney, Australia – the first semi-circulation of the globe, complete. Now, forty years later, he still resides in Australia, although many intervening years spent in a myriad of countries, some calm and safe – others, no more than war zones.

Made in the USA
Las Vegas, NV
23 May 2023

72468444R00173